PARRISH

SHANNEN CRANE CAMP

DEDICATION

For Ashlee, who loves these characters. And my writing group, who couldn't read this at night and let me know I'd done my job by giving them late-night paranoia. And, of course, for The Husband, who loves scary movies and haunted houses as much as me.

CHAPTER 1

"Did you die here?"

The empty room didn't answer me, although with the luck we'd had, I hadn't expected it to. The musty cold air left a sheen on my forehead, but I wasn't sure if it was the humidity or my own nerves.

"Did you read the notecards I gave you?" Jefferson asked in my earpiece, his thick British accent muffled by static. "There's some brilliant stuff on there." The static flared up, covering the rest of his dialogue.

"Look at the floor?" I asked, suddenly worried I had missed something.

"Number four!" he repeated.

I readjusted the earpiece, wondering if maybe all of the water was making it glitch and thinking, not for the first time, that anyone who didn't know I was wearing an earpiece would think I was completely nuts, talking to myself like this.

I thumbed through the soggy notecards, pulling them apart while clutching my flashlight, until I reached what I was looking for.

"I hope they've got some bathtub gin in this joint—I'm as dry as a bone," I deadpanned. "Seriously? Where do you come up with this crap?"

"That's how they talked, Sadie; it's not my fault it's ridiculous. I'm just being authentic."

"Nobody talked like this," I said, trying not to get too frustrated by our lack of preparation and the fact that, despite my protests, I was yet again being cast as the damsel in distress meant to lure the ghosts out to play.

I was a glorified earthworm wriggling on a hook.

"And I'm pretty sure the blonde wig isn't fooling anyone."

"Why not?" Jefferson sounded genuinely shocked in my ear, and I could only imagine his huge owl eyes getting even rounder.

"Because I'm Cuban! How many blonde Cubans were running around in the twenties looking for a drink?"

"At least one."

"This is stupid. I'm calling it, you guys. We've got nothing."

"What? No!" Deacon, Jefferson's cousin, whined over the earpiece.

I wasn't sure what he was so upset about—he had to have been just as miserable as me, sitting out in the freezing cold Jeep in one of Portland's famous rainstorms.

"Sadie, this place is supposed to be an absolute hotspot for activity," Jefferson insisted. "If we leave now, we'll miss our chance to be the first group to catch evidence on film."

"It's freezing, the floors keep creaking like they're about to collapse, and my lines wouldn't fool even the drunkest of bar patron ghosts." I rubbed my hands over the cold skin on my bare arms. How were people in the twenties supposed to stay warm in these skimpy dresses?

The getup Jefferson had given me was itchy and terrible. Plus it was purple. My least favorite color.

"Besides, I feel like Daphne on Scooby Doo in this ridiculous costume."

"Well . . ." Jefferson let his words trail off.

It was generally known that I didn't appreciate always being the ghost bait when I had actual ghost hunting skills that I could put to good use in the field. Instead of utilizing my abilities, though, these two crazy British boys had recruited me to dress up in ridiculous costumes and recite awful lines to try to get some activity stirred up. It was the worst ghost-hunting technique I'd ever seen, but Jefferson (our self-proclaimed leader and group-labeled sociopath) insisted that being the only group out there to do it gave us an advantage. I thought it just made us look like the idiots we were.

My "actual" ghost hunting skills were just yearning to be used. Of course . . . that was using the phrase "actual ghost hunting skills" very loosely.

I wished I could say I was an empath, who could sense emotions of ghosts, or that I was some sort of gifted hunter. But really, I just loved the paranormal.

That being said, I was also a normal human being, which meant when things got too intense for my liking, I leaned heavily towards the "flight" part of the "fight or flight" reaction.

It was embarrassing when it happened in front of the guys.

"You'd better not tease her or she'll quit, and it'll be you out there in a dress talking about bathtub gin," said Brighton, our fourth and final group member.

"Don't be ridiculous," Jefferson said. "Deacon's got much nicer legs."

"I could point out that you'd be a better fit for the dress," Deacon said.

"Yeah, but then who would run the equipment?" Brighton asked.

Brighton was sort of amazing with technology. She also happened to be terrified of ghosts, which made no sense since her hobby was ghost hunting. But this combination meant she always stayed in the van and operated tech.

"Touché," the guys said in unison.

"Wait, everyone shut up," I said to the empty room.

A loud beep came from the storage room of the abandoned pub we were investigating. "The shadow detector just went off," I said slowly.

"Which one is that again?" Deacon asked.

Deacon was a bit of a skeptic, which meant he didn't bother to learn about the equipment we used and constantly needed reminders about what each thing did.

"The one that detects shadows," Brighton said. "The answer's in the question."

Ignoring the banter in my earpiece, I shone my flashlight over the bar, the beam of light distorting and bending as it hit the rows of hanging wine glasses, sending shadows skittering every which way. The air around me grew cold (well, colder), and a chill ran down my spine. They were all signs that I was about to be monumentally scared by some unexplainable thing.

I used my free hand, which was amazingly steady, to turn on the audio recorder, and held the device out in front of me, squinting into the blackness ahead.

"Hello?" I called, the fear leaving me and the excitement taking over.

Maybe Jefferson's ridiculous lines actually did work.

"Who's there?" I called again, hoping that I was getting some good audio on the recorder, even if I wasn't currently able to hear the response.

I took a step forward on the creaky floors, hoping they would hold my weight in this condemned building. Secretly, I thought that was the real reason the boys made me do all the dirty work. I was short and skinny, and I was pretty much built like a twelve-year-old boy despite the grand total of twenty-one years I had under my belt. If one of those tall lanky guys came in here, they'd collapse the whole building with their clumsy tromping around.

"Did you die here?" I asked again, a smile beginning to spread across my lips at the thought that I might actually make contact with someone or something.

"Sadie!" Jefferson suddenly exclaimed in my ear as he grabbed my sides and made me jump a mile in the air.

He threw his head back and broke out into maniacal laughter. I grabbed a handful of his dark, curly hair and pulled as hard as I could, turning his obnoxious laughter into an exclamation of pain.

"What did you do that for?" he asked with a scowl, running his fingers through the untamable mess of hair he refused to cut.

I didn't bother answering, tired of babysitting the infamous Parrish cousins tonight. It was a wonder I hadn't killed them years ago.

"What's she doing, mate?" Deacon asked over the earpiece.

"Just walking away," Jefferson replied, sounding as puzzled and clueless as ever.

I shook my head in frustration, pulling off the less-than-convincing blonde wig (that wouldn't fool anyone) and running my fingers through my dark brown pixie cut, fluffing it up a bit.

The floor continued to creak under the clacking of my heels, but I had a point to make and that point could only be made with a fast-paced "angry stomp" out of the pub. I flung the front doors open with force, Jefferson hard on my heels, and slogged through the rain, jumping into the back of the old beat-up Jeep Wagoneer and gratefully accepting the big puffy coat Brighton offered me.

Brighton was the only sane one in the group, even if she was a walking contradiction. She looked like a typical high school mean girl, but she was the most bizarre blend of phobia-ridden beauty to ever walk this planet. Still, she had my back when the boys went nuts (which was every second of every day), so that made her my only ally in the overwhelming sea of crazy.

"I didn't come here to play pranks or feel like the butt of some anti-feminist joke. I came here to find evidence of the paranormal." I wrapped the coat tightly around my shivering form and stared at Jefferson.

He stood in the rain, not looking like he even noticed the torrential downpour that was soaking him through. His brow was furrowed and his dark green eyes looked intense as he tilted his head slowly to the side. It was a disturbing habit he displayed when thinking, and one that I had never quite gotten used to. There were a lot of creepy things about the boy, but his whole dark-and-twisty demeanor was the creepiest. He looked like a Tim Burton character come to life—tall and thin with abnormally large green eyes, which always made him look like he was staring into your soul. The fact that he also dressed like a Tim Burton character didn't really do much to deflect his unsettling nature, but I could ignore the dusty three-piece suits and skinny ties because as much as I hated to admit it, Jefferson had a gift. He was a good paranormal investigator . . . when he took things seriously.

The same couldn't be said of his cousin Deacon, but somehow I thought the Parrish boys would be lost without each other.

We sat in silence for a moment: Brighton staring at her computer screen and fiddling absently with her inhaler, Deacon watching the showdown, and Jefferson and me having a staring contest. I'm sure I just looked pissed, whereas he looked like a homicidal maniac.

Okay, that's unfair. Jefferson really was a nice guy. All four of us had met in college at a scary movie marathon one Halloween night, and, after confessing our love for the paranormal, it only seemed natural to form a group to go out and seek the "truth." But, Jefferson's being a nice guy didn't mean he wasn't also the single eeriest person I'd ever met.

"So, are we just going to keep staring at each other," Brighton asked, "or can we call it a night and go grab some Chinese food? Because I'm starving. Besides, I'm going to catch a cold in this weather," she said, taking a puff on her ever-present inhaler as though to prove her point.

Call me crazy, but I didn't really think ghost hunting was the best profession for an asthmatic with an anxiety disorder.

"Since the night's ruined anyway, I'd love to get food," Jefferson said much too brightly. He narrowed his owl eyes at me dramatically and walked toward the front of the Jeep with a poorly hidden pout.

Of course, he failed to mention that I had actually been investigating and he was the one who had ruined the night. And now that he was throwing a tantrum, Brighton and I would be forced to gather all of the equipment from the pub.

"Well done, mate," Deacon said to me, crawling out of the back of the Jeep to join his cousin in the front seat. "Now he'll be unmanageable all night."

~

It was nearly three in the morning by the time we pulled into the parking lot of our apartment complex. We all grabbed armfuls of equipment and carried them up the three flights of stairs that led to our adjacent apartments. Our wet shoes squelched on the linoleum floors and we were all completely exhausted from the disappointing night. Our oversized jackets did little to keep the cold from seeping into our bodies, and I could have sworn I felt my entire skeleton groan as I walked.

Brighton and I dumped the various cameras, cords, and audio recorders onto the Parrish boys' couch, which was already full of tapes from previous investigations that we still needed to go over. They were labeled with Deacon's untidy scrawl, sporting vague titles like "House with yard 1" or "Old snowman attic 8." To anyone else, his code wouldn't have made sense. Unfortunately, I understood it perfectly, and all it meant was that we had a lot of recordings to go over.

Being a paranormal investigator was a lot more work than I had originally thought, and regrettably, it didn't exactly pay well, which usually meant we were digging through our couches for grocery money.

"Better luck next time, right?" Brighton stretched her long arms high over her head and arched her back, which emitted a dull pop.

"Same time tomorrow?" Deacon asked, his blue eyes locked on Brighton's stretching form.

He wasn't exactly subtle in his love for her.

"I'm out," I said, cutting him off with a wave of my hand. "I've got a twelve-hour shift tomorrow. There's no way I can investigate all night after that." Just thinking about it made my body hurt. I wasn't even sure how I'd get up in the morning and manage to stay on my feet for all those hours of waiting tables.

"It's just as well," Jefferson said, leaning lithely against the door frame and blocking my escape route. "I can go over the footage from tonight's investigation."

"Don't you have work?" I asked, afraid of the response I knew I'd receive.

"I quit," he answered disinterestedly, picking at his fingernails.

"Jefferson!" I exclaimed.

I really was more of a babysitter than anything, which didn't make any sense, since Jefferson insisted on being the group leader. I mean, he even wanted to call us The Parrish Paranormal Investigators, which I wouldn't have agreed to in a million years.

"How are you going to pay your rent?" I brought a hand up to my forehead, unable to look at the train wreck of a man in front of me.

I could feel my Cuban temper flaring up. Or at least, I liked to blame it on the fact that I was Cuban.

"Deacon still has a job," he answered, nodding at his cousin. Deacon quickly pushed his thick black glasses up the bridge of his nose and straightened his posture a bit, trying to look much more responsible than he was.

"I do," he said with a sharp nod, obviously hiding something. I narrowed my eyes at the less stubborn of the Parrish boys, knowing I could easily get the secret out of him.

"Sort of," he added with a wince. "It's more of a freelance thing at the moment."

Brighton laughed. "They're going to kick you guys out of your apartment."

"And then they'll try to move in with us," I said, silencing her laughter.

"I don't think so," she said, turning her gaze on the boys. "Why can't you guys keep a job? It's not that difficult. You can't tell me that people don't work in England."

"It bores me," Jefferson said.

He had his huge eyes on me, gauging my reaction, I was guessing, but I knew he was just trying to get a rise out of me.

"Well, we aren't paying your rent," I said, "so you'd better think of something quick."

His lips tugged up in a slow smile.

"I mean it, Jefferson! We can barely pay our own rent, and all of this equipment isn't cheap." I motioned to the piles of cameras on their patched up old couch. "Besides, don't you guys have work visas or something you need to keep up on?"

"Dual citizenship," Jefferson stated simply, pointing to himself then Deacon with a proud smile, as if he'd even had anything to do with it. His mom had probably done it for them both. I shook my head. "Well, get out of my way. I need to get some sleep before I go to work tomorrow."

I stepped up to Jefferson, waiting for him to move. It was difficult to intimidate him when I could barely see over his shoulder. Being short was the worst.

Slowly, he leaned down so that we were face to face, his large eyes locked on mine and his lips still curled up in a smile.

"You know, if you'd let me set up cameras at your place like I suggested, I wouldn't have to worry about the two of you all alone over there," he whispered. "Or I could check for monsters under your bed." And at that suggestion he finally stepped out of my way, leaving me to wonder how he hadn't been committed yet. He had to have a couple of screws loose.

"Do you want some coffee or something?" Deacon asked behind me.

"It's three in the morning," Brighton said apologetically, following me out of the apartment and leaving the Parrish boys to do whatever it was they did in that place. They must have done something with all the free time that being unemployed offered. It wasn't like they were reviewing tapes like they should have been.

"Unbelievable." I sighed, closing our front door and dropping my coat on the ground.

Brighton quickly picked it up and hung it in the closet. She was a bit of a neat freak.

"I'm not his mother. I can't make his bed and pay his rent for him," I said incredulously, stripping off wet articles of clothing as I walked down the hallway to my room. My soaked twenties dress emitted a dull plop as it hit the floor.

"Leave it," I called over my shoulder to Brighton, who was still trying to pick up after me. "I'll get them in the morning."

I sat on my bed and created a snug little cocoon out of my quilt. "He's like a child."

Brighton perched on the edge of my bed, rubbing my quilted arm sympathetically. "They both are."

She looked like a blonde angel despite being waterlogged and exhausted. I just looked like a spiky-haired drowned rat, and somehow managed to look pale despite my naturally dark coloring.

It was infuriating.

We both sat there for a moment, having a wordless pity party over the fact that we had picked the most difficult friends in the world.

"They really are going to get kicked out of their apartment," I finally said. "I couldn't handle living with them full time. Please fix it, Brighton."

"I'll talk to Deacon in the morning before work," she promised, giving my arm one last reassuring squeeze before getting up to leave.

"Thanks."

"You try to get some sleep. No matter what you say, those boys are going to make us go investigating tomorrow."

I nodded my head somberly, giving in to my dramatic side and letting my lips pout a bit. Brighton rolled her eyes at me and closed the door, engulfing me in darkness.

It took a moment for my eyes to adjust, and even though I was exhausted and needed to wake up for work in just four hours, I let the night's investigation replay in my mind. Although I felt completely justified in my diva moment, I still couldn't help but worry that I'd botched an opportunity to finally have a successful investigation. Before Jefferson had ruined my attempt at connecting with whatever spirits might be lurking at the old bar, the shadow detector had gone off just one room from where I had been standing. I could almost hear it beeping in my empty room over the sound of the rain hitting my window.

An involuntary shiver crept through my body. No matter how excited I was to catch evidence of the paranormal, it was always a little unnerving to think that some unseen thing could be in the room with me at any given moment.

I pulled my quilt tighter around me and let my brown eyes roam the darkened room. Of course, everything looked like a human shape in the dark—my desk chair, a coat hanging on my closet doorknob, and some large dark object in the corner that I couldn't quite identify. My eyes stayed locked on the unidentifiable mass, and I held my breath without really meaning to.

The slightly skewed nature of the shadow reminded me of Jefferson and his creepy head tilt, and suddenly I was on my feet, running across the hardwood floor and flipping on my light switch.

A robe.

My robe on one of Jefferson's stupid camera tripods that I told him to stop leaving in my room. He left his stuff everywhere after an investigation, no matter how many times I scolded him about it. Although I guess it could have been worse. It could have been an actual camera and not just a tripod.

I really was his mother.

I pulled the robe off and tossed it on the ground with the rest of my clothes, walked back over to my bed, and sat down, grabbing my quilt once more and wrapping it around myself. Heaving a deep sigh and getting a grip on my shot nerves, I glanced at my nightstand only to notice something that hadn't been there only moments before.

A single key sat on the dark wood, shining in the semi-darkness. It wouldn't have been such an unusual thing, had it not been my mail key that was normally secured on my key ring and buried in my disaster of a purse.

I looked at it sideways and picked it up suspiciously, thinking it must have been Brighton's and deciding there was an easy way to get to the bottom of this particular mystery.

I dumped my entire purse over, spilling the contents on my quilt and rifling through my things. What I found left me breathless and slightly stunned. My mail key was missing from my key ring, but that hardly seemed important when compared to the envelope that had somehow appeared in my purse.

The envelope that had my name on it.

CHAPTER 2

My initial reaction should have been one of fear or shock. Instead, the only thought running through my head was, "Was someone just in my room while I was running around in rain-soaked underwear?"

Suddenly self-conscious, I grabbed a tank top and some shorts off my floor and pulled them on, looking over my shoulder every few seconds. My eyes darted around every dark corner of my room, but as little sense as it made, I was alone. I supposed the letter could have been placed in my purse while I was investigating, but I had dug through it on the way home, so it seemed like I would have seen it before then.

Goose bumps sprang up over my skin, though that might have had something to do with my poor choice of clothing on a rainy night. In my defense, I had grabbed the closest articles of clothing I could find. I wasn't going to be picky when I thought some creeper was watching me in my underwear.

When I was completely satisfied that I was alone, I sat back down on the bed—or rather, I jumped onto it, not wanting to get my feet too close to that unsettling space between the bed and the floor. I was still unnerved, but I was more curious about what was in the envelope that had mysteriously appeared in my purse. The handwriting on the heavy cream-colored envelope was loopy and well penned—something I never would have been able to do with my second grader handwriting.

I slipped my fingernail under the flap and slowly tore it open, trying to remember how long ago that whole anthrax scare had gone down. I had the letter pinched between my finger and thumb, when a loud knock on the front door tore me from my reverie.

Still holding the envelope and letter it contained, I opened my door to see Brighton poking her head out of her own room, looking rumpled and sleepy already. She had the unique gift of falling asleep in a matter of seconds no matter where she was, while I was a notorious insomniac.

"Who is it?" she asked, as if I would magically know the answer.

I shrugged and made my way down the hall to our front door, opening it without checking the peephole.

Jefferson leaned against the door frame, still wearing his vest, tie, and high top converse, and still completely soaked. I shivered just looking at him. He wore a grave expression, although with him, it was always difficult to tell. His face just looked like that most of the time. His eyes darted down to my bare legs for a split second, just long enough for me to realize I should have been wearing longer shorts.

Deacon stood behind him, wearing an old T-shirt and pajama pants, and with his skin looking even paler than normal.

"Are you guys okay?" I asked.

"What is that?" Jefferson asked, nodding to the envelope I hadn't realized I was still clutching.

"I don't know. I haven't had a chance to look at it yet," I answered, furrowing my brow at him.

"Then what is this?" he asked, pulling an identical envelope from his pocket with the name "Jefferson" written across the front.

"You got one too?" I was getting more and more confused and intrigued by the second.

Deacon wordlessly held up his own envelope behind his cousin, pushing his glasses up his nose with his free hand.

"Brighton, did you get one?" I asked over my shoulder, searching my roommate's hands but seeing nothing there.

"She probably fell asleep before noticing," Jefferson said dryly. "If you'd just let me set up security cameras in this place like I asked, we'd know where these came from."

I didn't bother telling Jefferson why him setting up cameras in our apartment was beyond the realm of normalcy. He wouldn't understand anyway.

"I'll go check," she said excitedly, running into her room. "Where will it be?"

"Try your purse, that's where mine was." I looked questioningly at Jefferson.

"Coat pocket," he said.

"Duffle bag I keep the cords in," Deacon added, flicking his own envelope with his fingers.

"I got one!" Brighton called, emerging from her room triumphantly and grasping her own cream-colored envelope.

The Parrish boys entered our apartment and we all sat around the coffee table in silence for a moment.

"You guys haven't opened yours yet?" I asked, to which both boys shook their heads. "What made you think we'd gotten them too?"

"Jefferson and I both get mysterious envelopes that somehow appeared on our person?" Deacon said skeptically. "How could that not have something to do with our weird little hobby?"

"Or someone is just playing a prank on us," I said, trying to sound lighthearted and failing miserably.

Jefferson didn't respond, but gave me a look that said that was the stupidest explanation he'd ever heard, his owl eyes extremely expressive in the dim apartment.

"Obviously the only thing we can do is open them to find out what they say," Brighton said, clutching her envelope in one hand and her inhaler in the other.

Jefferson nodded at me, wordlessly urging me to open mine first and making me uncomfortably aware of the fact that he had been staring at me this whole time. I took a deep breath and pulled the letter out of the envelope, looking around the room at my odd group of friends before reading aloud.

"To the Parrish Society."

I stopped reading abruptly and took a moment to look indignantly at Jefferson.

"We are not calling ourselves the Parrish Society," I said with a note of finality.

"Don't look at me," he shrugged. "I wanted it to be the Parrish Paranormal Investigators. The Parrish Society sounds like a funeral home or a cult."

"Or a combination of the two," Deacon put in, sitting as close to Brighton as he possibly could without actually sitting in her lap. "If the shoe fits," she said with a raise of her eyebrows and an amused grin.

I shook my head at them, internally vowing I'd return to the subject of this awful group name after I'd read the entire letter.

"After observing your activities of late, I have become painfully aware of two facts," I read, unnerved by the fact that someone had apparently been watching us. "The first is that you are terribly short on money and could use a boost in your current financial situation."

"Oh, I like this guy already," Brighton said.

"Guy?" I asked, raising my eyebrow and wanting to think it had been a girl watching us, especially if this person had somehow managed to sneak something into my purse without my knowledge.

"Or girl," she amended with a shrug.

"The second is that you are a group of talented young paranormal investigators whose talent is being vastly underutilized," I read. "I wish to correct both of these failings with a proposition that I pray you will accept."

"Write back and tell him yes," Deacon said immediately.

"You don't even know what he wants," I pointed out.

"I know he wants to give us money to investigate."

"There's no return address," Brighton stated, pointing at her own envelope.

"Finish reading," Jefferson said. His long fingers were pressed together, creating five tall steeples that he rested against his pursed lips.

"I have four different locations around the country, all with a dark past that seems to linger; their histories clinging to the locations themselves like the stains they are."

"Bit dramatic," Deacon said.

I ignored him and continued.

"If you can successfully identify the link between these four locations, utilizing your unique abilities, you will find your financial burdens to be nothing more than a distant memory."

"Done," Deacon said.

"Although the decision is yours to make, I'll assume, based on my own observations, that you will be accepting this job offer. Do not burden yourselves with finding a way to contact me. I'll be in touch with your first location within the next twenty-four hours. Sincerely yours."

"Sincerely yours, who?" Brighton asked.

"That's it," I said distantly. "It just says 'sincerely yours'. There's no signature."

Jefferson wordlessly took out his own letter and let his green eyes flick back and forth across the page.

"Mine says the same thing," he said, sounding a bit disappointed.

"Ditto," Brighton confirmed. Deacon simply nodded as he read his own letter.

"This has to be a joke, right?" I grabbed the blanket that Jefferson held on his lap and wrapped it around my shoulders. It was cold enough with our broken heater without the added chill of a mysterious business proposition.

"How did the letters get to us then, Sadie?" Jefferson asked, his voice sounding a thousand miles away.

"Maybe we just didn't notice them before?" I suggested lamely.

"I put my inhaler in my purse before I went to bed and didn't see anything," Brighton said. "But maybe I missed it?"

We all fell silent once more. It seemed we were all fairly certain the letters had come from nowhere, but the idea was much too ridiculous to comprehend. We were either dealing with a ninja or a ghost, and neither option seemed realistic, even in our line of work.

"Origin of the letters aside," Jefferson said, "Are we taking the job?"

"Who doesn't like a shady business proposition?" Deacon asked, obviously all in.

"We can't just rush in to this," I said, trying to be the voice of reason. "How are we going to afford to take the time off of work? I mean . . . for those of us who still have jobs," I added, giving Jefferson a meaningful look. "And if these locations are all over the U.S., how will we afford to travel?"

Jefferson pulled his worn wallet out and thumbed through the scarce money there. Among the crumpled bills I could see a dollar with "You owe me one" written on it. I'd given it to Jefferson ages ago when he'd needed some money, although why he'd kept it instead of spending it like a normal person, I'd never know.

"Pool our resources?" Brighton suggested.

Apparently she was all in as well.

"You mean ask our parents?" I didn't like that idea one bit.

My mom and dad had moved from Portland to Boston to be closer to my sister, and rather than looking like the less-than-favorite child, I decided to stay behind. I wasn't about to call them out of the blue asking for money, even though I knew they'd give it to me if I asked.

"Shawna's always good for a loan, right?" Deacon asked Brighton with a big grin.

"My mom's in North Carolina right now visiting her sister and my cousin," she answered vaguely. "Family emergency."

"Oh," he said, looking at the floor quickly and not asking her to elaborate.

"I just meant putting all our money together . . . but I guess that would turn into Sadie and me pooling our money, since you boys obviously don't have any."

Jefferson, who had been unusually quiet during the whole conversation, exchanged a look with Deacon, his lip curling on one side in a look of disgust.

"What?" I asked, looking back and forth between the two boys.

Deacon raised his eyebrows at Jefferson, who rolled his large eyes and shook his head, his dark curls falling into his eyes. They were having some sort of non-verbal conversation, leaving Brighton and me in the dark.

"What?" I asked again.

Jefferson rubbed the back of his neck, looking very put out.

"I'll get some money for us," he finally said with a deep sigh, his shoulders slumping considerably.

"How?" Brighton asked skeptically.

A grin broke out across Deacon's face, as if he suddenly found the entire situation overly amusing. "He has to talk to his mum."

CHAPTER 3

"Sadie?" a muffled voice called on the other side of the heavy door.

My breath came out in visible puffs in front of me and I closed my eyes against the sound, hoping I could block it out. The cool air danced across my skin, leaving goose bumps wherever it went and helping me to calm down.

A knock thumped, trying to pull me from my moment of peace, but I ignored it.

"Sadie? Did you get locked in there again?"

I emitted a deep exhale that turned into a grunt of frustration. "I'm fine, Steph. I'm just getting some vegetables for Dan," I called, lying through my teeth and figuring I should actually grab the vegetables in question if I wanted to look convincing.

It had been a long day at work, and when things got too overwhelming between the hot kitchen and the angry customers, I'd step into the freezer to cool off for a minute. I knew I still had some flour in my hair from the bag Dan had dropped when he slipped on a puddle I'd "apparently" forgotten to mop up, but I was too tired to dust it out.

Allowing myself one more long-suffering sigh, I grabbed a bag of chopped green peppers and opened the freezer door to see Steph standing there with a big grin on her face.

"Someone left something for you at the host's podium," she said brightly.

"A good something or a bad something?" I asked hesitantly. It was either a tip (unlikely) or a letter of complaint from the man I'd accidentally spilled soda all over.

Yeah . . . it had been that kind of day.

My feet hurt, my back ached, and I was only twenty minutes from going home to be bothered by two overgrown children about ghosts. Not that I minded the ghosts part—the overgrown children part was the kicker.

"A letter," she answered with an air of scandal, raising her eyebrows at me and handing the letter over before grabbing the peppers and turning to leave.

The envelope was thick and cream-colored, just like it had been yesterday. And just as before, it held only my name on the front. Suddenly I didn't need to sit in the walk-in freezer to feel cold. This letter was all it took.

"Steph, who left the letter?" I asked, holding my breath.

"I asked the hostess but she said it was just sitting on the podium. She must have missed whoever dropped it off," she said as she left, sounding incredibly nonchalant about something we never encountered.

I ripped the envelope open but stopped short of pulling the letter out.

"Should I wait for everyone else?" I wondered aloud, trying to ignore the eerie fact that our mysterious benefactor knew where and when I worked, and still hadn't been seen by anyone.

Shaking my head to clear my thoughts, I pulled the letter out, discarding the envelope in the garbage can. I took a breath to steady my nerves before looking over the note.

"Southampton, England. May 27th, 1936."

I read it again, raising an eyebrow at the lack of information. If this person wanted us to accept their offer, they weren't exactly doing a very good job with the whole "work orientation" thing.

I racked my brain, trying to find what this ambiguous clue meant. It didn't seem like a historically important date from what little information I remembered from my history classes.

"You can't come back here," I heard Steph calling in a panic, snapping me out of my thoughts.

"Sadie!" Brighton said, sprinting around the corner and almost tripping in her heels.

Jefferson and Deacon were right behind her, Deacon looking excited and Jefferson looking like his normal intense self.

"Did you get one?" she asked, panting and clutching her own envelope against her hot pink blouse.

"Yeah, but I have no idea what it means." I grabbed Brighton's wrist and directed them out the back door so Steph didn't have a panic attack.

It was rainy in the alleyway, but at least we'd be able to talk in private and not sound like a bunch of nut jobs to any eavesdropping restaurant workers.

"Did you get our funding?" I asked Jefferson, who had his chin tilted toward his chest so that he was looking up at me through his eyelashes.

He turned his head to the side and cracked his neck loudly before answering, not caring that the longer he took to answer a simple question, the longer we'd be standing out in the rain in a dirty alleyway.

"I acquired sufficient monetary resources," he answered in his thick British accent, talking like a legal disclaimer so that we wouldn't press him further on the matter.

That was fine with me.

"I've already gotten work off." Brighton beamed, even though she probably shouldn't have been so excited about missing work for something that would most likely leave us broke.

Or more broke than we already were, I guess.

"Me too," Jefferson said, looking over at me and letting his lips pull up into a smirk.

Funny.

"I guess this means we're really doing this," I said, not sure how I felt about that fact. "Do we have any idea what this first clue means, though?"

Brighton and Jefferson both wordlessly pointed to Deacon, who looked proud of himself.

"The Queen Mary," he stated simply, wiping his hands on his gray T-shirt.

I let my mouth open in a look of shock. The Queen Mary was kind of the golden goose of paranormal investigation, or at least it was to me. Living in Oregon, I was so close to it, but had never gotten the chance to actually visit the ship that was supposed to be haunted. This new job wasn't looking so bad all of a sudden.

"That's not even that far!" I exclaimed.

"We're not going to the Queen Mary," Jefferson interrupted, sounding like I had missed something obvious.

"What are you talking about?"

"Jefferson seems to think the clue is referring to the port the ship originally sailed to when it departed from England on May 27th, 1936."

"In New York," he confirmed with a slow nod.

"That's ridiculous," I told him, wondering how he could ever think that. "It's obviously referring to the ship itself, which is in Long Beach, California, so that's where we'll be going."

"You're not the group leader," he said.

"You're not the group leader either," I snapped, tired of him trying to pull nonexistent rank.

"It is called the Parrish Society," he stated evenly with a grin, trying to get under my skin.

"Just because a letter called us that doesn't mean it's our official name."

"Yeah," Deacon said, surprising me with his agreement. "Besides, if we're the Parrish Society, I could be the leader."

"We are not calling ourselves the Parrish Society," I said. "And we're going to Long Beach."

"When did she get so bossy?" Deacon asked Brighton.

"Actually, Sadie," she began, "I kind of agree with Jefferson. I think the clue might be referring to the port in New York."

I narrowed my eyes at Brighton for her disregard of our unspoken "never agree with a Parrish" rule.

"Sadie, are you going to collect your tips before you clock out?" Steph called out the back door, saving Brighton from my glare.

"Since you guys drove all the way down here, you might as well stick around and give me a ride home," I said, figuring we could revisit this discussion later—after I gave Brighton an extensive lecture about agreeing with Jefferson.

I narrowed my eyes at the Parrish in question before walking back toward the restaurant.

"Go ask for time off," Jefferson said. "We're leaving for New York tomorrow."

~

That night, I lay in bed with my eyes trained on the ceiling, my normal insomnia making it impossible to sleep despite an exhausting day at work. Somehow I'd managed to take the next two weeks off of work, though I could tell my manager wasn't happy about it, and part of me worried I wouldn't actually have a job when I got back.

And all because of a stupid letter that we probably shouldn't be trusting in the first place.

It wasn't good when your only proof of something's validity was the fact that you couldn't prove where it had come from. That didn't exactly bode well.

My suitcase sat at the foot of my bed and I played with a loose string on my quilt, balling it up in my fingers and then untangling it, only to repeat the action again and again. Something wasn't sitting right with me. Insomnia kept me up at night, but it didn't give me the sinking feeling in my stomach that I couldn't quite get rid of.

New York wasn't right. I was sure of it. We were supposed to investigate the actual Queen Mary in Long Beach, although I wasn't sure how to convince Jefferson and Brighton of that, since they knew how much I'd always wanted to investigate that location. If I said anything, they would just think I was making excuses to see the amazing and unsettling ship.

A creak in the floorboards startled me, and I sat bolt upright in bed, looking around the room like I had the night before. Tonight I didn't see anything out of the ordinary, but my nerves wouldn't let me lie back down and try to sleep. I needed to do some research of my own to convince my friends that we needed to go to California tomorrow, not New York. The only problem was that Brighton and I had left our laptop in the Parrish boys' apartment so that they could review footage on it.

Pulling an oversized sweater on over my tank top and shorts, I gingerly let my bare feet touch the wood floor in my bedroom, willing myself to stay still for a moment. It was a primal and childish fear to worry about that space underneath your bed, but I always hated planting my feet right in front of it, sure that one day a hand would reach out and grab my ankles. Forcing myself to sit like that for a moment was my own form of therapy—of facing my irrational fear.

After several seconds (and no ghoulish hand grabbing my ankles to pull me violently under the bed), I stood and walked quietly through our apartment, grabbing my key to the boys' apartment on my way out. No matter how much they annoyed me, it was nice having them so close. Maybe "nice" wasn't the word . . . it made things convenient, anyway.

Trying desperately to be quiet, I turned the key in their lock and entered the dark apartment, closing the door and standing still for a moment to let my eyes adjust from the bright lights in the hallway between our apartments. The boys' place was chronically messy and always smelled like cinnamon for some unexplainable reason, but they kept the computer in the living room, so it was relatively easy to find. I picked my way across the hardwood floor—stepping on countless shirts that I hoped were clean—until I reached the desk and started up the computer.

I didn't think it would be all that hard to make a case for myself. After all, why in the world would a ship port be haunted? It made much more sense for the ship itself to be haunted. Pulling up countless search tabs, I tried to find anything helpful.

There were pages and pages of ghost stories from tourists about the Queen Mary: people who claimed to see the footsteps of children in the now empty pool, ghostly figures wandering the long hallways, and sounds of a party that didn't exist. The more I read, the more I was convinced we needed to go to the ship, but I couldn't find anything to make my case against New York.

Trying a different strategy, I looked up the maiden voyage of the ship, hoping it would shed some light on its first destination.

"New York," I whispered into the darkness. The glowing computer screen blinded me and made the rest of the room pitch black and impossible to see. "All it says is New York," I repeated in annoyance. "What port did it sail in to?"

"I'm sure Deacon knows," Jefferson whispered in my ear, so close to me that I wasn't sure how I hadn't heard him breathing before.

I spun around in the desk chair so fast that I bumped heads with him, although my smarting forehead didn't stop me from smacking him across the arm as hard as I could. He backed away from me, mumbling something under his breath and holding his forehead in his large hands.

"What is your problem?" I whispered harshly, angry at his lack of normalcy. "You scared me to death."

"Obviously not," he retorted, pulling up a chair beside me and still rubbing his forehead. "I was just watching you for a while to see what you were up to."

"Why can't you just be normal?" I asked him.

"I'm not the one popping into someone else's apartment at three in the morning without permission."

He had a point.

"Not that this is the first time you've done this," he went on, confusing me to no end.

"What are you on about now?"

"You know, the late night chats you randomly decide to have at the most inappropriate times?" he said.

"Yeah, you must have been dreaming. That's never happened," I promised.

I think I'd know if I stooped to the level of coming to Jefferson for "late night chats," unless I was sleepwalking or something.

"I was looking for a way to prove you wrong," I said primly, resisting the urge to rub my own sore forehead.

"That's kind of a fool's errand," he said, though he rested his elbows on his knees and leaned closer to the computer screen as if he were interested in what I had found.

I noticed, with some surprise, that he was wearing a collared shirt with the sleeves rolled up to his elbows, and slacks. Did he just sleep in his Tim Burton attire? The boy was seriously weird.

"Jefferson, you know the Queen Mary is way more likely our destination than the port it sailed into. It doesn't even make sense for us to travel that far."

"Go on," he said.

Was Jefferson Parrish actually admitting that I might be right? Because letting me go on seemed dangerously close to possibly agreeing with me.

"Let's say I'm wrong about Long Beach," I began, excited to make my case. "Doesn't it make more sense to go there first anyway to see if that's where we're supposed to be instead of driving all the way to New York only to find out we're wrong? California is so much closer."

He stared at me for a long time in the darkness, his huge, unblinking eyes reflecting the computer screen. If I hadn't known any better, I would have thought he had somehow managed to fall asleep with his eyes open. I almost opened my mouth to speak, but he finally blinked and shifted his weight, letting me know he wasn't completely vacant in there.

"If you think that's what's best, Sadie, I trust your opinion," he said.

"Really?" I asked skeptically. "Because that doesn't sound like you."

I knew I was being a brat, but he was always making my life difficult—it was nice to return the favor every once in a while.

"You haven't led us astray before," he said with a shrug. "Besides, I kind of ruined our last investigation when you almost had something. I figure I owe you one."

He was right. He did owe me one. But it was weird to hear him admit it out loud. What had gotten in to him?

"Plus after the incident last week I really owe you one," he said, looking like he didn't think he was at all in the wrong for making himself a key to our apartment, letting himself in, and then putting locks on all of our windows.

Because that was a totally normal neighborly thing to do.

"Okay," I said slowly, and a bit more suspiciously than I had intended.

"You should get some sleep. We have a long day ahead of us," he said, standing to leave. He placed his hand on my shoulder and gave it a quick squeeze before walking away. "And don't forget to turn off the computer. Without jobs, I'm not sure how we'll pay the electricity bill."

I stared straight ahead at his retreating dark form with a puzzled expression, touching my shoulder that he had grabbed and wondering what in the world had just happened.

CHAPTER 4

"I love road trips," Brighton said for the millionth time.

It hadn't bothered me the first time she'd brought it up, but ten hours into our twelve-hour drive, it seemed a bit excessive. Not to mention the fact that being stuck in Brighton's Jeep with the Parrish boys for so long had completely shot my nerves.

At first, the two boys debated the merits of provoking ghosts while investigating versus asking planned-out questions for them to answer. That had quickly escalated into Deacon getting mad at Jefferson and saying that the only reason his mom had given them money was because she liked Deacon (which was a complete lie) and felt bad that he had to live with Jefferson (which was probably true). Eventually, both boys grew tired of arguing and fell asleep in the back seat, with Deacon snoring lightly and Jefferson's head tilting to the side in an extreme angle that made it look like his neck was broken, his limp head bouncing up and down with every bump we drove over.

"They're kind of cute when they're sleeping, aren't they?" Brighton asked, turning around in the passenger's seat to look at the boys. "You know, when they aren't opening their mouths and making you want to kill them? They enjoy picking on you a little too much."

"Just tell Deacon you want to marry him already," I said with a snort.

Brighton grinned and threw a magazine at me which I easily ducked.

"Driving!" I shouted.

"What about you and Jefferson?" she asked, waggling her eyebrows at me conspiratorially.

"Wow. Yeah, that's the last thing on earth that will ever happen," I said emphatically. "Ever!"

"Why?" she asked, as if she even needed to.

"Are you kidding? This isn't rocket science, Brighton. Jefferson is like Sherlock Holmes."

"Sherlock Holmes is sexy," she said, sounding much more like the popular girl she looked like and less like the agoraphobe she was.

"I mean, Jefferson's all about the work. I don't think he even likes girls."

"Well, he doesn't like boys."

"I don't think he likes anyone who's alive," I said. "He likes ghosts. And that's beside the point."

"What is the point, then?" she asked, looking like she was enjoying this conversation way too much.

I wasn't sure what she was getting at. It wasn't like it was a big secret how little Jefferson and I liked each other.

"I can't stand him because he's weird and creepy, and he thinks I'm only good for dressing up in stupid costumes to lure the ghosts out." I wasn't sure why we were even having this conversation. All I was trying to do was make Brighton admit she had a thing for Deacon. "And I'm pretty sure his idea of being romantic is getting a lock of my hair and turning it into a diamond necklace."

"What?" Brighton asked.

"Yeah. He actually asked if I had any qualms about giving him my hair because he, and I quote, 'knows a guy' who can turn it into a diamond."

"Gross."

"That's what I said. So no," I insisted. "There's nothing going on between us."

"Whatever you say, chief," she said with a knowing smile.

"Did you get permission from the people at the Queen Mary to do an investigation for the next two nights?" I asked, changing the subject from the awkward turn it had just taken.

"Yeah, I thought they'd say no since I'm sure they get lots of investigators down there, but they actually gave us a discount on our rooms."

"Really?" I asked.

Jefferson had managed to borrow some money from his mom, but we were still extremely tight on cash. The gas required for the old, less-than-economical 1989 Jeep Wagoneer was enough to drain our money without even considering the hotels we'd need to stay in.

"I mean, they had guidelines of where we could and couldn't go, but they were actually really nice about the whole thing," she said happily, much too awake for how long we'd been driving. "Since we saved so much money on the rooms, I got four separate ones in different parts of the ship. I figured we could cover more ground if we weren't all right next to each other."

Even though I knew she was right, my stomach sank at the thought of sleeping on the Queen Mary by myself for two nights. I wasn't all that scared of ghosts during investigations, but trying to sleep alone in a haunted place was a whole different story.

"I guess we should set up cameras in our rooms while we're sleeping," I said, swallowing hard. "Just in case?"

"Yeah, I'll basically be sleeping with my inhaler the whole time," she said, somewhere between panic and excitement. "But how amazing is it that we actually get to investigate the Queen Mary?"

"It's a dream come true," I admitted. "Although I still wish there was some way to find out who sent those letters. Are we nuts for going on this trip just because we got random letters from some random person?"

"Honestly?" she said. "I think we just needed an excuse to do a massive investigation. If the letters hadn't come, we would have found some other reason. This way we have a fun mystery to solve on top of the investigation."

"That's one way to look at it."

Brighton's levity didn't silence my fears, but it did stop me from brainstorming with her over where the letters could have possibly come from and how we were supposed to get the rest of our clues.

"We should probably paint our Jeep green and blue," she said randomly, after a long silence that left me suddenly feeling tired.

"Not funny," I responded, any further arguments about making us more like Mystery Inc. cut off by a massive yawn.

Brighton nudged me with her elbow. "Why don't you pull over and I'll drive the rest of the way."

"I'm fine," I lied, my eyes burning from exhaustion.

"Well, then stop at this gas station, because I have to pee."

I knew she was lying, but I obliged, knowing she could whine very convincingly when she wanted something.

"You should grab a soda or something while I'm in the bathroom," she said, her voice sounding unnatural.

I laughed. "I can tell why they leave the acting to me on these investigations. You can drive. I won't fight you."

"Oh good, we're switching things up," Deacon suddenly said from the backseat. He got out of the car and waited by the passenger's side door.

When had he woken up?

I looked over at Brighton with an exasperated exhale before realizing that if she was driving and Deacon was in the front seat, I'd be in the back with the long-limbed Jefferson, unlikely to get any leg room to myself. He looked like a spider all crumpled up in the tiny back seat.

"I take it back. I want to keep driving," I said quickly.

The look Brighton was giving me told me that my protests were futile.

I sighed deeply and resigned myself to my fate, taking my place in the back seat and sitting as close to the window as I could. Jefferson had somehow managed to sleep through our entire stop, and his head was now slowly drooping closer and closer to my shoulder. I'd wake him up before I let that happen.

Smashed against the window with my chin resting in my palm, I wondered how I'd gotten suckered into this entire trip and hoped it wouldn't prove to be a huge waste of time.

We'd seriously need to step up our game if we wanted to find what we were looking for.

~

"We're here!" Brighton and Deacon shouted in unison, waking me with a jolt.

My eyes snapped open and it took a minute for me to remember where I was; the darkened Jeep proved to be more disorienting than I would have thought.

"I don't make a very good pillow," Jefferson said right beside me, and I instantly realized—much to my mortification—that I had been sleeping on his shoulder.

At least he was nicer than me, I guess.

"You know . . . being so boney and all?" he elaborated. "Not that I minded."

I sat up quickly and rubbed the side of my face, feeling the indent of his sleeve seam there.

"Sorry," I mumbled.

At least in the dark he wouldn't be able to see how red my face was.

"Look at it," Brighton said excitedly, pointing out the front window at the large ship in front of us.

The Queen Mary was about ten times bigger than I had imagined it, and ten times more oddly placed. Wedged in downtown Long Beach, it seemed uncomfortable with the restaurants just across the bay and the city all around us. Everything in Long Beach was too modern to house this historic ship.

A string of lights illuminated the top of the smokestacks and ran down to the tip of the ship, silhouetting our first amazing location in a magical way. I could feel my heart picking up the pace a bit, and suddenly I wasn't worried that I'd be too tired to do some investigating tonight. I couldn't wait to see what mysteries were lurking inside.

"I guess we'll check in and then start setting up?" I asked excitedly, my exhaustion completely gone.

"We're investigating tonight?" Brighton asked, her voice taking on the whiny quality that had threatened to escape earlier.

"Of course we are," Jefferson said, looking over at me with an expression of disbelief.

It was always scary when I agreed with one of the Parrish boys. Still, if doing so meant I got to investigate on the Queen Mary tonight, I'd take it.

"If we don't do it tonight, we'll only have one night left," I said, not understanding how Brighton could even think of sleep right now.

"Being so tired, would it even be worth it to set up tonight? We might miss important evidence if we're sleepy," Deacon said, glancing at Brighton and obviously hoping to score some brownie points with the not-so-secret love of his life.

Just telling both of them that they liked each other would save me a lot of fights like this where Deacon would side with Brighton to impress her and make my life infinitely more difficult.

"We might miss evidence if we're tired while investigating tonight," Jefferson began, and sadly enough, I knew exactly where he was going.

"But we'll definitely miss evidence if we don't investigate at all." I wanted to gag over the fact that I had just completed his sentence.

Now Brighton really wouldn't let up on my non-existent crush.

She squinted her eyes and nodded her head a few times, probably trying to find some way out of this investigation and into a warm bed. In the end, her excitement over our mystery must have won out because she said, "I'll give you two hours."

CHAPTER 5

"Do these lights have to be on?" I asked the empty hallway, feeling underwhelmed by the lack of creepiness in this coveted location.

"It's still a hotel, Sadie. They have to keep the hallway lights on all the time," Brighton said in my earpiece, stationed safely in her hotel room with a pile of computers linked to our cameras.

The lack of fear I felt might have also had something to do with the fact that I knew Brighton was seeing a live feed of the camera I held. Nothing too bad could happen to me while I had someone else with me virtually.

The long hallways of the ship, while too well-lit for my taste, were impressive to see. From my position at the back of the ship, I could see all the way to the front, the hallway bowing down in the middle, then gradually rising back up to form a cupped shape. The maroon carpet muffled my footfalls as I walked toward a staircase, glad that the ship was so empty on a weekday; it wouldn't have been fun to try to explain my old-fashioned attire to one of the hotel guests.

At least vintage was back in style, right?

And with the vast amount of space we needed to cover on the ship, it was nice that Jefferson, Deacon, and I could all investigate simultaneously. In most cases, we were investigating a small home or building, and more than one person at a time inside would mean too many footsteps, voices, and unidentified noises that we'd have to throw out as tainted evidence. But in large locations like the Queen Mary, we could have all three of us out at once, connected to each other via earpieces.

It was fantastic.

Holding my handheld camera steady in one hand and clutching my flashlight (that I sadly didn't need) in the other, I walked down the staircase, hoping the lower I went on the ship, the more I'd find.

"This is Sadie, on the Queen Mary. It's about 2:30 in the morning on September third. I'm just entering the C deck," I said, tagging the camera footage so we'd have some sort of reference when we went back to review.

"R deck," Jefferson corrected in my earpiece.

"What?" I wondered how he knew where I was, and why he seemed to think R came after B in the alphabet.

"It's not called C deck anymore. It's R deck now," he said.

I would have argued with him but it was pointless to argue with a Parrish. Even if they were wrong, they wouldn't let up until you gave in to their opinion.

I could hear Brighton typing away on her computer from her room that I'd already forgotten how to get back to.

"He's right," she said.

Traitor.

"Fine," I said. "This is Sadie, on the R deck. Making my way toward the front of the ship."

"The bow," Jefferson corrected.

"Actually I prefer stem," Deacon said.

"You mean stern?" Brighton asked.

"No, I mean stem."

"Okay, you guys seriously need to shut it. I can't concentrate with so many people talking in my ear," I said, shaking my head to clear the voices.

"Go ahead Sadie, take the earpiece out if it bothers you," Jefferson challenged and I could hear the grin in his voice.

The boys would never let me live down the only time I'd taken my earpiece out because I was frustrated with their banter. I'd ended up getting lost in the old schoolhouse we were investigating and was too scared to find my way back. It took an hour for Jefferson to come find me, though I suspected it was because he hadn't really been looking.

"I'll refrain this time," I said. "But only because this place is like a maze."

Brighton snorted but didn't comment. It was easy for her to be all smug when she was safe in her room. Somehow I didn't think she'd fare quite as well if she was forced to walk the halls of the Queen Mary by herself.

"Don't you have some Beethoven to be listening to, Jefferson?" I asked, hoping I could silence him.

"Already done," he answered shortly.

Jefferson insisted on listening to Beethoven's Symphony No. 7 in A Major before every investigation to get him pumped. Personally, I didn't see how that song could pump anyone up, but who was I to argue?

"Pity," I said as I continued to descend deeper within the ship.

At the bottom of the staircase, I was met by two beautiful gold-clad double doors. The swirling designs looked like vines, growing right up the entrance, with pictures in the middle of each swirl.

Clutching my camera and flashlight in the same hand, I let my free hand trace the pictures gently, the cold metal reminding me of just how real this place was, and how amazing it was that I was actually investigating the Queen Mary. My fingers wandered down the gold curves until they curled around the long door handle.

"This is Sadie, about to enter the pool area," I said almost reverently. The pool was the most active spot on the ship, where hundreds of people had claimed to hear children playing.

"Uh, Sadie," Brighton began, but I ignored her, pulling the heavy door with force.

Unfortunately, it didn't even budge.

Thinking I must have tried to open it the wrong way, I pushed my weight against it, hoping it would move this time. It didn't so much as shift.

"I can't get in," I said.

"That's what I was going to tell you," Brighton said. "The pool is one of the off-limits places."

"Wait, what?" I asked, not understanding that logic at all. "How are we supposed to do a paranormal investigation if we can't even investigate the most active spot on the ship?"

I turned away from the doors and looked around for another way in.

"It's a liability," Brighton said. "The pool doesn't have any water in it. They can't have random people tromping around it in the dark. What if you fell in and broke your neck?"

"That's ridiculous," I said, not willing to have my plans thwarted by a few legal technicalities like possible death or dismemberment. "I'm finding a way in."

"Here we go," Deacon said, the exasperation thick in his voice.

I very blatantly ignored him and made my way around the misnamed "R Deck," searching for any way in. There was no way I'd come all this way only to miss an opportunity to explore the one space I'd always dreamed of seeing.

"This is Jefferson on B deck. September third, at about a quarter to three."

It always took a bit of getting used to, suddenly hearing someone talking in your ear when you were completely alone in a scary space. In a way, it made the experience less frightening. Knowing one of the Parrish boys could begin speaking at any moment meant I was less startled by any unexpected sounds I encountered during our investigations.

Trying to ignore Jefferson, I continued to search for a way in to the one location I simply had to see.

It didn't seem to matter how determined I was though, no matter where I looked, every door that led to the pool area was locked.

"I think I found something," Jefferson said suddenly, sounding much more enthusiastic than I had ever heard him.

"What?" we all asked from our various locations around the ship.

"Voices," he said.

I instantly forgot about my previous mission. "I'll be right there."

~

Because of the labyrinthine nature of the ship, it took me a good ten minutes to make my way back to Brighton's room where we were all meeting. I was the last one to enter the small cabin and when I did, I forgot all about looking at Jefferson's evidence.

"You have a window?" I asked.

I had been gypped on the room selection. It was a small porthole that could barely count as a window. Still, it was much better than the tiny, windowless cabin in the middle of the ship that I was staying in. A room with no windows brought out the closet claustrophobic in me.

"That's nothing," she said with a smug grin. "You should see my bathroom."

I let out an indignant sound as I turned on my heel and walked the two steps it took me to get to her bathroom in the minute cabin.

"Bloody women," Jefferson muttered. He was hunched over one of the computers with his headphones on, trying to find whatever voices he'd heard earlier.

"This is so much nicer than my room," I said. "You have an option for salt water in your shower?"

"Those don't work anymore," she answered with a giggle. "They just keep those old knobs on there for looks. Besides, I wouldn't want to shower in whatever salt water is surrounding this boat."

"Can you imagine?" Deacon asked, perched on the bed beside Brighton. "All that water sitting stagnant under the ship for who knows how long? You'd probably get botulism showering in that."

He gave a little shudder at the thought, even though I wasn't so sure you could get botulism from a shower.

"Even if the salt water knobs don't work, your room is way fancier than mine," I said, taking in the original woodwork and gold embossed details of the cabin.

"Shouldn't have made me pick the rooms," she said, throwing me a quick wink. "I made sure mine was in the most structurally sound part of the ship. No one's falling through *this* floor."

"I found it," Jefferson cut in.

I was sure he hadn't heard a single word of our conversation. He was in the zone.

Unplugging the headphones from the computer, he alienated the section of audio, looped it, and cued it up for us.

"This is Jefferson on B deck. September third, at about a quarter to three," his recorded voice said, instantly bringing me back to that space outside of the pool.

"I didn't have a camera with me," he said as we listened. "Just the audio recorder."

I heard a few muffled footfalls on the carpet over the ambient sounds that suddenly seemed deafening. How could a lack of noise be so grating to the ear?

"I stopped right there," he narrated, his large eyes focused on the wall. "And in a second you'll hear it."

Over the constant hum of the recording, I heard what sounded like glasses clinking. I looked over at Jefferson, who met my eyes and nodded, indicating he'd heard it too, and while I looked down to concentrate on the rest of the recording, he kept his eyes locked on me. Making sure I heard the voice, I guessed.

There was the sound of fabric rubbing against the microphone, and a split second later a low and almost inaudible sentence could be heard.

"No way!" Brighton exclaimed. "Play it again."

Jefferson didn't need to be told twice. He immediately cued up the recording to the exact place the sentence began, this time closing his eyes as he listened.

There was no mistaking the fact that the cadence and tone of the sound was a spoken sentence, but it was nearly impossible to decipher what it was saying.

"I can't make it out." Deacon squinted his eyes through his glasses, as if somehow that would help him. "One more time, mate." Jefferson played the clip again, this time with all of us holding our breath as we listened, the volume turned up so loud that the ambient sound hurt my ears. The beginning of the sentence was practically a lost cause, but the last four syllables gave me hope and I immediately brought my finger up to my lips, not wanting the group to say anything while I picked the phrase out of the jumble of words. I could almost make it out.

"Meeting her there?" I asked.

"Meeting her there," Brighton repeated as Jefferson played the recording again.

"Or we might be grasping at straws," Deacon said. "And it's just something else."

"I shouldn't have said anything," I said guiltily. "That was probably the worst thing I could have done because now that's all you'll hear when you listen to the clip."

"But that's not a problem if you're right." Brighton was practically beaming. "I can't believe we've been on this ship for two hours and we've already gotten a solid EVP!"

"And you wanted to go to bed," I said.

"You were right, I was wrong," Brighton said.

"You're the best, we're the worst," Deacon added.

"You're smart, I'm dumb," Brighton continued, reciting the same bit I'd heard a million times before.

"You're—"

"Okay, apology accepted," I interrupted, knowing the two of them could go on like that forever.

"And just for those who might not know . . . EVP is . . ." Deacon let his words trail off.

"You seriously need to learn the lingo if we're going to keep you on this team," I said. "Electronic voice phenomenon."

"We really caught evidence," Jefferson said quietly, looking awestruck. "We really did it. We found something."

He looked over at us and let out a short laugh, the smile lingering on his lips. Plugging the headphones back in, he pushed play on the computer and closed his eyes, listening to our discovery over and over again.

"He's like a kid on Christmas," I said, shaking my head.

It was the happiest I'd ever seen Jefferson.

"This doesn't really help us figure out where we're supposed to go next, but we have another entire night here to gather more evidence." Brighton pulled her knees up to her chest, looking quite proud of our accomplishment. "And tomorrow night we'll have hours and hours to investigate."

"Not to mention setting up the cameras in our rooms tonight," Deacon added.

"Oh . . . right," I said, almost forgetting for a moment that I'd be sleeping in my creepy windowless room alone.

Odds were I wasn't going to be doing much sleeping, no matter how tired I was from the long drive from Portland and the investigation.

"We only have like, four hours, until the sun comes up," Brighton said. "You'll be fine."

Again, it was easy for her to say, in her nice fancy room.

"I don't have windows in my room," I reminded her. "It'll be pitch black in there at noon." I was trying to act put out, but in all honesty, I was scared out of my mind.

"Oy," Deacon said, hitting his cousin on the arm and bringing him out of his apparent state of ecstasy.

"What?" Jefferson asked, looking genuinely confused, as if we had just woken him from a nap.

"We need to sleep," Brighton said. "And you guys are all sitting on my bed."

Deacon and I stood to leave, but Jefferson continued to sit there with the headphones in his hand, looking like someone had just run over his puppy.

"But the sound clip . . ."

"It'll be there in the morning, sweetie," Brighton said, patting his shoulder sympathetically and slowly taking the headphones from his fingers.

"I'm sure I can figure out the rest of the sentence if you just give me a minute," he tried again, almost pleading.

It was like watching a little kid attempting to get out of bedtime.

"We have a long day ahead of us." I grabbed his hand and pulled him up off the bed. "And you need to leave Brighton alone so she can get some sleep. You know how she gets when she's tired."

"I heard that," she said, though she was already falling back into her pile of fluffy pillows with a smile on her face.

"But the tape," he tried again, furrowing his brow in a way that was actually pretty adorable.

Not that I would ever admit that to anyone.

"Come on," I said, still holding his hand and pulling him out of the cabin. "Don't forget to set up your camera," I called to Brighton before closing the door and finally releasing Jefferson.

"What deck are you on, Sadie?" Deacon asked. "I'll be a gentleman and walk you to your room." He grinned at me with the same goofy grin he usually wore.

"I'm on B deck," I told him, widening my eyes theatrically. "You know, the one where our awesome group found a voice?"

"And caught it on tape," he added, sounding slightly less skeptical. "But forget that. I'm on this level. You can walk yourself down."

"You're so gallant, Deacon," I said, sarcastically. "I'm sure Jefferson would be happy to go with you, since he's also on B deck."

I looked over at the other Parrish boy, who seemed dazed by our discovery. He still wasn't listening to a word we said. He just stood there pulling on his suspenders and staring off into space.

"On second thought, you might have to walk him to *his* room. I'm not sure he even knows where he is right now."

"Great." I sighed. "Night, Deacon."

"Night, Sadie." He gave me an apologetic look and parted ways at the staircase.

"Come on, you useless boy." I grabbed Jefferson's hand once more and led him down the staircase to the empty B deck, feeling like the silence was eerie, no matter how good it was for our investigations.

"What room are you in?" I asked him, looking at the plaque on the wall that listed the room numbers.

"Huh?" he asked, raising an eyebrow at me as if he just realized I was there.

"Never mind." I pulled his room key from his vest pocket and located the number on it. There was no way I'd get any help from him tonight. He was too excited about our discovery. I was excited too, of course; I just happened to be human and couldn't run on zero sleep after a long drive.

I practically dumped him in front of his room, handing him the key card and giving him a skeptical look.

"You do remember how to use this, right?" I asked.

"Funny," he said after an unnaturally long pause. "I'm an expert with keys. Hence how it was laughably easy for me to get one to your apartment."

I ignored his statement, like I usually did.

"I'm just down the hall if you need me," I said, turning to leave and trying to focus on how tired I was, rather than how scared I was to be in my hotel room alone.

"Sadie?" Jefferson asked, stopping me before I'd gotten far.

"Yeah?"

"We actually did it," he said, the smile back on his face. "We found evidence."

I smiled over at him. I knew he was frustrating and annoying most of the time, but I just couldn't help it—his excitement was infectious.

"We're kind of great, huh?" he asked, still smiling.

"Yeah, Jefferson," I said. "We kind of are."

CHAPTER 6

It was amazing how loud silence could be.

Compared to the average person, I was pretty tough when it came to facing paranormal activity. I mean, I'd made it my hobby to willingly walk into haunted locations and ask ghosts to come talk to me. But lying in bed with my covers pulled up to my eyes, I was feeling a lot less tough than I wanted to now that I was without the earpiece that linked me to my friends.

My room was pitch black except for the small flashing red light on the camera I had aimed at my bed. When it blinked on for just a second, I could briefly see my room in the dim crimson glow, the light illuminating the darkest corners.

Since I couldn't seem to sleep, I somehow ended up counting seconds between flashes of light. It usually ran about ten seconds from blink to blink, and I found myself holding my breath in those ten seconds of darkness, just waiting for that split second of illumination to reassure me there was nothing in my room.

The worst part of the entire situation was that my being terrified was being caught on camera at that very moment, so I had to at least pretend like I wasn't scared out of my mind. I also had to think about how exhausted I would be tomorrow if I didn't get any sleep tonight. We had a full night of investigating ahead of us, and knowing the Parrish boys, they'd want to scope things out during the day as well, which meant I'd get absolutely no sleep.

"I could listen to music," I whispered to the dark room. Maybe putting my headphones in would help me sleep.

At least then I wouldn't have to just lie there and wait for the sounds of a ghostly laugh or creaking floorboard.

I leaned over and let my hand roam over the nightstand, feeling for my purse. The bed sheets ruffled as I moved, but the sound was magnified in the crushing silence of the room. When I finally made contact with my monstrously big purse, I let my fingers explore the bottomless interior until I successfully pulled my phone and headphones from the mess.

I sighed deeply, wishing I wasn't such a baby, and rolled back over in bed, staring at the indistinguishable ceiling. I turned the phone on, the screen practically blinding me in the darkness as I scrolled through playlists, looking for a song. Somehow, my mellow sleep mix didn't seem like it would do the trick tonight. I'd need something a bit louder; something that would drown out the nonexistent noises I would invent. Maybe some Panic! at the Disco.

Just as my finger hovered over my favorite band's name, I heard something—a sigh that materialized in the corner of the room near my bathroom door.

Had I been a normal person, I would have bolted out of bed and turned on the light immediately. Instead, I slowly pulled out my headphones, stayed frozen on my back, my eyes as big as Jefferson's as my phone light turned itself off and I counted seconds in between camera flashes.

I held my breath for ten seconds, my eyes locked on the direction the sigh had come from as I waited for that red camera light to ease my overactive imagination. My phone was in my shaking hands, but in my panic, I couldn't quite remember how to turn the flashlight on so I stayed still.

I felt my eyes drying out as I kept them open in the darkness. I felt my pulse in my fingertips where they were pressed against the phone. I felt the hair stand up on the back of my neck.

The only sound I could hear in the dark room was my own heart. All I could think was, *This is the longest ten seconds of my life.*

And then the red light flashed on, revealing nothing more than an empty corner of the room and proving to me just how crazy I was.

The breath I held came out of my mouth in a huge rush, relief and warmth flowing through my body as I put my earbuds back in. I had to laugh at myself; it was the only way I'd keep from being disappointed in what a baby I'd been. At least on camera the boys wouldn't be able to tell I'd been holding my breath and counting seconds, so I had that going for me.

Illuminating my phone screen once more and blacking out the world around me, I pushed play on "Nearly Witches," a song that was probably a terrible choice for my current situation. Still, I loved a good ironic twist.

Smiling to myself and ready to give sleeping my best try, I rolled over onto my side, facing the closed bathroom door. I could do it. I could close my eyes and go to sleep now.

Except just as I was about to give in to my exhaustion, the light in the bathroom turned on.

~

"Jefferson!" I banged my fist on his door frantically, looking over my shoulder every five seconds.

I would have been worried about waking other hotel guests up but the ship was practically empty during the week, and I wouldn't be surprised if there was no one staying in the rooms between Jefferson's and mine.

"Jefferson!" I yelled again, continuing to pound my fists on his door. I shivered in my tank top and shorts. I really needed to get new pajamas.

"What in the world are you doing, you crazy woman?" he asked, opening his door. He rubbed sleep from his eyes with the back of his hand. "Have you lost your bloody mind?"

He was actually wearing pajama pants and a T-shirt.

"There's something in my bathroom," I said, looking over my shoulder again.

Somehow I had convinced myself that a ghost would come gliding down the hallway at any moment in a blood-soaked dress, ready to take my head off with a sword . . . or was I mixing ghost stories there?

"Sadie, if this is about some spider, I swear I'll kill you and won't feel the slightest bit of remorse." Sadly, I believed him.

"Jefferson." I grabbed him by the shoulders and looked up at him intently. "I think it's a ghost."

His green eyes widened considerably at this simple statement and suddenly he didn't seem so annoyed that I had woken him. Instead, he closed the door behind him and ran down the hallway at full speed, his bare feet sounding loudly on the floor.

Flying up to my already open door, he stepped into my room, keeping the light off but taking my room camera off of its tripod and slowly panning around the darkened space.

"It turned my bathroom light on," I said, standing close behind him.

"It's off now," he whispered reverently.

This was what he lived for.

"It must have turned it back off again?" I guessed.

"Hello?" he called quietly, taking one step toward the bathroom door. I was forced to come with him since I was grasping his T-shirt like my life depended on it.

Silence.

"Do you want to talk to us?" he asked, and for the first time since we'd started our group, I wanted to tell him to stop provoking the ghosts.

There was no way I'd sleep now that I knew the ghosts had chosen my room to stay in.

"You don't have to be afraid."

At first, I thought Jefferson was talking to me, before realizing he was speaking to whatever disembodied spirit was floating around in my bathroom.

Another step toward the door with me grabbing Jefferson's arm now, and still more silence.

"We don't want to hurt you. We just want to talk to you."

"I don't," I mumbled, earning a shushing noise from Jefferson.

He stopped in front of the door, his hand outstretched slightly as if he might open it, but his body was frozen in place. We were both silent, listening, as we held our breath.

"Did anything else happen, Sadie?" Jefferson whispered to me.

"I heard a sigh right by the bathroom door," I said, glad that the light from the hallway was streaming into the room now so that we weren't in complete darkness.

"Before or after the light turned on in the bathroom?"

"Before," I said with a short humorless laugh. "I was out of here in two seconds after the light in the bathroom turned on."

"Why?" he asked, looking completely baffled.

"I was so excited to tell you," I said.

"Right," he responded, not catching my sarcasm at all. "Okay. Here we go."

Stretching his hand those last few inches, he grasped the doorknob and turned it slowly, pushing the door open with a creak worthy of a horror movie. It swung open into the darkened bathroom, but if we were expecting bloodstained mirrors and corpses in the bathtub, we were sorely disappointed.

"Huh," I said. "It's empty."

"What did you expect?" Jefferson asked, managing to sound condescending and amused all at the same time.

We both walked into the small dark bathroom, and even though I wasn't nearly as scared as I had been a moment ago, there was no way I was letting go of Jefferson's arm, no matter how embarrassing it was to be grasping it so tightly.

"Just because we don't see someone here doesn't mean they aren't with us."

Great. Creepy Parrish Number One just ruined my already slim chance of sleep that night.

"Hopefully we'll have picked up some audio," he went on, completely unfazed by the possible ghost in the bathroom.

Like I said, he may have been infuriating, but he was good at what he did.

"You had the camera recording when the bathroom light turned on?" he asked.

"Yeah, I did, but I doubt it picked up the sigh. Just the light."

"Good work," he said with a nod. "And for the record, I don't think you're only good for dressing up in costumes to lure ghosts out."

"What?" I asked, completely confused by his statement.

"What you said in the car on the way here," he said.

I narrowed my eyes at him in the darkness. "You were supposed to be asleep."

"I like to pretend to be asleep so I can listen to the more interesting conversations sometimes," he said, as if this were okay to admit.

Suddenly, I had to take a mental recount of the conversation I'd had with Brighton to make sure I hadn't said anything too embarrassing. I wasn't quite sure what I would have said, since there was nothing to say on the subject of Jefferson and me. But still, I didn't want him misunderstanding anything.

"I just don't want you thinking I don't value your skill," he said, actually being incredibly nice, even if he wouldn't look at me while complimenting me. "Of course, coming from the weird creepy one, I guess that doesn't mean much."

My face instantly went red as he repeated my own words back to me. Oops. I guess I had said something embarrassing in the car.

"I didn't mean that. I was just . . . kidding," I finished lamely. Jefferson smiled over at me to show he didn't care one bit about me calling him creepy. Something told me he embraced it. It worked for him.

"Well, sadly, I think whatever was in your bathroom is gone now."

I didn't think it was all that sad, but I nodded in agreement. Even with the lack of obvious ghosts in my room, I wasn't going to be sleeping that night, but it did make me feel better to know that someone had come to check things out.

"Thanks for letting me know," Jefferson said, handing the camera over to me and walking out of the bathroom.

"Anytime," I answered, pretending like I had gotten him because I was concerned he'd miss evidence and not because I was two seconds from passing out from fear.

"I'll see you in the morning. I've got an idea for how we can get into the pool area, so be ready for that."

"I was born ready," I said with a yawn.

Maybe I would be able to fall asleep after all.

"Goodnight, Sadie," he said, turning to leave and stopping again abruptly. He turned on his heel to face me once more, scrunching up his nose and staring at me guiltily.

"What?" I asked, checking behind me for the ghost.

"I don't have my room key."

"You have got to be kidding me," I said slowly. "Well, you're not sleeping here. Go find Deacon."

There was no way I was letting Jefferson sleep in my room, no matter how helpful he had been tonight. Of course, sending him away to his cousin's room did mean I'd be on the B deck all by myself, and something told me that wouldn't exactly be conducive to sleeping.

"He's going to be mad if I wake him up."

Seriously? Was he really thinking I'd ever let him sleep in here? I wouldn't even let him sleep in the bathtub.

"I'll wake him up for you," I said, dragging him by the hand once more and leading him up the stairs to Deacon's room.

Luckily, we didn't see anyone in the hallways, since we were both barefoot and under-clothed. It probably wouldn't have looked great.

I knocked on Deacon's door, Jefferson's hands on my bare shoulders as he hid behind me.

For someone so brave, he could be a real baby sometimes.

The door swung open forcefully and Deacon stumbled out without his glasses on, mumbling a few incoherent curses under his breath.

"What in the bloody—"

"Jefferson locked himself out of his room and has to stay in yours tonight," I said, cutting Deacon off before he could finish his inappropriate sentence.

I pushed Jefferson into the room and began walking away from the Parrish boys.

"What were you guys doing?" Deacon asked, his voice indicating that he thought our night's activities were a lot more scandalous than they actually were.

"Our job," I called back, passing the staircase and continuing straight on down the hallway.

I had given up on the delusion that I was brave enough to sleep in a room by myself, and there was no way I was going to face tomorrow on no sleep. Coming to a stop in front of Brighton's door and trying to ignore the highly inappropriate questions Deacon was aiming at his cousin down the hall, I knocked loudly, hoping my friend's ability to sleep through anything wouldn't prove true tonight.

Surprisingly, she answered the door only seconds after I'd knocked, holding her inhaler and looking pale.

"I can't sleep alone in that room," I admitted in embarrassment.

"Oh good!" she said, pulling me into her room. "I was just about to come to your room and say the same thing."

CHAPTER 7

"I still don't understand why you guys couldn't have just asked the guy at the front desk for a room key last night," Deacon said, still sore about being woken up.

"It was late," Jefferson answered absently. "I didn't think about it."

He was back in investigation mode, staring at the split screen that held all four tapes from our rooms last night. Brighton wore headphones to keep track of the audio, and, as it was, Jefferson and I were running late for his "brilliant plan," whatever it might be.

"Van would have given you a key," Deacon went on as I finished fluffing up my pixie cut and doing a once-over in the mirror.

It was always nice when we weren't doing a night investigation because I could wear normal clothes. Jefferson had told me to dress like a tourist today, but I just took that to mean "dress in what you would normally wear," so I sported a mustard yellow tank top, black skinny jeans, and yellow ballet flats. He wore dark brown corduroys and some old band T-shirt he'd borrowed from Deacon, and therefore actually managed to look normal.

I had to admit, it was kind of nice to see him in something other than his trademark old fitted slacks and a white button-up shirt.

"Who is Van?" I asked, washing the hair gel from my hands.

"The guy at the front desk," Deacon said. He furrowed his brow at me.

"We caught the light turning on in your room," Jefferson said over his shoulder.

"We also caught you running away faster than I've ever seen anyone move," Brighton added with a laugh.

"Shut up, it was scary," I said, trying to look hurt.

Deacon and I made our way to the monitors to see what they were talking about, and sure enough, the light under the bathroom door flickered on, and I ran for my life, making it across the room in one second flat.

"Nice form, mate," Deacon joked, nudging me with his elbow.

I rolled my eyes at him but didn't respond.

"You also see the light turn off just before we come back in," Jefferson said.

He was much too happy about all of this. Granted, I was excited that we'd caught evidence, but it wasn't exactly comforting to know that the activity had decided to localize around my bathroom for some reason.

"I guess tonight we'll need to set up a camera in the bathroom to see if we catch anything," I said. "But for now, we need to let Deacon and Brighton go over everything. We have some mysterious appointment to keep."

"What are you guys doing?" Deacon asked.

Maybe he'd get it out of Jefferson, since he definitely wasn't telling me anything.

"Getting into the pool," he answered with a wide grin.

He was definitely proud of whatever scheme he'd concocted. I just had to hope it would actually work, because if it didn't, I was about two seconds away from breaking down the doors into the pool area to investigate.

"Bring cameras," Brighton said, handing each of us a tiny camera—one with night vision capabilities and one thermal imager.

"You guys all seem really optimistic that we'll actually be able to get into the pool," I said suspiciously. "What do you know?"

"They trust me, love," Jefferson said. "Now let's go."

~

I had to laugh. The fact that our big sneaky plan for getting into the pool area on the Queen Mary was to go on the "Ghosts and Legends Tour" was a little idiotic. If we were trying to be important and respected paranormal investigators, we weren't doing a very good job.

"I'm glad you're so brilliant," I said to Jefferson as we walked through the ticket area and waited with a small group of tourists in a cold metal room on the ship.

"What are you talking about?" he asked, seeming puzzled as usual.

"I guess technically you're right; we will get into the pool area by doing this. But getting to walk through it and actually investigating are two completely different things."

"We're going to investigate, Sadie. Just calm the classic Cuban temper for two seconds and follow my lead."

"I'm sure your next move is brilliant," I said, my words still oozing with sarcasm.

"Hello, everyone." A young man walked into the room and shut the heavy metal door behind him so that we were instantly engulfed in a muffled silence. "My name is Van and I'll be guiding you through the more . . . sinister parts of the Queen Mary today."

He spoke in a way that I'm sure he hoped was slow and menacing, but just ended up being a bit cheesy.

"Van works at the front desk," I whispered to Jefferson, who had suddenly stepped behind me.

"Why do you know that?"

"I'm just repeating the useless information your cousin fills his head with." I watched as he dug around in the pockets of his corduroy pants for something. "Although I'm not sure how he has any room to store these facts when his head is so full of important information like Brighton's favorite yogurt flavor."

Jefferson stifled a laugh behind me, and as I looked back at our tour guide, I realized he was staring at me.

In fact, everyone in our group was staring at us.

"Sorry, what?" I asked, thinking they must have asked us a question.

"We were just asking what brave souls have decided to join us on our journey today," the tour guide repeated, trying to keep the overly dramatic eerie tone to his voice.

Apparently, everyone had introduced themselves but us.

Suddenly I felt Jefferson's arms encircle my waist from behind as he bent over and rested his chin on my shoulder. His cinnamon smell hit my nose instantly. Had we not been surrounded by sweet families on vacation, I would have punched him right then and there.

"We're on our honeymoon," he said, his voice so sickeningly in love that it made me queasy. "But someone can't wear her ring because her dope of a husband got it a size too big and had to send it to the jewelers."

I glanced down at Jefferson's left hand that was currently resting on my stomach and noticed a small gold band on his ring finger. When on earth had he gotten that?

"Isn't it still so funny to hear, honey?" he asked me, forcing me to look over at him and try not to appear too uncomfortable with how close our faces were. "Husband," he repeated, looking like he was relishing in the title.

The entire group was silent, watching us with knowing smiles on their faces (except for the tour guide who looked annoyed with our fake love).

"It still seems unreal," I said through clenched teeth. I tried to keep a forced smile in place and refrained from squirming out of Jefferson's grasp.

"I can't believe it either, dear," he said, giving me a squeeze and resting his cheek against mine.

The tour guide cleared his throat and continued on with his spiel.

"I'm going to murder you in your sleep," I whispered to Jefferson in a singsong voice, still smiling as our tour guide talked.

"I can't wait, petal," he answered. He leaned over and kissed my cheek.

Yeah, he was definitely a dead man.

"If you'll all just follow me," our guide said, ushering us through a door and beginning what was sure to be the most awkward hour of my life. "Stay close together. I wouldn't want to lose any of you to the spirits who may join us."

We made our way through various parts of the ship, with ghostly sound effects and staged water leaks popping up at unexpected moments. Had I not been so mad at the boy who was currently holding my hand and occasionally rubbing my back lovingly, I probably would have thought the tour was pretty cool. Unfortunately, I was too busy not killing Jefferson to pay any attention.

"This next room is one of our most famous on the ship," our guide finally said, flipping off a light switch and turning on his flashlight in the pitch-black room. There were no windows to let in even the smallest bit of illumination. "The pool area has been host to a number of sightings, ghostly encounters, and paranormal activity."

"We're here," I said over my shoulder, unable to contain my excitement despite the fact that Jefferson was, once more, hugging me from behind and invading my personal space bubble in a way that he would definitely be punished for once the tour was over.

"Just stick close to me," he whispered in my ear.

"I don't really have a choice when you're hanging all over me, now do I?" I asked, still keeping the overly sweet lilt to my voice.

"Just wanted to show everyone how young and in love we are," he said, matching my fake tone almost perfectly.

"You're sure doing a good job of acting like you enjoy being this close to me," I said.

"I just can't keep my hands off you, Sadie," he said without an ounce of sincerity.

The tour group began to move again and I was aware of the fact that I'd missed everything our guide had said. It was a pity, really, since I was genuinely interested in the various claims in the pool area. I'd read most of them online, but it was always fun to hear them from someone who was paid to know their stuff front and back.

I tried to walk with the group, but Jefferson's hold around my waist tightened, forcing me to stay behind with him. I was pressed tightly against his chest in the darkness.

The beam of our tour guide's flashlight moved farther and farther away until finally he and the entire group passed through a door, closing it behind them and leaving us in a darkness so complete that I couldn't see my hand in front of my face. Jefferson instantly let his hands drop from my waist and I heard a ruffling sound before his own flashlight popped on, giving us a small glow that only stretched a few feet.

"I'm pretty sure our tour guide can count, so I give us five minutes tops to do some investigating," Jefferson said from somewhere behind the flashlight. A tiny red light suddenly came to life out of thin air, indicating he'd turned his camera on.

I followed suit, taking the camera out of my purse and turning on the night vision capabilities. I may not have been able to see, but at least I could sort of make things out in the viewfinder.

"Did you bring an EMF reader?" he asked, his voice suddenly so close that I jumped.

"Yeah, hold on."

It was difficult enough holding on to the camera when I couldn't see where I was going, but holding two handheld objects was going to make the whole navigating-in-the-dark thing kind of difficult.

"What does it say?" Jefferson asked, barely giving me time to turn the EMF reader on.

"Wow," I said, giving a little whistle for effect. "The electromagnetic field in here is at a point one."

The beam of his flashlight bobbed up and down as he walked away from me. "Why does that impress you?"

He should have warned me we'd be walking around in the dark. I would have packed my own flashlight.

"It doesn't. I'm actually surprised it's so low."

From the spastic movements of Jefferson's light, I could see that we were only a few steps from the empty pool, which looked much too deep for comfort. The room was set up like an atrium, with the pool in the center and a second story balcony lining the walls. There was a small, straight waterslide that didn't look even close to being safe, and the tiled staircase our tour group had climbed to leave the room sat just to my right.

Jefferson shone his flashlight in my eyes. "Why are you just standing there? We only have a few minutes."

"I don't have a flashlight. I'm not walking around here in the dark. I'll probably fall in the pool and die."

He let out one long-suffering sigh before lowering the light from my eyes and approaching me, clicking on another small flashlight and handing it over. It was difficult to juggle all of the equipment in my hands, but I managed to shine the light at the EMF reader, thinking that was the most important thing to see at the moment.

"Hello?" I called, getting right down to it, since Jefferson seemed to be waiting for me.

My voice echoed around the tiled room, coming back to me with a distorted quality. I heard a few drops of water and aimed my flashlight at Jefferson to see what he thought. His head was tilted to the side as usual, but his large eyes were closed as he listened.

"There's no water in the pool," I whispered. "Should we be hearing water?"

"We are on a ship," he said. "I wouldn't say hearing water is all that special when you're on a ship."

I shrugged in the darkness and looked back down at my EMF reader that sat stubbornly at a point one.

I sighed at our bad luck. This place was supposed to be full of paranormal activity and we might as well have been standing in the middle of a Wal-Mart.

Shining my light over at Jefferson, thinking he'd have some great insight into our problem, I found him walking away from me.

Straight toward the empty pool.

You know, the one he'd surely fall into and die?

Yeah. That empty pool.

I sprinted over and pulled him away from the edge. "What are you doing? Are you a complete lunatic?"

"I thought I saw someone," he answered.

"Oh, did you now," I shot back. "So you thought it would be a good idea to fall into an empty pool and die?"

"I forgot the pool was there," he said, though I didn't understand how that could be true.

He was just mental.

"Do you know who sent us?" Jefferson suddenly called. "Can you tell us anything about our employer?"

I forced myself to stop babysitting Jefferson and looked back down at the EMF reader, which had just inexplicably jumped up a few notches.

"Point two," I said.

I wasn't sure why, but the electromagnetic field in the room had just gone up. Had we been in a modern home or hotel where an air conditioner might have kicked on, I would have thought nothing of it. But standing in the dead spot that was the pool area, it gave me pause. There weren't any electronic devices here to alter our EMF reading. There was a security camera I was sure, but even that wouldn't have made the levels jump around.

"Are you the one we're supposed to be looking for?" Jefferson went on.

"Point three."

I couldn't hear any disembodied voices and I couldn't feel a sudden chill in the air, but something was definitely happening.

"Did you die here?" he asked.

"Point four," I whispered.

I let my eyes wander from the EMF reader for a moment, scanning the room that suddenly felt much more interesting than it had only moments before.

"We heard someone say yesterday that they were meeting a woman somewhere," Jefferson said. "Are you the one he was meeting?"

"Point three," I said. "Try something else."

"Did you know the man we heard on B-deck yesterday?"

"Point five," I said, a grin beginning to form on my lips.

"Is he the one we're supposed to find?"

"Point six."

We were both silent for a moment, listening to the still air around us with wide eyes.

"Where can we find him?" Jefferson asked after a moment.

"Point seven," I whispered, trying to keep my voice low in case we caught a disembodied voice on our recording.

Silence again.

I could only hope we were catching something on our camera that we just weren't hearing at the moment.

"Point five," I said, wondering why our friend was suddenly leaving us.

"Can you tell us who the man is we're trying to find?" Jefferson attempted.

"Point four."

"Who are you?"

"Point three."

"Why is it going away?" he asked me, somewhere between frustration and panic, his British accent much thicker than normal.

There was no way he was going to lose such a unique opportunity.

"Sadie, what do we do?" he asked, coming to stand by me so that he could watch the EMF reader.

I wasn't sure why he was asking my opinion. I was the one who had bolted from my room the last time I thought I'd encountered a ghost.

"Do something," he practically pleaded.

"The man we're looking for," I began, not sure if this would work. "The one we heard on our recording last night . . . is he the one who turned on my bathroom light?"

I heard a small sound of either excitement or shock from Jefferson as he nudged me with his elbow and gestured toward the EMF reader in my hand, whispering reverently, "Five point oh."

CHAPTER 8

"Hello?" a panicked voice called as the lights in the pool room suddenly popped on, practically blinding Jefferson and me.

I grabbed our cameras and quickly shoved them in my purse and pulled him into a hug, trying my best to look scared.

Our tour guide rushed down the stairs, looking immensely relieved to see us while the rest of the group stood near the exit, craning their necks to see if either of us had fallen into the pool and died.

"You guys walked away too fast," I whimpered, looking as pathetic as possible and tightening my arms around Jefferson.

He patted my back reassuringly and made soothing shushing noises.

At least we were good actors, right?

"It was so dark, and we couldn't figure out where you'd gone," I said, throwing a few well-placed sniffs in there for good measure. "It was so scary."

"It's okay," Jefferson said reassuringly. He turned to the tour guide. "How do we get out of here? I think I need to take her back to our room. She's obviously upset." He injected just enough unspoken blame to make the tour guide uncomfortable.

"Of course. I'm so sorry miss," he said, reaching out to touch my arm but thinking better of it when Jefferson gave him a chilling look. "If you'll follow me, there's an exit right over here."

"Thank you," I said, sounding delicate.

We followed our guide, Jefferson keeping his arm protectively around me, until we walked into the main part of the ship where I'd been investigating the night before.

"Will you be all right?" the guide asked us.

I didn't answer him but nodded somberly, keeping my eyes locked on the ground.

"Thank you for your help," Jefferson said, indicating that the conversation was over.

The tour guide looked between us once more, probably trying to figure out if he was about to be sued or not, before nodding once and turning back toward the rest of his group. We watched him go in silence, trying to keep our faces straight even though I could see Jefferson's lips tugging up in one corner with every step the guide took away from us. When he finally closed the door behind him, I burst into a laughing fit, resting my head on Jefferson's chest and trying to catch my breath.

"You're completely ridiculous," he said between his own bouts of laughter. "You know that, right?"

"At least I'm convincing! Can you imagine if I was a bad actress?"

"We'd be thrown off the boat and possibly arrested," he agreed with a nod, giving my side a squeeze before dropping his hand from me. "I may be 'the weird creepy Parrish,' but at least I'm good in a tight spot. Deacon would have pleaded guilty right then and there."

"Would you give it a rest and stop being so put out about that innocent little comment? Besides, who said being weird and creepy was a bad thing?"

I arched an eyebrow at him before walking back toward Brighton's room.

"Oh, I see," he said, following close behind. "You meant 'weird and creepy' in a good way. Silly me."

"Anyway," I said pointedly, drowning out any further complaining from him. "Can you believe what just happened? I mean, I'm a little creeped out about the ghost in my bathroom, but still. We actually made contact with a spirit! We talked to someone who's died and we got actual responses from them."

"I wonder if we picked up any audio on the cameras," he said hopefully.

"There's only one way to find out."

I pushed open the wedged-open door to Brighton's hotel room with gusto, walking at full speed until I stopped in my tracks, causing Jefferson to crash into me from behind.

"Oh hey!" Brighton said, much too happily, trying to scoot away from Deacon without being obvious about how close they had been when I'd first walked in the room.

I couldn't be sure of exactly what I'd seen, but the way they'd jumped apart when I pushed through the door was enough to make me suspicious. Deacon's trying to discretely retract his hand from Brighton's leg was even fishier. I'd have to wait until the boys left before pressing her for information, but something was definitely up with Brighton and Deacon.

"Why did you stop so fast?" Jefferson complained. "You could have warned me at least."

"What have you guys been up to?" I asked accusatorially.

Brighton widened her eyes and put on her brightest smile. "Just going over the evidence from last night again."

Liar.

"Oh good. Do you have anything new to show us?" I was matching her too-happy tone, trying to make this as awkward for her as possible. It was just too fun to pick on her when I got the chance. It almost made up for the stupid costumes she let the boys dress me up in for our night investigations.

"Didn't really find much," Deacon said, keeping his eyes trained on the ground.

That confirmed my suspicions at least. There was definitely something going on between them.

"Jefferson and I have some footage to show you guys . . . I mean . . . if you don't have other things to be doing, that is."

"Let's see it," Brighton said too quickly, scooting over and making a spot for Jefferson and me to sit in between them.

I rolled my eyes but sat on the bed with them, connecting the camera to Brighton's computer.

"It was pretty amazing," Jefferson confirmed, squeezing in between Deacon and me and putting his arm around my shoulders. "Plus Sadie confessed her undying love for me and . . . well . . . we have an announcement," he said with a fake catch in his throat, holding up his left hand to display his fake gold wedding ring.

"I still can't believe you brought props for your stupid plan." I searched for our footage on the camera.

"Okay, now you have to explain," Brighton said with a giggle, looking at Jefferson's ring. "No way! Is that real gold?"

"Of course not," I said to her, leaving the footage for a moment to look down at Jefferson's hand. "Wait. Is it real?"

"It was my dad's," he said with a shrug, removing his arm from around my shoulder and suddenly looking uncomfortable.

"And you just carry it around with you?" I asked.

I knew Jefferson's dad had died when he was young and that his mom was some kind of rich widowed socialite back in England, but he never really talked about his parents much. The one or two times I had heard him mention his dad, though, he spoke about him with a reverent pride.

"Did you find the footage?" he asked, his voice sounding off.

"Not yet, but I'll keep looking," I said, swiveling back toward the screen and ignoring the awkward turn our conversation had just taken.

"So, what did you need the ring for?" Brighton asked.

"Sadie and I pretended to be married and on our honeymoon for the tour," Jefferson said, letting the smile return to his face, though it didn't seem natural.

"No," I said. "Jefferson pretended we were married and used that as an excuse to assault me the whole time we were on that stupid tour."

"Assault?" Deacon asked, suddenly interested.

"I may have been a convincing newlywed husband," Jefferson elaborated with a wink.

"Okay, you and I are definitely talking later," Brighton said.

"Yeah, we definitely are," I said back to her meaningfully, shutting her up on the subject.

"Well played, mate," Deacon said to his cousin.

I shook my head and tried to block out the conversation happening around me, pushing the playback button on the camera in my hand, anxious to see the evidence we'd caught.

"Oh no," I whispered.

"What?" Jefferson asked darkly, already knowing the answer.

"Our footage is gone."

"How is that even possible?" he asked, leaning over me to scan through the tape himself. "What happened? Did you record over it somehow?"

"No!" I stated emphatically, knowing the last thing I needed was an angry Parrish on my case. "The camera was turned off when I pulled it out of my purse. The record button couldn't have even been pushed by accident."

I took Jefferson's camera from him and tried to bring up the video he'd caught, hoping we'd have at least some sort of evidence. But just like my camera, his was blank.

"Did you push record when we started the investigation?" he asked.

"You saw the red light on my camera. And besides, yours doesn't have any footage either."

Not taking my word for it, he took the camera back from me and scanned through it, trying to find any hint of our investigation.

"This can't be happening," he said, shaking his dark curls into his eyes and breathing deeply.

"How could our footage have been erased?"

"Didn't you guys say you found something? Can a spirit do that? I know they can drain batteries, but can they completely erase camera footage?" Deacon asked.

"I've heard of cases like this before, but honestly, I just always assumed those people didn't know what they were doing so they made up some story about a ghost to cover their tracks." Jefferson was still breathing deeply. He looked like he was two seconds from throwing a chair through a window. "I guess it is possible."

"That's kind of good then, right?" Brighton offered, quickly going on when Jefferson gave her a death glare. "I mean, you can tell us what happened so we know, and now you have evidence that you really did make contact."

"Our lack of evidence is our evidence?" Jefferson asked.

"Yeah," she said, sounding less sure of herself now.

Jefferson took a steadying breath before continuing, obviously trying to calm his temper. "Brighton, we had video evidence of the electromagnetic field fluctuating as we asked questions. Now all we have is a blank tape and our word that it happened. Which evidence do you think is better?"

"This is just motivation to get an even better experience on tape tonight," I said, trying to be the peacemaker.

Jefferson was quickly falling into one of his moods and I knew he'd be absolutely impossible to work with if he pouted all night. I had to find a way to twist our current predicament so that it didn't seem so dire to him.

"Who cares about that EMF reading? I bet tonight we can get an actual EVP."

"You think we're going to catch a voice?" he asked, still skeptical.

"We already know where to look. We just have to figure out the right questions to ask."

"And where do we look?" he asked.

He still didn't want to accept that his life wasn't ruined.

"My bathroom."

CHAPTER 9

"Not the most comfortable place to investigate, is it?" Deacon asked, readjusting his position on the edge of the bathtub.

"I'm not sure all three of us really need to be in here," I said. "And I don't think I need to be dressed up for tonight's investigation."

I knew it was futile to try to protest the costumes, but it was always worth a try.

Tonight, I wore a long powder pink satin dress with a shawl collar and sleeves. The hems of the skirt and the sleeves were trimmed with a ruffle and the entire dress had little flowers embroidered on it.

Needless to say, it was *not* the type of thing I'd wear if I had a say in the matter, and I still didn't understand why they made me wear the costumes when it was obvious they would all look better on Brighton and her perfect everything. No ghost was going to believe that a short Cuban girl with a pixie cut was actually someone who belonged in their time period.

"You aren't dressed up," Jefferson said, tossing a dark wig at me. "Yet."

"You're the worst." I fixed the curly brown shoulder-length wig on top of my head, feeling a little less conspicuous now that my hair matched the time period. "How on earth are you even affording all of these wigs and costumes?"

Jefferson looked down at the ground, tapped his finger against his knee, looked back up at me and said, "It's better if you don't know."

I don't know why I'd expected a normal answer from him.

"And how do you know my dress size?" I continued, determined not to be derailed by his cryptic answers.

"Again, it's probably better if you don't know."

I looked up at Deacon, who gave me a "What can you do? He's crazy" shrug, like we should all just keep indulging the obvious shadiness in the room. I mean, I wasn't sure what else we could do. Jefferson was a riddle that was probably best left unsolved. It was like turning over a rock. You never found candy under the rock. Just creepy crawly things you didn't want to know about.

"And again I say, do all three of us really need to be in here? It's a little cramped." I thought a subject change was in order. Especially after my mind had started thinking of all the ways Jefferson could have gotten my dress size without me knowing.

Each idea was worse than the last.

"It's not that bad," Jefferson said, nearly knocking over one of our cameras with his elbow.

We were completely surrounded by technology in the already tiny bathroom, and the various devices were all perched much too precariously. It didn't seem like a good idea to balance an expensive EMF reader on the faucet of the sink.

"Do we have everything we need?" Deacon asked.

"You've got the EMF reader, two cameras, and an audio recorder for any possible EVP," Brighton said over our earpieces. "I didn't give you the shadow detector, laser grid, or the REM pod since I figured the space is too small for that anyway."

"It's like you guys are speaking a different language," Deacon said. "I'm just going to make up my own names for these things. From now on the EMF is the electronic measurement finder."

Brighton giggled. "That's basically what it does, so feel free to call it that."

"This is definitely enough equipment." I pulled on the overly frilly sleeves of my dress, trying not to shiver. My thin dress didn't do much to protect me against the chill from the cold toilet seat lid I was sitting on, despite the fact that I'd kept my jeans on underneath it.

"Let's get right down to it, then," Jefferson said. He turned off the lights and cast us into darkness. "Jefferson, Sadie, and Deacon in Sadie's bathroom on the Queen Mary. September fourth at 11:00 p.m."

We all sat there for a minute, listening to the silence and hoping some foreboding sound would suddenly materialize. Jefferson stared straight ahead, his large owl eyes focused on a spot on the wall, while Deacon grinned from ear to ear, staring at my dress in obvious amusement. I stuck my tongue out at him while Jefferson wasn't looking.

"Very professional," Brighton said over our earpieces.

Right. She could see us. Oops.

Deacon made faces back at me, trying to get me to laugh.

Jefferson didn't seem to notice our goofing off. He was in his "serious paranormal investigator" mood. Of the many moods he had, this one was probably the most manageable.

"Is there anyone here with us?" he asked.

Silence.

"What's the EMF reader looking like?" Jefferson asked me, forcing me to actually do some work.

"It's sitting at a point two. Nothing too exciting."

He sighed in annoyance but wasn't about to give up that easily.

"Why are you following Sadie?" he asked the dark bathroom.

"Because Sadie's a babe," Brighton said, making me laugh and earning a dirty look from Jefferson. Either he didn't agree or he was tired of our goofing around. Kind of the pot calling the kettle black, if you asked me, since we probably would have made contact in the pub in Portland if he hadn't decided to scare me and ruin everything.

He let his brow furrow as his lips pouted a bit. Taking pity on him, I tried to rein our antics back in.

"Were you on the Queen Mary on its maiden voyage?" I asked the dark bathroom. I paused long enough for an unheard answer that the equipment might pick up. "Do you want us out of—"

My words died instantly as I heard a noise.

"Did you guys hear that?" I asked.

Deacon shook his head in confusion.

"I did," Jefferson said, staring intently at me. "I can't make out what it was though."

"It kind of sounded like a kid whining. Or maybe . . . an animal?"

"Because those sound the same," Deacon said.

I ignored him. "Play the tape back, Jefferson. Let's see if we caught it."

He obediently played the sound in question once more, turning the volume up all the way on our recorder. We could hear a muffled, high-pitched sentence but, as usual, I couldn't decipher what it was saying.

I couldn't quite understand why, but the voice made the hair on the back of my arms stand up. This childlike sound made me feel uneasy. Looking around the cramped bathroom, I could see I wasn't the only one. Deacon had stopped making faces and Jefferson had his eyes closed, trying to figure out what was being said.

"Play it again," I said.

The voice materialized once more as the recording was played, and though I still couldn't fully understand the sentence, two words were undoubtedly clear to me.

"I heard stuck," I began.

"And pool," Jefferson finished.

"It sounded like a little kid," Deacon said sadly.

It wasn't exactly a happy thing, trying to communicate with the dead. But finding paranormal evidence of children always cast a bit of a shadow over our group. Death was sad. But the death of a child was a whole new level.

"I'm turning on the K2 meter," I said, holding the small handheld device in front of me and powering it on. "If you can hear me, I don't want you to be afraid of us," I spoke as if I were talking to a child. "This device I'm holding in my hand has lights on it. If you come up and touch it or make a loud noise next to it, the lights will light up and we'll know you're trying to talk to us."

"Can you touch the device?" Jefferson asked, his talking-to-children voice not as comforting as mine.

Glancing at the two Parrish boys, I began to wonder if it really was a good idea to have all three of us in the bathroom at once. I mean, if I were a little ghost child, I wouldn't want to hang out in a bathroom full of adults.

"I think you both need to leave so I can do this on my own," I said.

"What?" they both said together. Deacon sounded confused but Jefferson sounded annoyed, as if I were trying to steal his glory.

"You can still watch from Brighton's room, I just don't think a kid is going to talk to us when there are so many people in here."

Jefferson didn't say anything, but I could tell he agreed. Reluctantly, he rose to his feet and nodded to his cousin, indicating he should listen to me.

"I'll be on the mic, so ask any of the questions I feed you," he said.

"Yes, sir."

I refrained from smiling at Jefferson's sudden burst of authority as the boys shut the door behind them, leaving me on my own.

Taking a deep breath, I let myself get back into the zone and hoped we hadn't scared the child off completely. Assuming, of course, that it was an intelligent ghost and not just a residual haunt, which simply left a trace behind, replaying the same sentence over and over like a broken record.

"Okay, now that it's just the two of us, can you come up and touch this device to let me know you're here?" I asked, holding the K2 meter out in front of me and holding my breath.

For a moment, nothing happened, and I began to lose hope. Maybe I was alone. Then suddenly, a rainbow of lights lit up across my palm, and the breath I had been holding escaped my lips in a rush, a smile creeping over my cheeks.

"That was so good," I said.

"No, she's only asked one question," Brighton said in my ear. "Calm down, you insane Brit."

Deacon and Jefferson apparently had arrived at out little command central.

Jefferson must have jogged down the hallway to get there so fast.

Crazy Parrish.

"I want to play a little game with you, okay?" I asked.

Jefferson was making a racket in my earpiece as he tried to grab the microphone from Brighton, but I ignored him.

"I'm going to ask you some questions. If the answer to those questions is yes, I want you to touch the device to make it light up, just like you did before. If the answer is no, don't touch it at all. Do you understand?"

The lights on my K2 reader lit up instantly, making my stomach do a flip. Some girls got butterflies from boys—I got butterflies from a paranormal question and answer session. My mom would never get grandkids from me at this rate.

"This is amazing," Jefferson said in my ear. "Good call getting us out of there, Sadie."

I wanted to answer him, maybe point out the fact that he had just complimented me, but I also didn't want to confuse whoever I was currently making contact with, so I just smiled, hoping he'd pick up on the appreciation. After all, it wasn't every day a Parrish was nice to you.

"Were you a passenger on this ship?" I asked.

Lights.

"Great!" I said enthusiastically, encouraging this child to continue talking to me. "Are you the one who's been trying to contact us?"

The K2 didn't light up instantly, but I waited for a moment, thinking my new friend was just a bit slow to respond.

"That's a no," Deacon said in my earpiece, after almost half a minute had passed.

"Okay," I said. "Do you know the person who's trying to contact us?"

Lights.

"What is the EMF looking like?" Jefferson asked.

"It's at a one point oh," I answered, trying to decide which direction I should take my questioning. "Is there someone trying to contact us?"

Lights.

"Ask about the pool. What were they saying about the pool?" Jefferson said, making me want to rip the earpiece out. It was much too confusing having him shouting instructions while I tried to sound friendly and to not freak out over the fact that I was actually talking to a ghost.

"Earlier, when those boys were in the room with me, we thought we heard you say something about the pool. Something about being stuck." I paused, wondering if I was on the wrong path with these questions.

I knew what I wanted to ask next, but I wasn't sure if I should. It wasn't exactly helping us find whatever it was we were sent to the Queen Mary to find, but I couldn't just ignore the fact that I was actually making contact with a spirit. I had to follow the line of questioning all the way to the end.

"Did you die in the pool?" I asked.

I could hear Brighton mumble something to the Parrish boys, but I was too focused to make out what it was. The lights in my hand did nothing. I waited for a moment longer, just to make absolutely sure the answer was a no.

To my relief, the lights stayed dark. At least this ghost wasn't quite as tragic as I had originally thought.

"Are you staying on the Queen Mary?" I asked.

It seemed odd for a ghost to attach itself to an area it had visited briefly in life. Typically, we saw entities attaching themselves to the place they'd died.

But the lights illuminated. So, for some reason, this child had come back to reside on the Queen Mary in the afterlife. And they were still here. Maybe they'd come back to the Queen Mary because of fond memories from their lifetime.

I licked my dry lips, unsure of how to proceed.

"Whatever it is we're looking for . . . is it in the pool room with you?" I asked, before I could really think about what I was saying.

The bathroom light suddenly clicked itself on.

Before Brighton, Jefferson, or Deacon could say anything, I was out of my hotel room and running down the hallway.

CHAPTER 10

I pulled the ridiculous pink dress over my head and tossed it on the ground, glad that I had kept my jeans and tank top on underneath the costume.

"Where did she go?" Deacon asked over my earpiece.

I raced down the stairs on bare feet, tossing the wig on a chair. I had kept the K2 meter with me, but abandoned the cameras in the bathroom, leaving everyone in Brighton's room blind.

"Jefferson, where are you going?" Brighton called

"We finally have some direction," I said, walking right up to the doors to the pool. Even though it made no sense, I could hear splashing and children laughing behind the doors. I knew the doors were locked, but that didn't stop me from pulling on them as hard as I could, desperate to get inside.

"Sadie!" Jefferson yelled from down the hall, running toward me and looking concerned. "Sadie, stop!"

"I can hear them in there. Jefferson, they're in the pool area. They're in there with whatever it is we need. We aren't crazy for coming out here. There's a clue in there. We have to get it," I said, shaking the doors once more as I strained to break them open.

Jefferson grabbed my hands, pulling them forcefully away from the doors. "You're going to break the bloody doors and get us kicked out before we get our clue." He looked over his shoulder before kneeling down in front of the door.

"What are you doing?" I asked, thinking he was wasting valuable time.

Jefferson didn't answer me. Instead he pulled a rolled up leather container from the pocket of his suit coat. It looked like something Brighton would keep her makeup brushes in, and as he sat it on the ground, he unrolled the bundle in dramatic fashion.

Jefferson loved to be dramatic.

"Jefferson, what is that?" I asked, this time a bit louder so he'd stop ignoring me.

"Just keep watch," he instructed, pulling a small metal object from the bundle.

"You know how to pick a lock?" I asked skeptically. "Why do you even have that on you? Why didn't you use it before?"

He began working on the locked door. "This is my emergency kit," he answered, though his voice sounded distracted.

"And you just carry it around with you?" I asked.

"Not the emergency kit," Deacon grumbled in my ear.

"What?" Brighton asked.

"Jefferson, put that thing away before you get arrested," his cousin said, not bothering to answer us. "You know what that looks like when people see it."

I raised my eyebrows, looking down at the bundle with new eyes and not quite liking what I saw.

"What exactly do you keep in your emergency kit?" I asked, raising a lip at some of the questionable things I was seeing, the most troubling being the small glass vials labeled "bleach" and "chloroform."

"Normal things. In case of emergency."

"Like?" I pressed, since he wasn't going to willingly give this information up.

"Zip ties. Rope. Lye. Bleach. Lock picking kit. A tiny bit of chloroform."

I let my mouth drop open and wondered if I should bother rebuking him or just try to stay out of his way in case he decided to use his "emergency kit" on me.

"That sounds more like a serial killer's kit," Brighton said, so that that I didn't have to.

He had to know we were all thinking it.

"You'd be surprised at how similar the two kits are," he mumbled, still completely unconcerned with this new disturbing revelation. "Got the lock." He rolled up his "emergency kit," and placed it back in his suit pocket.

We opened the double doors to the pool and Jefferson pulled a well-hidden flashlight off the wall and located the light switch quickly to illuminate the room.

I would have bothered asking how he knew where to find the flashlight and light switch, but he'd probably just answer me by saying it was better if I didn't know.

"Hello?" I called in the empty echoing room. "Is anyone here?"

"Sadie, you know there's no one here," Jefferson whispered. "At least not anyone who's going to come right out and answer you."

As crazy as it sounded, I could have sworn I saw a shadow move in the doorway of the changing room. And from the experiences we'd been having on this ship, I couldn't ignore that as a coincidence.

"Hello?" I called, ignoring Jefferson and running into the changing room attached to the pool area.

Despite the lights being on and having Jefferson in the vicinity, I suddenly felt an eerie dread spread through me, stopping me in my tracks.

"Sadie, it's only a matter of time before someone figures out that we've broken into the pool. I'm sure they have security cameras," Jefferson said, joining me in the changing room.

"He's right, Sade," Brighton said over my earpiece, scaring me. I had totally forgotten they were listening in.

"Jefferson, there's something in here. I can feel it."

Jefferson didn't say anything but walked in front of me protectively, looking around at the empty stalls of the long changing room.

"Hello?" he whispered.

I couldn't tell if he was as nervous as me or if he was excited by the strong feeling of dread that seemed to permeate this room.

"Sadie."

"What?" I asked.

"What?" Jefferson said back to me, looking utterly confused.

"Why did you say my name?"

"I didn't," he said, giving me a you-might-be-unstable look.

"Is she losing it?" Deacon asked.

I pushed past Jefferson, walking through the long changing room and coming to a stop in front of the stall the sound seemed to come from—one with a small crack in the tile that didn't match the rest of the tiles around it.

"Probably," Jefferson said back, coming into the stall with me. "Stand by."

"That tile doesn't match the rest. I need a bobby pin or something," I said to Jefferson. "I'd bet you anything there's something hidden in here."

"I've got a knife," Jefferson answered, pulling a pocket knife from his slacks.

"I would ask why you have a knife, but given the 'emergency kit' I just saw, the knife is the least of my worries," I said, worrying—not for the first time—that Jefferson might one day lose it and chop us all into tiny pieces for no reason at all.

Putting aside my worries for the moment, I took the knife from him and lodged it into the gap in the tile, managing with no small effort, to pop the tile itself out.

"At least we've managed to rack 'destruction of public property' up on our quickly growing list of crimes tonight," Jefferson said.

"As if you care."

"I don't," he agreed. "I'm just glad my fake wife loves minor crimes as much as I do."

I ignored him. I usually did. And instead, I dug my fingers into the small space behind the tile, making contact with a small folded up piece of paper.

It took a few tries to dislodge it, but when I finally pulled the paper from its long-time hiding spot, I felt a rush of pride.

I'd done this.

I'd used whatever meager ghost hunting skills I had and had actually found us a physical clue.

"How did you find that?" Jefferson asked, his cheek practically pressed against mine as he tried to get a closer look at the paper.

"This is it. This must be what we were sent here to find." I handed the knife back to Jefferson. "This is why the kid led me to the pool area. Why they called me over to this stall."

"What is it?" Brighton and Deacon both said in my ear.

"Stand by," Jefferson said again, his already abnormally large eyes even bigger in his state of excitement. "Is it a note? The paper doesn't look all that old."

I turned to face him with my back against the wall, trying to ignore how close we were all of a sudden. I wasn't quite sure why I picked that exact moment to look down at his lips, or why I suddenly found myself so distracted, but a man's voice calling out in the darkness made me jump so violently that I almost dropped the paper I was holding.

"Hello?" the voice called again.

My first thought was that a ghost had followed us in here, but my paranormal brain quickly gave in to my logical brain that told me we were in big trouble.

Just as Jefferson had predicted, the man from the front desk had been watching the security cameras and was now running in to find out why two kids had broken into the pool.

"Give that to me," Jefferson whispered, pulling the paper from my hand and placing it in his pocket.

He put his arm around me and ushered me out of the stall, confusing me to no end before I remembered our little act from the tour earlier. It also didn't escape my notice that he pulled the gold wedding ring from his pocket once more and slid it on.

Why the boy kept a wedding ring in his pocket, I'd never know.

"Are you sure you heard them in here, darling?" he asked me.

"Darling?" Deacon repeated in disgust.

"They're married, stupid," Brighton said.

"Excuse me, but what are you two doing in here?" Van, our tour guide from the ghosts tour asked. He looked like he thought dealing with a crazy woman twice in one day was way beyond his pay grade.

"I thought I heard children playing in the pool," I answered, trying to look fragile. "I swore I hear them and I was so worried they'd gotten locked in here, just like I did on the tour, so I forced my husband to break in so we could get them out."

The damsel-in-distress act seemed to work wonders when confronted with young men.

"Darling, why don't you go sit down outside for a minute," Jefferson said, giving me a meaningful look that I didn't quite understand.

"I'm fine," I said back to him, not wanting to leave.

"Trust me. Go sit outside."

"Fine," I mumbled, dropping the act the second I passed the tour guide.

I sullenly walked into the hallway and fleetingly wondered if Jefferson was murdering our poor tour guide and hiding his body somewhere. I then had to wonder what kind of weirdo that made me, since I had stopped for a split second and seriously considered, maybe, possibly, sort of kissing that sociopathic boy just because we'd found physical evidence of paranormal activity.

Jefferson was saying something to the tour guide, but I was too lost in my own self-analysis to listen.

Kicking at an uneven spot on the carpet and silently blaming Brighton and her crazy theories for my odd moment of insanity, I heard a giggle over my earpiece.

"What?" I asked them.

"Jefferson is telling that guy that you have night terrors and sometimes see things that aren't there," Brighton informed me.

"I know he's good at what he does, but I'm going to kill that Parrish one day," I said, just as the Parrish in question joined me in the hallway with Van.

The desk clerk gave Jefferson an understanding nod before turning to lock the door once more, and Jefferson put his arm around my shoulders, guiding his "unstable wife" up the stairs.

"Are you guys on your way back?" Deacon asked in my earpiece.

"Almost there," Jefferson confirmed.

Neither of us spoke to each other, which was fine by me. I didn't need a lecture about jeopardizing our investigation with my sudden burst of enthusiasm over possibly finding a clue. Of course, that was what had led us to the paper in the pool, so it seemed like any argument against me would be a moot point.

My guess was that the paper was the only thing that kept Jefferson from scolding me as we approached Brighton's room, but even so, I was gearing up for a fight, knowing I was in the right on this one.

Stopping outside her door, Jefferson turned to me, locking his intense eyes on my face. He pulled his earpiece out and turned it off before reaching up and pulling mine out as well. I looked at him questioningly but didn't speak, knowing it was best to let Jefferson play out whatever weird act he was putting on.

"It's really good that we found this note," he said slowly, keeping his voice quiet so that Brighton and Deacon wouldn't hear us on the other side of the door.

"But?" I prompted, knowing I was about to get in trouble.

"No but," he said. "I just want to stress to you how dangerous it can be to go running off after ghosts. I know you were excited, and your skills paid off. But you have to be careful."

I balked slightly at the unexpected kindness, almost at a loss for words. Was Jefferson really concerned about my well-being? And more importantly, had the world's least controlled man told me to have more self-control?

"I know it can be exciting sometimes," he went on, sounding much too human. "Making contact with the other side. But you still have to take your own safety into account."

"But they wanted us to find this paper, Jefferson," I said, interrupting his rare moment of sweetness. "They led us to the pool to help us. I can't just ignore a clue that's literally been handed to me."

"Just please promise me you'll be more careful in the future. Try to show a little restraint."

"Really?" I asked. "You're going to lecture me on restraint? The guy with the shadiest 'emergency kit' I've ever seen?"

Jefferson opened his mouth to speak, but shut it again. My guess was that he had something rude he wanted to say to me but just didn't feel like fighting with me anymore.

"Right," he finally said. He turned away from me and pushed the wedged-open door to Brighton's cabin, leaving me to glare at his back before following him inside.

"Have you looked at the paper yet?" Deacon asked. Brighton was sitting in her normal position on the bed, surrounded by computers and Xanax.

"Of course not," Jefferson said, sounding indignant that Deacon thought we'd look at our clue without him.

I sat next to Jefferson but tried not to touch him, still a little miffed about our disagreement. Really, he had been making sure I was okay and I should have appreciated that. But the fact that all three of my friends thought I was slightly crazy for doing what needed to be done to find this clue made me mad. Where would we have been if I hadn't been so "unrestrained"?

"This note," Jefferson began, looking down at the crisp white paper and studying it. "Looks brand new. I'm not sure it's our clue."

I sighed. "Just because it's new doesn't mean it's not what we were sent here to find."

"Well, don't just sit there," Deacon practically shouted. "Read it."

Our anticipation was suffocating.

"I need to go and collect my sweetheart," Jefferson began.

"A love letter?" I asked.

Jefferson ignored me and continued reading. "Eva lost her job last year after the tragic passing of the woman of the house, Alice Littlefield. I'll be in touch when I can."

We were all silent for a moment.

This sounded like a clue, but why was an old love letter written on a brand new sheet of paper?

"Texas," Brighton said, pulling us all from our silent reverie.

"Texas?" I repeated, looking over at her questioningly.

"The Littlefield house in Texas," she elaborated, holding her phone up to show me an image of a beautiful Victorian home. "Alice Littlefield died in 1935, one year before the maiden voyage of the Queen Mary. This was her house."

Brighton was hovering somewhere between excitement and an anxiety attack as she grinned at me.

"This is a real-life, honest, legitimate clue," she said. "We found a clue."

I tried not to smile, since I was still put out by the little lecture that Jefferson had given me, but I couldn't help myself. Brighton was right. We'd somehow managed to not only make contact on the Queen Mary, but we'd found the clue that would lead to our next location. Suddenly our wild goose chase didn't seem so crazy.

We had found what we were looking for. Not only were we on the right track, but we'd also made contact. A spirit had led us to our clue. And yet, I was uneasy by the newness of the paper, thinking something wasn't adding up.

Why would a note from the 1930s be written on new paper? Was someone following us around and planting these clues for us?

"You did it, Sadie," Jefferson said quietly, not looking at me as he spoke.

I couldn't tell if he was actually congratulating me or if he was being sarcastic, but I didn't really care.

"We're paranormal investigators," I said to the group with a small smile. I'd try to figure out my timelines later since I didn't feel like putting a damper on our victory by bringing up the new piece of paper.

"We investigated," Deacon said with a little nod.

"And found evidence," Brighton added.

"And now we know where we're going tomorrow. Perfect. I'm going to get some sleep," Jefferson said abruptly, standing from the bed and leaving the room without another word.

"What's his problem?" Brighton asked.

"He's Jefferson," I answered, as if that should be all the explanation she needed. "If he's not switching his personality every five seconds, he's not being himself."

I did have to wonder if our two-sentence disagreement might have set him off, but the interaction was so brief I couldn't imagine him being that put out by it.

"You should probably go talk him off of whatever ledge he's on," Brighton said to Deacon.

"Not likely," he answered with a laugh. "I'm going to bed. If you guys want to deal with Jefferson's dark and twisty place, be my guest, but I'm not touching that with a ten foot pole."

"Coward," Brighton said to Deacon's retreating form before adding, "Leave it to the Parrish boys to ruin a perfectly good night with their psychosis."

~

"Did you kiss Deacon?" I asked Brighton as we lay side by side in her bed.

I wasn't going to pretend I could spend the night in my room alone again, so I'd admitted my own cowardice and asked if I could stay in her room again for our last night on the ship. I'm sure Jefferson would have made fun of me, but no one had seen him since he had turned dark and broody.

"Let me sleep," she mumbled, halfway between dreams and wakefulness.

"If I don't get to sleep, then neither do you."

She groaned at this exclamation and rolled over on her side so that her back was to me. My insomnia was bad enough on a normal night, but being on the Queen Mary combined with the emotionally charged day I'd had meant I wasn't going to be getting any sleep that night. Of course, Brighton could sleep anywhere, but I wasn't about to let her off the hook after I'd caught her in a "compromising" situation with Deacon.

"I'm sleeping in the same bed as you. You can't really avoid the question." I nudged her in the back with my elbow.

She grunted, but finally rolled onto her back, joining me in staring at the ceiling.

"Think about who you're talking to," she said simply.

"You guys looked pretty cozy when I walked in."

"Yeah, and maybe something would have happened if you didn't have terrible timing," she said. "But we're talking about Deacon Parrish."

"So?" I asked.

"So, the boy can't talk to anyone of the female gender unless it's one of us," she explained. "He's not exactly the type to make a move."

"Maybe that means you have to make the move," I said.

"The girl who can't order her own food at restaurants because she's scared to talk to people? Yeah. That's not going to happen."

"If you're both such chickens, how did Deacon end up with his hand on your leg and his face about two inches from yours?" I asked in a conspiratorial tone.

Brighton just laughed at this question, making me want to hear the explanation even more. She reached over to check the time on her phone, knocking over about ten prescription bottles in the process and sending her anxiety medicine skittering across the nightstand.

"He pretended to be pointing something out on the screen," she said, still laughing. "And apparently that meant he had to lean really close to me."

"Those Parrish boys think they're pretty smooth," I said. "Jefferson and his whole stupid idea that we needed to pretend to be married."

"Yeah, what was that about?"

"Don't get me started on how little sense that boy makes," I said with a sigh.

We fell into an uneasy silence, thinking of the burden of a Parrish, before Brighton voiced something that had been bothering me.

"So, Texas," she said.

"Are we crazy for doing this?"

"You already asked me that," she pointed out.

"But the further into it we get, the more I'm starting to think we're crazy."

"I would agree, if we hadn't found a clue. If we've found what we're looking for, doesn't that mean we're not crazy?"

"Okay maybe not crazy. But out of our league, definitely."

"We're a little out of our league," she conceded. "But this is how we're making it into 'the league.' This guy chose us for a reason."

"That's another thing," I began.

Brighton cut me off. "No, Sade, we don't know who sent the letters. Yes, it's creepy. Yes, we should be kind of cautious and probably shouldn't expect to actually get money out of this. And no, I don't care."

"Well, that settles that issue then," I said. "At least Jefferson's mom is funding this little project."

"Sounds like he has some mommy issues," she agreed with a yawn.

I was losing her to sleep.

"And daddy issues," I said. "Who carries their dad's wedding ring around in their pocket?"

"If mommy and daddy issues were all Jefferson had, we'd be fine," Brighton said distantly. "But we have to worry about those multiple personalities of his that are going to snap one day and kill us all."

"Yeah," I agreed half-heartedly. "That'll be a fun day."

"So much fun," she answered, and I knew I had lost her.

Jefferson's mood swings were the least of my worries when compared to the monumental task of linking four haunted locations together for an unknown benefactor. Yet as I lay there, listening to Brighton gently snoring beside me, I didn't think of the job ahead of us. Instead, I thought of the crazy Parrish boy who was somehow the glue of our dysfunctional little group.

And that did nothing to comfort me.

CHAPTER II

The sunflower yellow polish on my toenails shone in the sun as my feet dangled out the window in the back seat of the Jeep. Even with the wind blowing through the open window, it was still like a sauna in the dumpy old Jeep with no air conditioner.

"I don't know that you're really allowed to have your feet hanging out the window like that," Jefferson said, his shaggy curls blowing wildly around his face.

"Quiet," I replied. "I'm concentrating. These nails aren't going to paint themselves."

I had my body parallel to the back seat, my back leaning against Jefferson's shoulder for support as I let my wet toes dry out the window, the wind pounding against them forcefully. Deacon and Brighton had claimed the front of the Jeep for this leg of the trip—Deacon piloting our massive hunk of junk like a captain and Brighton insisting a bug was going to hit my feet if I didn't pull them inside.

"Sade, you can't paint your nails in a moving car," Brighton singsonged from the passenger's seat.

"I'm actually highly impressed by the skill being displayed back here," Jefferson said, as I finished up my fingernails.

The drive from the Queen Mary to the Littlefield House was about nineteen hours long and our group, in our overly confident state, had decided to make the drive in one day—though that may have had more to do with our limited funds when it came to hotel rooms than the actual desire to be stuck in a Jeep together for nineteen hours.

The long trip had awakened a keen desire to find anything to entertain ourselves. As we slowly descended into boredom-derived madness, I'd decided to paint my nails in the failed hope that it would pass the time.

"Do you always color coordinate your nail polish with your clothes?" Jefferson asked disinterestedly.

I didn't think he actually cared, but at this point, any conversation was good conversation.

"I just happen to wear a lot of yellow." I stuck my tongue out the side of my mouth as I concentrated on not painting my entire finger.

"I guess at least if you spill it, it won't be noticeable," he replied with a yawn. He picked a loose thread off my grey and yellow striped shirt and placed it on my jean shorts.

I rolled my eyes.

"Let's play the cinema game again," Deacon suggested, obviously desperate for a distraction. He was met with a resounding chorus of nos and groans.

"We can talk about our clue again," Brighton said.

Jefferson rubbed his temples. "I'd rather play that rubbish cinema game than dissect those three sentences one more time."

"Ellen Page," Deacon said excitedly, apparently needing no more prompting to begin playing.

"I just think it would be wise to have some idea of what we're looking for when we get to this place," Brighton said, ignoring Deacon's game.

"*Inception*," Jefferson answered.

Apparently, the Parrish boys were playing the game by themselves.

I screwed the cap back on my nail polish. "I think we should try to figure out who Eva was," I said to Brighton.

"Leonardo DiCaprio," Deacon said.

"I'd start the questioning with her," Brighton suggested. "Maybe ask if she's still in the house or ask if any presence there knows who she is. It sounds like our mystery is surrounding whoever came over on the Queen Mary and this woman."

"*Romeo and Juliet*," Jefferson said, confusing me for a moment as I thought he was talking about our case and not his stupid game.

I blew on my fingernails. "We'll have to ask the people at the Littlefield House if they know anything about an Eva."

"Claire Danes," Deacon shouted after a moment.

"I already did. They said they don't have anything about her in their records except for a small document stating that she was some kind of maid or servant for Alice Littlefield."

"Stardust."

"So, our mystery man came over on the Queen Mary because his girlfriend Eva was suddenly unemployed after her employer died," I said. "But why did he get here a whole year after her death?"

"*Stardust*?" Deacon asked.

I glanced over my shoulder at Jefferson, who looked at me with a sly smile. He was winning at their little game. The Parrish boys were nothing if not competitive.

"Maybe he couldn't get enough money to come over right away?" Brighton asked. "Or he had to take care of some business first. I mean it's not like he could just buy a plane ticket online and fly over an hour later."

"Robert De Niro. Ha!" Deacon said triumphantly.

"Brighton, does he have his phone out?" Jefferson asked.

She and Deacon exchanged glances but didn't say anything.

Jefferson sat up abruptly, pushing me up in the process since I had been using him as a human backboard. He craned his neck over the front seat and pulled Deacon's phone out of his hands.

"It's very dangerous to surf the web and drive, cousin," Jefferson said darkly, though I could see his lips curling into a smile.

He was being "funny" Jefferson, not "I might snap and kill everyone in this Jeep" Jefferson.

"You need to lean back—trying to sit up like this on my own is an ab workout I'm not fond of," I said, reaching behind my back to push Jefferson against the seat so I could lean against him again while my toes finished drying out the window.

"I'm guessing the people at the Littlefield House were okay with us investigating?" I asked Brighton.

"So, here's the thing," she began.

"Brighton Gilbert, we are not breaking into this place to investigate," I said. "It's a school. They'd have on-campus security on us from the second we got in there."

"That's not what I was going to say," she said, stopping my accusation before it really took flight. "I may or may not have let the university think that we were part of a historical society doing research for an important scholarly project. But that's not important. What I was going to say is that this building is owned by the university now and they're doing some kind of Founder's Day town thing for the next week. They need the building for that."

"So how do we investigate if they're using the building?" I asked, trying to ignore the fact that she had definitely lied to the school to get our investigation approved.

"We only have tonight to do it," she answered.

"Tonight?" I repeated. "Tonight?"

"I think we only have tonight to investigate. Is that what you heard, Jefferson?" Deacon asked, making fun of me.

"Brighton, we already had to leave at five this morning, with only a few hours of sleep, to get to this place by midnight, and now this is the only chance we have to investigate?"

Even though we had taken shifts sleeping in the car, we were all exhausted. We'd already spent our nights on the Queen Mary investigating, and with our early morning departure time, we were barely functioning. There was no way we'd be able to conduct a successful investigation on such little sleep.

"It gets worse," she said with a wince.

"How could it get worse?" I asked.

"Our funds aren't stretching quite as far as I'd hoped."

"It's this brute of a Jeep," Deacon said knowledgeably. "It can't handle driving so far. It's sucking up gas like it's the end of the world."

"And what does that mean for us?" I asked.

"It means we have to share a hotel room tonight. And it's not the nicest place I've ever seen."

"We may get botulism staying there," Deacon added.

"What is it with you and botulism?" I asked him. "Everything is going to give us botulism."

"Okay, fine, we'll probably get athlete's foot from that place." He grinned. "Is that better?"

"What time will we get to Austin?" Jefferson asked, back to being all business.

"Originally I was thinking one in the morning," Brighton began.

"But thanks to my superb driving skills, we've managed to make up some time and we should be there around eleven," Deacon finished.

"That's not a terrible timeframe," Jefferson said with a nod, shifting his long limbs behind my back.

"I'm declaring tomorrow a 'no drive day,'" I said. "We can use the time in the hotel to go over footage and sleep until they kick us out."

"Sounds like a good plan to me," Brighton said.

I appreciated her support, especially since she didn't need a hotel room to sleep in. I could drop her into a dumpster and she'd sleep just fine. Well . . . except for the germs.

"I don't know why you guys are complaining so much anyway," Brighton went on. "You get to go into the Littlefield House to investigate. I'll be stuck sitting cross-legged in the back of this tiny Jeep with all four of the monitors. At least you get to stretch your legs a bit."

She did have a point. I felt bad that Brighton was always stuck in the small confines of the back of the Jeep. Unfortunately, until we could afford a nicer van (which probably wasn't going to happen any time soon), it was our only option.

"At least you're small," Jefferson said, tilting his head to the side and cracking his neck.

"Thank you for that," I said, finally pulling my feet inside of the Jeep and rolling up the window.

"I quite enjoy being your seat," he said with a smirk.

I grimaced. "I was talking about the neck cracking right in my ear. How long until we get there?"

"About six hours," Brighton answered with a sigh.

"Does anyone have a sleeping pill I could borrow?" I asked sarcastically.

"I've got some Xanax," Brighton offered with a laugh. "It always puts me to sleep."

"Being alive puts you to sleep," Deacon pointed out, quite accurately.

"Touché."

"I've got a brilliant idea on how we can pass the time," Jefferson said, instantly making me wish I hadn't said I was bored.

Whatever his idea was, it was sure to be monotonous and awful.

"Let's go over your lines for tonight."

CHAPTER 12

The Littlefield House was an amazing sight. As much as I'd loved investigating on the Queen Mary, the ornate details of this historic home continually distracted me while I was supposed to be asking ridiculous questions to any disembodied spirits that might be lurking about. Even though the paranormal-nerd in me ruled most of my life, my appreciation of historic buildings sometimes got in the way of investigations.

We'd managed to make it to Austin by ten at night, giving us about six hours to investigate before we had to pack up and be out of there. We'd already spent a good five hours checking claims from the docents, conducting question and answer sessions with empty rooms, and trying to get Deacon to take the investigation seriously. That count didn't even include the nine minutes of Beethoven Jefferson insisted on listening to before the investigation. I'd somehow managed to convince the Parrish boys that I didn't need to wear some ridiculous old-fashioned dress for this investigation, and instead remained in my striped shirt and jean shorts. The questions, though, I couldn't seem to get out of.

"Why am I asking about the Great Depression?" I asked, waiting for a response from Brighton, Deacon, or Jefferson, who were all stationed in the Jeep outside.

We'd been taking turns investigating all night, and now that I was inside for the second time, I was starting to think the location was a bust. We hadn't found a single scrap of evidence, let alone a game-changing clue.

"I was trying to think of relevant things that happened in 1935," Deacon said in my earpiece.

"Yeah, well, I'm going to ask normal questions for once to see if that gets us anywhere."

"Might as well," Jefferson said, his voice muffled by the static of the earpiece.

He was in a foul mood because we'd already used up most of our investigating time that night and still hadn't managed to find anything. He was quickly losing hope of locating our next clue and his hopelessness was starting to turn him into "dark and twisty Jefferson."

"Go ahead and ask your question," Brighton said over the mic. "I'll try to cheer up the little ball of sunshine out here."

Jefferson didn't respond, but I imagined he was narrowing his huge eyes at Brighton for that comment.

Holding the K2 meter in one hand and my camera with a flashlight fixed to it in the other, I glanced around the beautiful space with its billowing drapes and gold carpets. Maybe I should have worn the dress Jefferson brought for me; I was very out of place in my jean shorts and yellow ballet flats.

"Is Alice Littlefield here?" I asked.

I was trying to block out the sounds of Deacon and Brighton whispering in my ear about how we should get an RV instead of a van when we became millionaires. It wasn't an easy task.

I was met with silence to my question, but held onto the hope that I might be picking up some unheard audio on the camera.

"Alice, if you're here, can you reach out and touch the device in my hand?" I asked. "It's nothing to be scared of. When you touch it, these lights will light up to let me know you're here."

Nothing.

"It doesn't have to be Alice," I tried. "If there's anyone here with me, they can reach out to touch this device."

Nothing.

"Or even yell really loudly next to it," I offered. "Anything to make it light up."

"I'm sure your desperation is very inviting," Jefferson deadpanned in my ear.

He was slowly trailing into "snide Jefferson"—one of my least favorites of his mood swings.

Trying to ignore everything else, I took a deep breath and closed my eyes, thinking I could will the ghost of Alice Littlefield into contacting me.

"Did anyone here know an Eva?" I asked, holding the K2 steady and stretching my arm out a bit further, as if distancing it from me would make it more accessible to them.

Still nothing.

"This is useless," Jefferson said. "We're almost out of time and we haven't found so much as a cold spot. This is a bloody waste of time."

"Maybe we'll find something when we review the tapes?" Brighton offered, sounding less than convincing.

"What are we supposed to do if we don't find anything?" he asked.

Brighton was silent for a moment, probably having a panic attack and grasping her inhaler to her chest. I wasn't about to let her be pushed around by Jefferson Parrish. She didn't need the added anxiety in her life.

"Stop pestering her, Jefferson," I said. "I'll call the university and see if we can reschedule after their Founder's Day events."

"And what are we supposed to do until then?" he asked, making me want to punch him in the face.

"Sleep for once? Review tapes? You pick."

"Unless you want to sleep in the car, we don't really have that option," he said, pointing out our unfortunate financial situation that I was desperately trying to ignore.

"Everyone just be quiet," I finally said. "I wouldn't be able to hear even if someone was trying to make contact with all of this background noise." I hoped that would be enough to quiet the insufferable Parrish.

I expected an immature, "You started it," but was gratefully met with silence. Satisfied that I had ended the argument, I walked into the main sitting room and perched on one of the old arm chairs, resting the camera on my lap and reveling in the silence for a moment.

When stuck in a Jeep with Deacon and Jefferson, silence was difficult to come by. They were either always bickering with each other or trying to make my life miserable, so I took this rare opportunity to let myself listen to the old house, hoping I'd hear something.

It was several minutes before the sound of Jefferson's voice startled me back into reality.

"I'm pretty sure she fell asleep."

"This place is ridiculously quiet," I said, ignoring his accusation. "I mean, in a house this old you'd expect some creaky floorboards or wind sneaking through loose window panes, but there's just nothing. We don't even have normal sounds to blame on the plumbing."

"There's nothing here," Jefferson said, still sounding like he was throwing a fit. "Unless we plan to tear this place apart looking for some rubbish hidden letter, I think we need to call it a night."

"We've still got about thirty minutes before they wanted us out," Brighton said, trying to save the situation.

"I'll have a go," Deacon replied, not waiting for Jefferson to shoot his idea down. "Sadie, come on out. I'm going to work my magic."

"Sure thing," I answered with a yawn, grabbing the equipment I'd been toting around and making my way out into the warm night air.

I gave Deacon a sleepy high five as he passed me on his way into the house, then jumped up into the back of the Jeep where Brighton was squished between monitors and piles of equipment. Jefferson sat on the edge of the Jeep's gate, his long legs reaching the ground where mine dangled like a child's.

He was wearing a sweater vest over his shirt and tie, and his curly hair was a mess where he'd apparently run his fingers through it over and over again. He stared dejectedly at the ground, not bothering to look up when I sat next to him.

I glanced back at Brighton with a questioning look. She simply looked at Jefferson and then back at me before rolling her eyes in exasperation. We were used to his extreme mood swings by now, but that never made them much easier to deal with. The fact that he was so easily defeated didn't do much to boost the group's morale.

"You should know better than anyone that some of our best evidence has come after we review tapes from our investigations," I said, resisting the urge to hit him.

It was amazing how often I waffled between the that and being his friend. I guess it wasn't really his fault he was weird. Somehow, his lack of awareness made him slightly more sympathetic in my eyes.

"Well, we'd better find something in the next few minutes because I'm not calling my mum for more money," he said, twirling the gold wedding ring around his ring finger.

"I'm sure we'll find something," I lied.

The truth was we had hit a wall and I knew it. Coming to the Littlefield House, I'd thought evidence would be a piece of cake. There were so many claims surrounding the location of voices and objects being moved that it seemed impossible to do an entire night's investigation without finding a single scrap of evidence. Yet there we were, cramped in the back of an ancient Jeep Wagoneer in the warm Texas night with nothing to show for our efforts.

"If we're going to get all of our stuff packed up, we might want to start now," Brighton said gently, trying not to set Jefferson off.

"I'll start turning on the lights," Deacon said over the speaker.

None of us actually said we were giving up, but we all knew that's what was happening. We could only hope we'd find something on our tapes and audio files, but if we didn't find a clue, we'd have no idea where our next location was and our search would have been in vain. It wouldn't matter that we'd found amazing evidence on The Queen Mary because we'd hit a dead end in Austin.

"I'll wrap cords," I said, hopping out of the Jeep and walking into the beautiful old house.

After a moment, Jefferson stood and followed, silently gathering equipment and pulling tape off the floors.

I tried to smile at our team when I passed them in the hallways, but I was just as dejected as Jefferson. The trip had ended in a failure, and now we'd have to return to our mundane lives of being broke in Portland. Somehow I'd have to start making up for the days of work I'd missed, too.

"I didn't think we'd fail," Jefferson said, suddenly beside me. "Especially not at our second location."

He didn't sound particularly angry. If anything, he seemed resigned. We both silently stared at the painting, not voicing our failure aloud any more than we needed to.

"We still have the tapes to review," I reassured him, glancing at him for just a moment to offer a half-hearted smile.

He returned it for a split second before his already round eyes suddenly grew even bigger.

I felt my blood run cold at the look of amazement he was now aiming over my shoulder, afraid for what had changed his mood so quickly.

"What?" I asked, looking at the painting behind me.

"The light," he said, opening the door to the fully illuminated closet. "The light popped on."

"Are you sure?" I asked. "I mean, I can see that it's on now. But you're sure it wasn't on the whole time?"

"This is our ghost's MO," he said, now openly grinning. "The directions to the next location have to be in here."

I squeezed my way into the tiny coat closet with Jefferson, determined to find whatever small clue had eluded us during our entire investigation. If this really was our ghost's way of directing us down the right path, I wasn't going to risk Jefferson overlooking something.

"Sadie, I appreciate your willingness to assist," he said, "but there really isn't enough room in here for both of us."

As it was, I had pinned him against the wall with my hip as I dug through dusty coats and boxes of old files. It looked like the closet hadn't been opened in ages.

"If you can't stand the heat, get out of the closet," I said.

"First, that's not how that saying goes. And second, I saw the light first, ergo, I should get to find the clue."

I straightened up and faced Jefferson, ready to list the many reasons why I was a more worthy candidate of the closet search (starting with my small stature), when the closet door slammed shut and the light turned off. I jumped about a mile in the air at the sudden burst of noise.

"Fine, I'll get out if you want me out so badly," I said, trying laugh at myself for jumping.

"Yeah, I wanted you out of the closet so I shut the door," Jefferson said, reaching out to open it. I could hear him trying to turn the handle a few times with no luck before turning to me, the dim moonlight from outside the house streaming under the door being the only thing reflecting on his eyes.

"I can't get it open."

"Don't be stupid," I said in annoyance, pulling on the string of the old light bulb that had chosen the worst possible time to burn out. Giving up on that, I fumbled around for my flashlight and clicked it on, just as the fact that we were trapped in the closet sank into my brain.

"You've got to be kidding me." I closed my eyes and took a few deep breaths, trying not to let my claustrophobia get the better of me. I was somewhere in a wide open field. No one was around me. I was free to walk anywhere I chose.

"Deacon!" Jefferson shouted. "Brighton?"

His voice shattered my self-made method of coping. "Please stop shouting," I said in a choked voice. I kept my eyes closed tightly. "Just . . . just be quiet for a minute, okay?"

"They have to know we're in here or they won't know to get us out," he said, his voice much too close to me.

I was suddenly aware of his heart beating against my cheek, the sound of his breathing, and the way his clothing rubbed with every miniscule movement. I began to sweat. Every sound seemed magnified in the small space and it only made the walls feel that much closer.

"Stop breathing," I pleaded, my heart rate picking up and my breathing becoming shallow. "Just don't breathe or move or . . ." My words trailed off as my throat caught.

"Sadie, you need to calm down," he said.

I felt him pull my flashlight out of my grasp and swore I could actually hear the blood flowing through his veins.

"You need to take a deep breath. You're hyperventilating."

"There's no deep breath to take," I said. "There's no air in here." My own heartbeat pounded in my ears.

I could hear my rapid shallow breaths as if they were being broadcast over a loudspeaker, and I was quickly growing lightheaded.

"What are you guys doing in there?" Brighton asked on the other side of the door.

"The door is jammed. Can you lot get it open?" Jefferson asked, his voice so loud and close that it was deafening.

"The power went out in the house," Deacon said, his footsteps on the carpet outside sounding miles away.

If I could just get on the other side of the door, I'd be okay. As it was, I felt like the walls of the closet were crushing me on either side, pressing up against my arms and burying me under the suffocating piles of old coats. I tried to back away from Jefferson but didn't make it an inch before my back hit the wall.

"I can't do this," I whispered.

"Can you please try to hurry and unjam the door?" Jefferson asked, his voice falsely calm. "Sadie's freaking out in here."

I heard Brighton mumble something to Deacon about me being claustrophobic, but I was too far gone in my panic to really make it out.

"Sadie, just hang in there for a second," Brighton said a little louder. "We're going to get a letter opener or something to unlock the door."

I knew she understood irrational phobias better than anyone in the world, since there wasn't a single phobia she didn't already possess.

"We'll be right back," Deacon called.

My chest rose and fell faster and faster until I didn't think I could possibly breathe anymore.

"Sade, listen to me," Jefferson said in a low, quiet voice, placing his hands on my arms and making me feel even more enclosed. "You need to calm down. I know you don't think there's any air in here, but just take a few deep breaths. Please."

I grimaced at his words and tried taking a deep breath, but ended up hiccupping instead, my brain fuzzy from the lack of oxygen in the closet. Jefferson turned off the flashlight and stuck it in his pocket.

"You need to try to focus on something else," he said, beginning to rub his thumbs over my arms in what was supposed to be a soothing way. "Think about all of the great evidence that's probably in this closet. We can explore it more once we get the door open."

"Why do you carry your dad's wedding ring around with you?" I asked, voicing the first distracting thought that came to mind.

It was all I could do. He stopped rubbing my arms but I didn't open my eyes to see his face. I didn't want to be reminded of just how small the closet was. I could already feel the walls against my sides and back, and Jefferson was pressed up against my front. There was no room anywhere. I could feel my breath come back and hit me in the face as it bounced off of his neck.

"It's the only thing I have from my father," he said.

I wasn't sure if I cared that he kept talking or not. All I could really focus on was the stale air and the bead of sweat that was slowly trailing down my temple.

"He died of cancer when I was really little," he continued, and I tried desperately to focus on his voice and ignore the pressure of the wall against my back or Jefferson's heart against my cheek.

"Sorry," I managed to choke out.

"My mum is really cold. Not motherly at all. But my dad was the warmest person in the world."

I tried to say something but my throat was too dry, so I continued to listen in silence, focusing on slowing down my breathing.

"My dad was a brilliant businessman and he was quite wealthy. When he died, all of that went to my mum, which was perfect for her. She wasn't really cut out to be a wife or a mother. She was cut out to be a rich socialite. Ingrid Temple, mother of the year," he said.

"And?" I asked, looking up at him as my eyes began to adjust to the darkness.

His hands left my arms and he brought them together in front of my chin in the small space, probably playing with the ring again, although I wasn't about to check.

"My mum couldn't stand having all of my dead father's things in the house after he died, so she sold all of his stuff," he said. "Didn't even keep a picture of him up. Although I did manage to lock his office and told her that if she broke the lock and went inside, I'd tell all of her socialite friends what a terrible mother she really was."

I could tell this was an extremely personal memory that he probably didn't want to share with me, and I wished I could tell him I was probably only hearing half of what he said, so his secrets were safe.

"I managed to steal his wedding ring out of her room one night and I've hidden it from her ever since. She thought she'd just lost it."

I managed to slow my breathing down, listening to Jefferson's voice right in front of me and focusing on the words he was saying.

"I know I kind of worship my father, but when you lose someone so young, you only really remember the good things about them, you know? But I'd rather put my dad on a pedestal than be like my mum, who finds any opportunity to bring up every fight they ever had."

"Why don't you wear the ring?" I asked, my eyes still closed as I continued to slow my breathing. "Why do you keep it in your pocket?"

"It never really fit me before."

"But it does now." I finally gained control over my breath, although I kept my eyes closed.

One thing at a time.

"This sounds ridiculous, but I just wasn't sure if it was okay to wear it," he said. "If I'm worthy to wear it. The odd Parrish kid who stole his dad's wedding ring and unsettles his family with his 'intensity.'"

He laughed, but it sounded hollow. I knew I should be comforting him when he was bearing his soul to me, but I was having a difficult time opening my eyes. It was the first time Jefferson had acted like a human being and I couldn't even enjoy it because I was terrified of the stupid closet.

I took two deep breaths, telling myself that when I opened my eyes I was going to concentrate only on Jefferson's face. I would try to read his expression and say something that would comfort him. I wouldn't pay any attention to the walls around me.

When I parted my lids and looked up at him, he wasn't looking at me. He was staring at the plain gold wedding band he had pinched between his fingers, his brow furrowed and his dark curls covering his forehead.

Ignoring my racing heart and the coats that engulfed me, I pulled the ring from his grasp and slowly slid it over his ring finger on his right hand. He let his large green eyes flick up to meet mine in the darkness, looking confused.

"It's never wrong to try to connect with someone you've lost," I told him, pursing my lips. "You shouldn't feel guilty for wanting to remember your dad."

I let my hand cup his cheek, hoping I was being at least a halfway decent friend and comforting him somewhat, since I was the one who'd forced him to reveal his sadness in the first place. I was sure he wouldn't have opened up like that to me if the situation hadn't been desperate.

He looked down at me with his big sad eyes, and I could almost understand where some of the mood swings came from. He was fighting an internal battle over his feelings toward his family. It was, unfortunately, something I did often, being the not-favorite daughter.

"I think it would make your dad really happy if you wore his ring," I finally said.

Jefferson's brows knitted together as his eyes roamed across my face. He looked like he might say something for a moment before his long arms encircled me and pulled me into him, engulfing me in a tight hug. He rested his cheek on the top of my head, my face slightly smashed into his neck, but even in the middle of my claustrophobic panic attack, I didn't mind.

I let my arms circle around his waist and held him like that in silence for a moment, rubbing his back soothingly. I wasn't really sure what I should say to him, but it felt like this silent gesture was better than any words I could offer.

I had to wonder if Jefferson's obsession with paranormal investigation came from his desire to connect with his father again, but that was a question I'd leave for another time.

"Thank you, Sadie," he said into my hair, still holding me tightly against him.

"It's just the truth, Jefferson." I pulled away slightly, looking up at him and feeling like I might almost understand the bizarre Parrish for once. "Thanks for telling me."

"Thanks for listening," he said with a small smile.

Then, the door swung open in a sudden burst of light.

Jefferson immediately dropped his hands from where they had somehow come to rest on my waist, and I pulled away from him as much as I could in the small closet, banging my elbow on the wall behind me and bringing my hand up over my eyes to shield them from the bright flashlight either Brighton or Deacon was shining into the closet.

As they lowered the light slightly, I was expecting a questioning look from Brighton or some inappropriate comment from Deacon, but instead, both of them stared at the back of the closet with open mouths. Jefferson and I followed their gaze curiously until we found the source of their wonder.

The back of the closet had a small panel of wood that didn't match the rest of the wall.

CHAPTER 13

"What is that?" Brighton asked, trying to get to the panel before realizing there was no possible way we could fit another person into the closet with us.

"Sadie, why don't you step out into the hallway," Jefferson instructed after clearing his throat. "Get some air."

As much as I wanted to see what was behind that mismatched panel, I didn't need to be told twice. I practically jumped through the open doorway out into the hallway that suddenly seemed so much colder than the cramped closet.

"Wait, don't touch it!" Brighton shouted, startling me. "You guys, this place is a historic site; you can't just rip down the walls. It's bad enough that we've blown the power."

"If you really think we're going to ignore the fact that a ghost led us to this secret compartment, you're mental," Jefferson said. He was, once again, taking no time at all to flip his mood like the light switch it was.

"A light turning on in a closet is not a ghost leading you to a clue," Brighton countered.

"You're right," Jefferson agreed, surprising me. "But a light suddenly turning off as a ghost locks you in a closet is another story."

Brighton was silent for a moment, narrowing her eyes at the impossible Parrish, while Deacon stood on the sidelines watching the whole thing unfold. Eventually, Brighton shook her head, glanced around the empty house, and then nodded at Jefferson.

"I'm pretty sure our time is almost up and I don't know when the docent will be here to lock up, so whatever you do, do it fast."

"Right," Jefferson said, turning to pull the panel away from the wall.

I stood on my tiptoes to see around Deacon's tall frame as Jefferson wedged his long fingers underneath the old wood and pulled as hard as he could. It didn't take much force before the panel popped off, releasing a little cloud of dust in the process. A small compartment lay behind the old wall, too deep and dark to see the end of it.

"I bet there are so many spiders in there," Brighton said with a shiver. Jefferson ignored her as he rolled up the sleeve on his white collared shirt and stuck his arm into the dark space. He immediately screamed out, causing all of us to jump. He laughed at how jittery we were.

"Very mature," I said. "Is there anything useful in there or did we just get stuck in a closet for no reason?"

"Feels like another letter. And a necklace of some sort."

"Hello?"

The four of us jumped even higher than we had when Jefferson had yelled, and I think, for a moment, we honestly thought the newcomer was a ghost. The small older woman who rounded the corner with her flashlight and grey tied-up hair, however, was slightly more frightening than a ghost as we stood in front of the closet we had just vandalized.

Deacon, who was much quicker on his feet than the rest of us, stepped forward to greet the docent, who had come to show us out and lock the building after we left. He used his frame to block her view of the giant hole in the wall.

"I'm so glad you're here," he said, trying to be charming.

At least this woman was far beyond dating range. Maybe for some reason that made her less intimidating to Deacon.

"Can you direct me to the fuse box?" Deacon asked. "We seem to have lost power."

"I was wondering why it was so dark in here," she said, failing to notice the nervous smiles our group wore. "It's right this way, dear."

Deacon threw us a look over his shoulder that said "hurry up" before the two rounded the corner. Brighton took a deep puff on her inhaler and closed her eyes. I could only imagine how painful it had been for her to refrain from using the inhaler while the woman was in the hall with us.

"We've got this," I said, giving her a quick pat on the shoulder. I turned to Jefferson. "Fix it!"

"You're so bossy." He slid the letter and necklace into his pocket and replaced the wood panel. It seemed to pop right back into place, luckily, and Jefferson quickly moved the coats on their hangers so that they covered the wall before stepping out of the closet and dusting his vest off.

He smirked. "And you doubted me."

"Let's just pack up the rest of our stuff and get out of here," I said. "Deacon can only distract a woman for so long."

"Ouch," Jefferson said.

"No, she's right," Brighton said, apparently regaining her ability to breathe. "I love him, but he's too scared of women. It won't take him long to realize that he's actually trapped alone with someone of the opposite sex and he'll start to freak out."

"Fair enough," Jefferson agreed.

~

"Boston isn't exactly a small city," Deacon said around a mouthful of noodles, passing the Chinese take-out box to me.

I scooped my own noodles out and shoved them unceremoniously into my mouth before passing the box on to Jefferson.

"That's what public records are for," I said. "We can check a census or something to see if there's any record of an Eva or Thatcher living in Boston around 1937."

"First names won't be enough," Jefferson said, passing the Chinese food back to Deacon after taking some. "We really need to figure out last names if we're going to narrow our search down."

"Well, we don't have last names," I said, "so I guess we just have to hope there aren't too many Thatchers in Boston in our timeframe."

We all sat in a clump on one of the full-size beds in the hotel room, a couple of Chinese food boxes between us as we tried to stick to our minuscule budget without starving to death.

I watched curiously as Brighton poked the contents of the take-out box with her chopsticks. "Brighton, what are you doing?" I asked.

"Trying to see if there are any noodles in here that you guys didn't get your germs all over," she answered in the most serious tone I'd ever heard her use.

"No one's touched this box yet," Deacon said, looking very anxious to deliver this good news. "You can have it."

"She bloody well can't." Jefferson snatched the unopened box from his cousin for a moment, before I was able to steal it right back and hand it to my germaphobe of a friend.

"Leave her alone, Jefferson," I said "Sure, she might die ten years sooner than the rest of us because all that hand sanitizer and clean water has killed her immune system, but at least she won't have to swap spit with us."

"Thanks for the help," she said sarcastically, although I noticed she didn't complain about getting her own box of food.

She'd probably starve before sharing food with someone.

"When will you treat us to a taste of your Cuban heritage by cooking something for us, Sadie?" Deacon asked.

"She rejects her Cuban heritage," Jefferson stated matter-of-factly.

I would have thrown him a dirty look, but he was right.

"Why?" Deacon pressed.

"Because her mum wants her to embrace it and she doesn't like her mum," Jefferson said.

"I can answer for myself," I said.

"Am I wrong?" he asked, raising a challenging eyebrow.

I didn't answer, but rolled my eyes at him, not wanting to give him the pleasure of knowing he was right.

The corners of his mouth tightened as he puckered his lips out in a self-satisfied smile.

He was the worst.

"Read the letter again, Sadie," he said, becoming serious once more. "There has to be some kind of clue in there that will narrow down our search."

I picked up the yellowed piece of paper delicately, not wanting to stain our only valuable clue. The necklace we'd found, which had the initials "E.C. and E.M." engraved onto the heart-shaped metal, had led us to another dead end. The letter was our only hope. Without this simple letter, we were stuck in Texas with no direction in our lives and no money in our bank accounts. With it, however, we were one step closer to solving our puzzle.

"I'm sure one day I'll understand why things had to end this way, Thatcher," I read. "I can only hope the beauty of Boston makes up for the sadness I feel in my heart."

It didn't matter how many times we read the crumpled up letter, it still didn't reveal any new secrets to us.

"We know she never sent him this letter," Deacon said.

"That's true," I agreed, not sure this really helped us. "Maybe because she went after him?"

"That's not really relevant though," Jefferson said. "We don't need to piece together their story; we need to find out where our next location is."

"But piecing together their story is part of that," Brighton insisted. "Our 'benefactor' said he or she wanted us to find the link between all of these places, and obviously Thatcher and Eva are the people we're following here. They are our link."

"Are we trying to solve their mystery?" I asked. A love story with a sad ending was not much of a mystery.

"There has to be more to the story," Brighton said, abandoning her food as her imagination kicked into overdrive. "Thatcher came all the way from England to see Eva after she lost her job. I doubt one year later he'd suddenly decide he didn't want her anymore. There must have been a reason he ended it so abruptly. Maybe because of the second set of initials on the locket Eva hid?"

"I think you've been watching too many of your Korean dramas," Jefferson said, taking the letter from my hand.

It didn't escape my notice that he still wore his father's ring on his right hand, and I couldn't help but feel a small surge of pride that I had convinced him that it was okay to remember his dad. The ring was a reminder that Jefferson was actually a human being underneath all of the mood swings and disturbing mannerisms.

"Mark my words," Brighton said. "You find the reason Thatcher left Eva so suddenly, and you figure out our mystery. And if it doesn't have something to do with this third player from the necklace, I'll share food with all of you."

I pondered this for a moment, wondering if it could really be that simple. Or not so simple depending on how you looked at it, since we had no idea who the other person on the necklace was.

"Do you think our benefactor knows the answer to this mystery?" I threw one of the empty Chinese food containers across the room and narrowly missed the trash can. "Or are they just hoping there is a link between these places? Because I'm going to be pretty mad if we're searching for something that doesn't exist."

"If it comes to that, I say we just make up a link and get our money," Deacon answered with a yawn. He took his glasses off to rub his blue eyes sleepily. "If we're going to head out early tomorrow . . . or today, I guess, we should get some sleep."

"Agreed," I said.

Our "no drive day" had been cancelled since we had a real clue to follow.

I had gotten almost no sleep on the Queen Mary, and sleeping in the car on the way to Texas hardly counted, so my eyelids were drooping before Deacon even made the suggestion to go to bed. No matter how cramped it would be with two incredibly tall Parrish boys in one full bed and Brighton and me in the other, I knew I'd sleep better tonight than I'd ever slept in my life.

CHAPTER 14

I stared at the dark ceiling in a silent rage.

Or at least, I tried to stare at the ceiling.

It was a bit difficult with Brighton's arm dangling over my face.

I'd already pushed her off of me five times in the last two hours, but no matter how thin and perfect my best friend was, she was a bit of a bed hog. Of course, the fact that she slept like the dead didn't help, because every time I rolled her over or pushed her arms off me, she'd just fling her long limbs out again and smack me on the nose.

I let out a little huff of frustration, trying to be silent in my anger so I didn't wake the Parrish boys. No matter how impossible they were on a daily basis, a tired Parrish was by far the worst kind to deal with.

Moving slowly to avoid rustling the covers, I turned over on my side, facing away from Brighton and finding an impossibly large set of green eyes staring at me. Needless to say, I jumped at the unexpected and unwanted company of Crazy Parrish Number One, lying on his side and watching me like a creeper.

"Why are you still awake?" I whispered in slight annoyance.

"You try sharing a bed with Deacon," he whispered back.

"Don't get me started. At least he doesn't beat you up all night."

"You have no idea. He's a sleep snuggler," Jefferson said with an exaggerated shudder. "I'm two seconds away from sleeping in the bathtub."

I smiled over at him, feeling like maybe Brighton's violent sleeping wasn't quite as bad as being "snuggled" by a Parrish.

We both fell silent again, me thinking about how grumpy I'd be in the morning since I obviously wasn't getting any sleep that night, and Jefferson staring at me as usual.

"You know how people say you're weird?" I asked him. He nodded, not even trying to deny it. "This is why."

"What did I do?" he asked defensively.

"Why are you just staring at me?"

"I'm not staring, I'm looking. There's a difference," he said. "And besides, why is it weird to look at someone? I think it's weird to avoid eye contact all the time like you do. That seems way more suspicious than someone who will look you in the eye."

"I don't avoid eye contact," I answered. "Your staring is much more off-putting."

"That's the problem with you and all of the 'normal' people, Sadie. You think it's weird to be yourself and act on normal impulses," he said, not convincing me at all. "Why shouldn't I look at you if I want to?"

"That, right there, is what I'm talking about. That's a weird thing to say. Why would you want to look at me?"

"Because I'm trying to figure out what you're thinking, since you're so opposed to the idea of just telling me what's on your mind. You bloody women," he said to himself, as if the female species plagued his existence on a regular basis.

"You don't need to know every little thought in my head, Jefferson," I said.

"At least I don't purposefully avoid eye contact with you. All. The. Time."

"I don't do that," I reiterated.

"I watch you, remember? I can tell that you're avoiding looking at me. When we were stuck in that closet, I think that's the first time you've held eye contact with me for more than a few seconds."

I stopped and thought back on our interactions. Most of the time I was annoyed with Jefferson because of his mood swings. Even when he was in a good mood, I spent most of my time getting ready to be annoyed with him for a mood swing that may or may not happen. He may have been weird but he was also observant, and suddenly I felt like a bad friend. He didn't deserve half of the attitude I threw his way. He was just so odd that I couldn't help it.

"I'm going to go sleep in the tub," Jefferson said suddenly, slipping out of the tiny bed and grabbing his pillow.

I wasn't sure if Deacon had tried to snuggle him again or if he just wanted an abrupt ending to our conversation, but either way, I didn't want to be the reason he woke up with a neck cramp and complained all day. I could only imagine Jefferson attempting to bend his spidery limbs into the small space.

"Wait," I called after him in a low whisper, untangling myself from Brighton's arm that had twisted around my neck in a forceful headlock.

I suspected she let all of her pent-up anxiety out at night, which resulted in the acts of violence.

"We can set up camp on the floor," I suggested. "It'll be a lot more comfortable than you trying to squeeze into the tiny tub."

He looked at me suspiciously.

"Just wait here," I said with a sigh.

He could be suspicious all he wanted—I just had to show him we were actually friends, no matter how mad he made me.

Grabbing every spare towel in the bathroom and all of our coats from the closet, I formed two lumpy piles of assorted soft items in the small space between the two beds on the floor and threw comforters over them, since Deacon and Brighton insisted on only sleeping with the sheets. Apparently Brighton had read that hotels never washed their comforters so she refused to use them, and Deacon copied her.

"Those comforters are probably full of bedbugs," Jefferson said, though he still climbed into the makeshift bed I'd made for him.

I was glad to see that he was, once again, wearing pajama pants and a T-shirt.

"Stop complaining. I'm being nice," I said, climbing into my own little bed. It was surprisingly a lot more comfortable than I thought it would be.

I formed a little wall of towels between us and prayed Jefferson was a less violent sleeper than Brighton. At least on the floor I had a lot more room to myself, even if it meant technically sleeping on the same level as a Parrish. We were still a few feet apart, so that was a plus.

"You wear a lot of yellow," Jefferson said out of the blue, eyeing the yellow tank top and shorts I wore.

He was lying on his side, still staring at me, but I didn't think telling him to stop would really do anything. I stayed on my back, looking up at the ceiling and avoiding eye contact . . . something I apparently did often.

"That's another weird thing to say," I pointed out.

"It was an observation. How is it weird?" he asked defensively.

He was mad that I was shooting down all of his attempts at small talk. At six in the morning.

"Because we weren't talking about clothes, or colors, or anything."

"You were looking at my pajamas and making some judgment in your head, so I thought I'd talk about clothes too," he said, very matter-of-factly. "Like how you're not wearing the purple pajamas today."

How on earth did he know I was thinking about his pajamas?

"You are one creepy boy," I muttered. I didn't think it was worth mentioning that I didn't own purple pajamas since it was none of his business.

"And you're impossible. All I say are nice or neutral things to you and all you say are mean things to me."

It was a simple enough assessment, but it still made me feel bad.

We were silent again for a moment. I wasn't sure if Jefferson was still staring at me or if he'd given up being creepy for the night, so after a moment I turned onto my side to find that he was, in fact, still looking at me. Of course.

"Yellow is my favorite color," I said. He was starting to make me feel guilty about being so mean to him, so I decided I'd play his game and have a weird Jefferson-esque conversation.

"Why is that?" he asked.

Of course, this would be a conversation he'd want to have in the wee hours of the morning, because what else could we possibly be doing right at that moment?

"It's bright and happy and full of life."

I let my tired eyes roam over the planes of his face. His sharp cheekbones and jaw caught the fading moonlight in a dramatic way, the straight edge of his nose throwing his face into sharp focus in the darkness. It was amazing how different he and Deacon looked in some aspects. They were both tall and thin, but Jefferson was all olive skin, dark eyes, and curly brown hair, while Deacon was pale with blonde hair and blue eyes. It didn't make sense to me that they were related.

"You're nervous about going to Boston," Jefferson said, catching me off guard.

I had gotten lost in studying his face and forgotten we were having a conversation.

I guess he was right—you could stare at a person in silence without feeling like a huge weirdo. It was possible to lose track of time trying to figure someone out based on the expression in their eyes or mouth.

"A little," I confessed.

"But not because of the investigation."

It wasn't a question. He knew enough about my family to know I had my own reasons for avoiding Boston. We may have never sat down and had a heart-to-heart about the reasons, but Jefferson was observant. He had picked up little bits and pieces of phone conversations and rants to Brighton.

"I just don't want my parents to find out I was in Boston and didn't come visit them."

"Or your sister," he added.

"Or her."

My older sister, Michigan, was my family's pride and joy, although I wasn't quite sure why. She was definitely the sweeter one out of the two of us, but she hadn't done anything extraordinary with her life to make her so much better to my parents.

"Could you be exaggerating your parents' bias in your head just a little?" Jefferson asked.

"They moved away from their hometown just because Michigan got it into her head that she wanted to live in Boston," I said. "Honestly, I think she moved there to get away from their smothering, and they still preferred to live by her instead of me. And to top it all off, she's a liar anyway. She'd constantly tell my parents about all of these horrible things I'd supposedly said to her that I never actually did. And when I'd confront her about them, she'd stick to the lie and insist I'd said everything she'd told my parents. Right to my face. She'd flat out lie."

I felt a little bad complaining about my parents and sister to Jefferson when he'd told me about his cold, gold-digging mother and his dead father, but I couldn't help myself. My family was a sore spot.

"At least they didn't name you Michigan," he joked.

I found that I was smiling in spite of myself. "That was all my mom. She's this crazy Cuban woman who went from being Yaraina Vasquez to Yaraina Smith. I think to spite the fact that my father's family changed their Cuban last name to something boring and American when they moved here, she decided to name her first daughter the weirdest thing she could possibly think of."

Jefferson let a small smile cross his lips. An actual smile.

"Good thing you weren't born first, huh?"

"My dad had a lot of say over my first name, which is good, since I'd probably have ended up being named Colorado or something."

"Your mother sounds charming," Jefferson said.

"She's nuts," I assured him.

"I think she sounds great," he said again.

He didn't state outright that I was lucky to have a loving mother, even though I could read the subtext pretty plainly.

I guess the fact that he hadn't come right out and said it was an improvement toward becoming normal.

"It's late," I finally said, stating the obvious.

"What time does the hotel kick us out?" Jefferson asked.

"Eleven, I think."

"At least we'll get some sleep now, thanks to your genius." He smiled at me appreciatively.

"I do what I can." I yawned, pulling the probably filthy comforter up to my chin and closing my eyes.

"Good night, Sadie," Jefferson said after a moment.
"Good night, Jefferson."

CHAPTER 15

"You have to take a picture."

In my half-awake, half-sleeping state I heard Brighton and Deacon murmuring about something. I hardly cared what it was. I hadn't gotten nearly enough sleep and was determined to drown them out at all costs.

"You know she'll kill you for this, right?" he asked with a nervous laugh.

"But they're so cute," she responded.

I could feel the pressure of an arm lying over my own with a hand resting along my jawbone, and I could only guess who it belonged to. Hearing the camera on Brighton's phone snap a picture, I knew it was too late to avoid the embarrassing situation, so I kept sleeping, not caring that Jefferson had his hand resting on my face like some poorly posed photo in a magazine.

He could have had his foot in my mouth for all I cared. I was too tired to do anything about it.

"Should I pick up some breakfast before we start packing?" Deacon whispered.

"That would be great!" she said. "I'm going to grab a quick shower before Jefferson wakes up and hogs the bathroom trying to style his mass of curls."

"I'll see you in fifteen," Deacon said, leaving the hotel room in relative silence.

As exhausted as I was, I couldn't seem to force myself back to sleep, though I was lazy and refused to actually get out of bed when I had another fifteen possible minutes of good rest before I'd be forced awake.

I kept my eyes closed as Brighton rummaged through her bag and eventually went into the bathroom, closing the door behind her and turning on the shower.

A moment later I felt Jefferson move beside me.

"Sadie?" he whispered quietly.

I wasn't sure why, but I kept my eyes closed and my breathing slow.

I felt Jefferson's thumb trace a light line down my jaw, running back and forth across my skin. I tried desperately to be annoyed or creeped out by his behavior, but some small part of me felt content to stay there, so I kept my eyes closed, still pretending to be asleep.

There was something liberating in the guise of sleep. It was like running an experiment where you got to watch the results unfold without the test subject knowing they were being observed.

After a moment, his thumb trailed over my lips in the lightest of touches and I knew my goose bumps would give me away, so I shifted my weight, hoping that the signs I was waking up from my fake sleep would deter any further physical contact from Jefferson . . . partly because it was totally weird, and partly because I wanted to keep pretending I was asleep so he'd keep his thumb running over my lips. That was a dangerous thought to have.

Luckily, the second I shifted my weight and let out a sigh as if I were waking up, he pulled his hand away from me quickly, just like I'd wanted him to. Sort of.

"Sadie?" he said again, this time a bit louder.

"Hmmm?" I answered, slowly opening my eyes. My intention was looking at the ceiling, although I stole a quick glance at Jefferson first.

His curls were sticking up in an unruly coif, but he looked well rested. A lot more well rested than I felt.

"We should probably get ready to leave," he said after a moment, his voice husky from sleep.

I let my eyes wander back to him and found that he was, as usual, looking at me, though his large green eyes were now trained on my lips, which made me infinitely more uncomfortable. And slightly curious. But mostly uncomfortable.

"I'll go kick Brighton out of the shower. Besides, we're sleeping on all of the towels, so she might have a nasty surprise when she gets out." I was unsure of what else to say. "Is it okay if I shower first?"

"I've got to map out the next leg of our trip anyway," he responded. He stood up and started gathering various papers and maps, suddenly out of whatever spell he'd been in.

"Sounds like a plan," I said, slightly confused by his behavior.

If I was being honest, though, it wasn't Jefferson's behavior that had me worried. It was my own.

He was Jefferson Parrish. There was no way on earth I should have been okay with him touching me. He was hardly human on a good day, and there I was, finding myself sad that we weren't in close quarters anymore. I actually had to resist the urge to go stand next to him, just so we could be close again. It was ridiculous and slightly insane. Maybe being around the Parrish boys for so long had finally unraveled my mind.

I grabbed some things out of my bag, but found myself unintentionally stopping to stare at Jefferson. He was sitting at the small table hunched over a piece of paper, writing like a madman. He puckered his lips for a moment as his pen hovered above the page, anticipating what he'd write next.

Suddenly he glanced over at me. "Hey, Sadie?"

I looked down in embarrassment, startled out of my little episode. "Yeah?" I tried to be nonchalant as I gathered the rest of my toiletries.

He grinned. "You're staring at me and it's really weird," he teased.

My cheeks instantly flushed and instead of saying something witty back to him like I should have, I grabbed two towels and darted into the bathroom, shutting the door behind me and wishing I could crawl into a hole and die.

"That had better be Sadie or there'll be a dead Parrish in about five seconds," Brighton called from the other side of the shower curtain. She turned off the water and poked her head around to see who it was.

"You need a towel and I need to get away from Jefferson, so I come in peace." I threw the towel at her and busied myself with brushing my teeth to give Brighton some privacy.

"Right. Jefferson," she said, her voice irritatingly slow.

"Don't even." As I spoke with a mouthful of toothpaste, I dripped a glob onto my yellow tank top.

I was horrified by the spikey mess that was my hair, so I avoided looking in the mirror until I could shower and make myself look decent.

It didn't really help that Brighton stepped out of the shower, fully clothed in a cute pink shirt and skinny jeans, looking like a model, even with wet hair and no makeup.

I rinsed my toothbrush. "Did you put your clothes on in the shower?"

"Yeah."

"That's quite a skill," I said. "You didn't get your clothes all wet?"

"I have social anxiety disorder, Sade. Do you really think I could have survived a high school PE class if I didn't know how to change in the shower?"

She did have a point.

"Here's your mirror, by the way," she said, handing me an ornate, sliver, antique hand mirror.

One of the few I'd brought with me.

I collected antique hand mirrors.

Well . . . maybe collected was the wrong word. I was sort of a hoarder. I wasn't sure if the obsession had sprouted from some weird Bloody Mary infatuation. Or maybe just the idea that so many people had looked into these mirrors for so many years. It felt like keeping a piece of their historical reflection.

Which sounded crazy. Probably because it was.

Of all the not-normal things I couldn't seem to stop myself from taking an interest in, the mirror thing was maybe the weirdest. Although my newfound admiration of Jefferson Parrish was high up on that list.

I hadn't even known Brighton knew about me bringing some of my mirrors with me. I kept the weird obsession pretty well hidden.

"Where did you get this?" I looked suspiciously back and forth between her and the mirror that I finally took from her outstretched hand.

"You asked me last night to put it in the bathroom for you," she said, sounding completely unconcerned.

It was like Michigan putting words into my mouth all over again.

"I never told you to do that."

Brighton shot me a sideways glance that said I might just be crazier than her. "Maybe you were too tired to remember. But you definitely said, 'Brighton, there's a silver mirror in my bag. Can you put it in the bathroom for me?' I mean, I thought it was a weird request, but I obliged."

I opened my mouth to protest since I 100% hadn't said anything even close to that, but she quickly cut me off in favor of a topic she thought was more interesting than this phantom mirror requester.

"So, are we just ignoring the fact that you slept with Jefferson, then?" she asked, toweling off her hair and getting out her makeup bag.

I quickly put my hand over her mouth in case Jefferson was lurking outside the door, which—let's be honest—he probably was. "I didn't sleep with him."

"But you slept next to him," she said, removing my hand and wiping my "germs" on her pants.

"That's definitely not the same thing," I said. "And besides, I wouldn't have had to sleep on the floor if you weren't beating me up all night."

She nodded solemnly. "I'm a violent sleeper. So how did the two of you end up sleeping on the floor?"

"It's not some big scandal, Brighton. I was just tired of being hit and he was tired of Deacon trying to snuggle him."

Brighton's eyes became almost as big as Jefferson's at that statement, and I knew I'd said exactly what I needed to in order to steer the conversation away from my taboo sleeping arrangement.

"Deacon was trying to what?"

"Didn't you know? Apparently Deacon is a sleep snuggler."

Brighton giggled at this revelation, grinning as she applied her makeup. "Well, that's adorable."

I had to refrain from making a comment about how she probably already knew he was a sleep snuggler, since that would inevitably turn right back around on me and we'd be talking about Jefferson again.

"I don't know why you're even bothering with makeup. You know we're going to be in the jeep for fifteen hours today, right?"

"And yet it's ten o'clock and we're still in the hotel." Brighton sighed, finishing up her mascara and looking even more perfect than before. "We really need to get a move on or we'll probably break down at two in the morning in a strange place and get robbed."

"Stop hogging the bathroom and go take a Xanax," I joked, shoving her toward the door as she tried to apply her lip gloss.

"See, you joke about that, but that's exactly what I'm going to do," she said as I locked her out of the bathroom.

"Have fun, crazy," I shouted to her.

~

"Jefferson?" I rested my chin on the steering wheel of the Jeep, trying to stay awake while I drove.

"Ten minutes," he said in a low monotone. His British accent much thicker when he was tired.

"What?" We had much more than ten minutes left in our trip.

"Until we stop to eat." He gave a deep sigh. "Blimey, I'd kill for a custard cream right now."

Apparently, the act of speaking was too much for him. We had been in the car for thirteen hours and I had a sneaking suspicion we were about two seconds away from having our own version of *The Hunger Games* in the car.

Brighton would probably win by blowing up her inhaler and creating a Xanax bomb that would render us all useless.

"Do you think the Jeep is making a funny noise?" she asked for the billionth time.

"There's nothing wrong with the car," Jefferson snapped.

"Calm down, mate," Deacon said, trying to come to Brighton's defense even though his heart wasn't in it.

We were all too worn out by the drive to express much emotion.

"I swear it's been making a clicking noise since we last stopped," she went on.

"Would someone please just sedate her so we don't have to deal with a full-on panic attack," Jefferson said.

"Okay, I know you aren't a human being," I said, "but you need to tell the scientists who made you to do a better job of programming compassion into the next version."

"You're a regular stand-up comedian, Sadie," he muttered.

I gritted my teeth against his insults, refusing to engage. There was no good way to deal with Jefferson when he was in a mood like this. Literally an hour before, he'd been joking around with us and acting totally manic over the clue we'd found in Texas. Now he was sitting in the passenger's seat with his head resting against the window, looking like he wanted to kill someone as he poked his fingertip with his pocket knife over and over again. A little shudder passed through me at the sight of the sharp metal making contact with his skin, so I tried not to look at him, concentrating instead on the freeway signs that would direct us toward the next exit.

"We need to get gas and fill up the Jeep," I said, trying to find a distraction.

"Ouch," Jefferson whispered as he drew blood from his finger.

Apparently, he hadn't expected to cut himself when he'd become stab-happy five minutes earlier.

"Will someone please take Jefferson's knife away?" I asked. "I fear for everyone's safety."

Deacon shifted as if he would take it, but one look from Jefferson put him right back in his seat.

Yeah, we definitely needed to get out of the car. Crazy Parrish Number One was losing it.

"We've only got about seventy dollars left in the budget for today," Brighton said, trying to break up the awkward silence that had just fallen over us.

Brighton hated awkward silences.

"That should be fine. I mean we're not exactly eating gourmet food," I replied.

"That's for gas and food," she corrected with a little wince.

"Will that even fill up this beast?" Deacon asked.

"Probably not," she answered.

"We could always go dumpster diving for food," Jefferson said with a grin.

We all swiftly and loudly gave an audible dissent to that idea.

Then we fell silent again—slaves to our unfortunate financial situation. I wanted to point out the fact that we wouldn't have so many money problems if the Parrish boys could just hold onto jobs, but it didn't seem like a wise thing to do when Jefferson was holding a knife.

Really, what I needed was a solution that could stretch our money as far as it could go and distract Jefferson from his dark and twisty place. It should have been difficult, but I was a little ashamed at how quickly I thought up a plan—and how happy the plan made me, although I'd never admit it to anyone.

I turned off the freeway and pulled into the parking lot of a fast food place. "We might be able to make this work."

"How?" Brighton asked.

"Can I borrow your ring?"

She looked at me skeptically, but slid the simple silver band with its pink stone off her finger. The second I put it on my ring finger, her face lit up with realization.

"Jefferson, how would you feel about being married to me one more time?" I asked. It wasn't the best plan, but it was better than starving.

"Nothing would make me happier," he said in a completely serious tone.

I instantly regretted my decision.

"You two go get the gas and pick us up here when you're done," I instructed, getting out of the car.

Chances were, it wouldn't even work and we'd just have to dip into tomorrow's food fund, but it was always worth a shot.

"I don't know what you're up to," Deacon said, "but make sure you take good pictures." He threw his cousin a wink.

This was definitely a bad idea.

"So, married people eat free?" Jefferson joked, instantly turning into the lighthearted version of himself.

"Just shut up and follow my lead," I said. As we walked into the restaurant, I laced my fingers through his and put on a bright smile.

There was a small line, which was surprising, since it was a little past midnight, but being one of the only stops off the freeway I guessed it was normal. We got in line and I decided to lay the groundwork for our story, making sure to remind myself over and over that I wasn't going to enjoy this . . . mostly because I sort of was enjoying it.

Turning around, I wrapped my arms around Jefferson's neck and smiled up at him. He looked a little confused for a moment before shrugging his shoulders and sliding his arms around my waist. Apparently it didn't take much for "Fun Jefferson" to just roll with the punches.

Keeping my smile in place and talking through gritted teeth, I let my fingers play with his curly hair.

"Don't ruin this by speaking or calling me some ridiculous pet name, Jefferson Parrish, or you'll be the reason we all starve tonight."

He smirked at me infuriatingly. "I love you too, cupcake."

He was definitely going to ruin it.

"I can help the next person in line," the teenage boy said slowly, obviously not too thrilled to be working so late at night.

Jefferson tried to move toward him but I stood my ground, my back turned to the boy. Not thinking nearly as much as I should have been, and wondering why I thought I could make a good plan I wouldn't regret after a long day of no sleep, I stood up on my tiptoes and lightly touched my lips to Jefferson's.

It was hardly a kiss, although the boy at the register wouldn't be able to tell, and after the brief contact (that was definitely not a full kiss), I let my nose nudge Jefferson's for a moment, making sure I kept my eyes closed so I wouldn't be too aware of the fact that I had sort of just kissed a Parrish. I was pretty sure kissing was anti-Parrish rule number one.

Jefferson's hands were grasping my waist so tightly that I could barely breathe, and I could only assume it was from the shock of what I'd just done. It wasn't my fault—I had to show the worker that we were so madly in love that we couldn't be bothered with simple things like ordering our food.

"I can help you when you're ready," he said again in the same dry tone.

I finally opened my eyes and looked up at Jefferson for a split second—long enough to see that his huge owl eyes were bigger than ever and his breathing was deep—before turning around and pulling him up to the register with me.

I put my smile back in place and tried to look annoyingly flustered. "Sorry about that," I said breathlessly. "We just got married, like, literally a few hours ago."

The boy didn't even look up from his phone as his thumbs flew over the screen. I had sort of kissed a Parrish and the stupid worker wasn't even looking at me.

"We lost track of time at the reception, so we're just on our way to the hotel now," I went on, trying to be overly loud to get this boy's attention.

It didn't do any good, of course. His eyes were still locked on his screen.

"So, we thought we'd stop here and get some food," I said, even louder this time. "You know . . . because we just got married?" "That's great. Go ahead and order when you're ready," he said, still not looking up from his phone.

I let out an indignant sound, furious that my attempt at making a clever plan like Jefferson had on the Queen Mary had backfired. Now all I had was a sort-of kiss with a Parrish, and that awful Parrish here to witness my failure.

"I'll order for us, love," Jefferson said in that overly sweet voice, winking at me.

He proceeded to order our food and then paid the boy with a large chunk of the money we had allocated for the next day. All I could think about was how I would explain my failure to Brighton and Deacon, or better yet, how Jefferson would elaborate on the real story to make it that much worse.

As soon as the boy left to get our food, Jefferson wrapped his arms around my waist again, coming very close to getting a good slap in the face.

"I just figured you'd want to keep up the charade so we wouldn't have to tell that boy you lied to him to try to get free food," Jefferson said, having way too much fun with this.

His large hands rested on my waist and I tried to glare at him while I ignored the butterflies in my stomach.

Stupid, stupid butterflies.

I narrowed my eyes and tried to look intimidating. "I hate you so much right now."

I was pinned between the tall Parrish and the food counter, so there wasn't a whole lot I could do in the way of intimidating him, but that didn't stop me from trying. It was seriously frustrating that he was always one step ahead of me at this stupid fake marriage game. We definitely needed a new plan or I'd always be playing catch-up and looking like an idiot.

"Your food is ready," the boy called to us, plopping it onto the counter unceremoniously before walking away without a second glance in our direction.

Just as I was about to turn around and take what should have been the spoils of war, Jefferson leaned over and kissed me.

Actually kissed me.

It was not the barely-a-kiss tiny peck I'd placed on his lips. He actually pulled me into him, pressed his lips firmly against mine, and kissed me good and well. It felt like my heart had fallen into my stomach and my rage had bubbled over all at the same time. I could feel the counter digging into my back from the force of the kiss. There wasn't much that was gentle about Jefferson.

After a five-second grace period where I allowed myself to guiltily enjoy the feeling of being wrapped up in his arms, I pushed Jefferson away forcibly, putting enough drama in it to be believable to both him and myself.

"What is your problem, Jefferson?" I whispered with as much venom as I could muster without attracting too much attention.

"What?" he asked, looking honestly confused at my anger.

"What do you mean, 'what'? Why did you do that?" I asked, still keeping my voice low.

"You kissed me first."

He said it so matter-of-factly that I realized he really didn't see anything wrong with what he had just done.

"I thought we were kissing now. I thought that was our new thing," he said with a shrug, picking the food up off the counter and beginning to walk away with it, forcing me to jog to catch up to his long strides as he left the building.

I knew he understood why I was angry, and if I was being way too honest with myself, I couldn't really get mad at him for guiltily taking advantage of an opportunity the way I had only moments before. But that didn't stop me. I was a notorious hypocrite.

The air outside was warm on my skin, although my face was already bright red from the range of emotions surging through me all at once.

"Don't walk away from me," I said, running into the tall Parrish as he stopped dead in his tracks on the sidewalk, waiting for Deacon and Brighton to return.

"There," he said. "I stopped."

I wasn't great at reading Jefferson since he didn't function like a normal person, but even I could tell by his dry tone that he was upset. Maybe I'd offended him because I wasn't thrilled that he had practically assaulted me in a fast food restaurant.

"Stop it," I said.

"Stop what, Sadie? You're so difficult to please sometimes."

"Stop pretending like you don't know how to be human," I said. "Stop acting like you don't know why that was weird in there."

"I did the exact same thing as you," he said incredulously. "I keep trying to follow your lead and yet I keep getting in trouble for it. Tell me how that makes any sense."

"Because we'd already lost at our own game in there. There was no need to keep pretending."

"You didn't kiss me because it was part of your little act," he said, looking over at me with an expression I couldn't quite read. He was either mad or indignant.

"Just stop talking," I said. "I'm tired of hearing your crazy theories."

"You didn't have to kiss me to make your act believable," he went on.

"I said stop talking," I snapped as Brighton and Deacon rounded the corner in the Jeep.

"Fine," he said. "I won't talk about it once we get in the car. I'll keep ignoring it just like you want me to because you don't like doing anything that someone could criticize you for."

I rolled my eyes at him and his holier-than-thou speech, but he grabbed my arm before I could open the car door.

"You kissed me for the same reason you were staring at me this morning," he said. "And just put yourself in my shoes for two seconds and think about how it makes me feel that you're putting up this much of a fight over something you so obviously feel."

And with that, he let go of me and got into the Jeep, leaving me standing outside and feeling like a horrible person.

CHAPTER 16

"There's always the Eva with no last name," Brighton said, but I was hardly listening to her.

I was lying on the bed in our hotel room in Boston, staring at the ceiling and trying to figure out when my solid day and a half of silent rage had turned into regret and guilt.

Jefferson and I hadn't spoken since our little fight in the parking lot just outside of Knoxville, Tennessee. If he had been a normal person, Brighton and Deacon definitely would have noticed his silence, but because he was infamous for his mood swings, they both just assumed he was in one of his depressed phases and left him alone.

Sadly, we'd been stuck in the back seat together for the rest of the night, me glancing over at Jefferson every once in a while and him very obviously avoiding eye contact. It was weird that the tables were suddenly turned. I was even a little hurt that he was no longer staring at me creepily.

Jefferson and I were both horrible insomniacs, which meant that I knew he'd been awake half of the night in Knoxville, and yet not once did he try to talk to me or even look in my direction. I actually found myself watching him that night, wondering why I was being so strange and trying to decide if I wanted to apologize or kill him with his own stupid pocket knife.

The worst part of the whole trip, however, had been when we'd made a stop to get gas eleven hours into our thirteen-hour drive to Boston and Jefferson and I had waited in the car. It was a pretty small space to be stuck with someone you weren't speaking to.

But as mad as I had been at him, right at that moment, as I lay on the bed with Brighton rambling about one thing or another, my rage was slowly cooling down and turning into guilt.

Maybe I did like being around Jefferson, no matter how weird he was, but that didn't mean I could ever be his girlfriend or something. How could you live with someone that unstable? There was no possible way to have a healthy, functioning relationship with a sociopath. Besides, no matter what he said, I didn't like him in that way. I was just fond of him as a friend.

But that didn't really explain the guilt. The guilt must have come from some Parrish mind trick.

"So, we'll stick with the no-last-name Eva?" Brighton asked.

"Mhm," I responded, furrowing my brow.

"Or we could just skip the whole thing and take the Jeep on a really long and pointless road trip," she went on.

"Okay," I agreed.

Maybe I felt guilty because I'd made Jefferson think I liked him and now he was upset with me. Or maybe I really did like him. But only a little bit. Like, out of morbid curiosity to see what it would be like to enjoy spending time with someone like him.

"And we can drive it down to North Carolina? I've got some family down there," Brighton said. "Isla would love it if we visited. She's got this hot doctor boyfriend I could introduce you to."

"Sounds good."

There was something so terrible about the idea of admitting to myself that I sort of liked Jefferson. The idea was just ridiculous. "And then we can drive to England and visit Deacon's family too."

"Yeah," I mumbled, brow still furrowed.

"Sadie," Brighton said loudly, pulling me from my inner turmoil.

"What?"

"I've been speaking nonsense for the past five minutes," she said. "You're not even listening to me."

"Sorry, I'm just really tired." I wasn't technically lying.

The sleeping arrangements hadn't gotten much better, and if I didn't get a decent night of sleep pretty soon, I'd have a mental breakdown.

Maybe that was it! I'd kissed Jefferson during a time of extreme mental fatigue. That explained a lot.

"Sadie!"

"What?" I asked.

"You're ignoring me again," Brighton said, matching my annoyed tone.

Apparently, she'd been speaking to me.

"Sorry, I was just thinking," I said.

At least I didn't have to deal with Jefferson today. He and Deacon had gone to the library to go through old census records and were texting their findings back to Brighton. She'd volunteered to go with Deacon but Jefferson had instantly stepped in, claiming he should go to make sure Deacon stayed on task. Translation: Jefferson couldn't stand to be in the same room as me anymore because I'd hurt his feelings.

"If just Jefferson was being weird, that would be normal everyday life," Brighton said with a sigh. "But you've both been totally awful to be around ever since Tennessee."

She was out of her comfort zone, pointing out that I was being annoying. Poor girl was too sweet for her own good.

"What's going on?"

I bit my lip to buy some time before responding.

What *was* going on?

"Jefferson and I had a disagreement."

"That's normal," she began. "The way you guys have been acting isn't. What happened?"

"I kind of sort of barely gave him the tiniest of baby pecks," I said with a wince, hoping I could downplay it enough so that Brighton wouldn't freak out.

I failed.

"You what?" she practically shouted. "You broke anti-Parrish rule number one!"

"You're one to talk."

"I have not," she said defensively. "I mean, I want to, but that's a whole other story. When did you kiss Jefferson?"

"I didn't kiss him," I lied.

She instantly gave me a look that said I'd better tell her the truth fast.

"When we were 'married' so that we could get free food, I gave him the smallest kiss ever. Honestly. It could barely be called a kiss."

"What did he say?" she asked, scandalized.

Now she was acting like the preppy cheerleader she looked like and not the asthmatic anxiety-ridden girl she was.

"He didn't say anything; he just kind of stood there in shock," I said. "And then after we were done pretending to be married, he kissed me."

"Just out of the blue?"

"Completely out of the blue," I emphasized. "I mean, we weren't even talking about our little act or anything and suddenly he kisses me."

"A real kiss?"

"A very real kiss," I said, still wondering if the memory made me want to smile or run from my own insanity.

"Is he a good kisser?" she asked with a wicked grin.

"Brighton! That's hardly the issue here," I said.

"I know, inner turmoil and all that." She waved her hand in the air as if my problems were trivial. "We'll get to it, I promise. I'll even help you figure out what you should do, but I have to know. Is Robot Boy a good kisser?"

"I'm not talking about this with you." I crossed my arms across my chest to show how firm my resolve was.

"I'll tell Jefferson you're secretly in love with him," she threatened.

"Fine! He's a good kisser, okay?"

"Oh my gosh." She giggled, putting her hand over her mouth like a little girl. "Good job, Jefferson. Where would he even learn to be a good kisser? Who would he possibly practice with? The boy hates people."

"Can we please get back to what's important?"

It took her a moment, but Brighton managed to calm her giggling fit and put on a semi-serious face.

"Sorry, proceed," she said.

"What do I do about Jefferson? He's all moody now. I mean, more moody . . . which is a pretty incredible feat for him."

"Yeah, he's been terrible lately," Brighton said. "Is that what you guys were talking about when we pulled up that night?"

"I was being put in my place for a bunch of stuff I didn't even think I was doing," I said. "We were having a good time pretending to be married and suddenly he has to call me out for leading him on or something."

I narrowed my eyes at the memory, my guilt starting to turn back into anger.

"He said I needed to put myself in his shoes and think about how it felt that I was so opposed to the idea of liking him."

"Did you?"

"Did I what?"

"Think about how that would make you feel," Brighton elaborated.

"He's Jefferson!" I practically shouted. "He doesn't care what people think about him."

"He cares what *you* think about him," she pointed out. "You might be the only person whose opinion he values. As much as I hate to admit it, I kind of agree with him. You're the only person he looks for approval from, so how do you think it makes him feel that you act like he's too weird to be datable?"

"Well, then, why is he so weird? If he cares so much, why doesn't he just act normal?"

"Sade, none of us are normal," Brighton said with a laugh, telling me this was obvious. "I have every phobia, anxiety disorder, and OCD issue in the world, but I'm also highly aware of the sad fact that people are nicer to you when you're pretty. It's unfair, but it's kind of true. And while it's great that people are nice to me, it's also really annoying that they get weirded out when they figure out I can't talk to them because I have social anxiety or when I pull out my inhaler. It's like I've suddenly become some alien species."

"But you still dress cute," I pointed out.

I couldn't understand why she'd do that if she hated the double standard so much.

"Yeah, because it's like a security blanket," she said. "If I didn't dress how people wanted me to, then I'd be openly ridiculed, which I'd never be able to handle. This way, if I don't talk to people, they just think I'm being a stuck-up pretty-girl snob instead of the neurotic mess I really am."

I didn't respond, but looked up at the ceiling in silence instead. I really wanted to be mad at Brighton for sticking up for Jefferson when she should have been validating my opinions, but somehow I knew she was right.

Jefferson was very anti-normal because he didn't think it was fair to be held to an arbitrary societal standard, and there I was, trying to force it on him constantly. Of course Brighton would stand up for him, since she was the biggest walking contradiction of them all.

"I still don't know how I feel about the fact that he kissed me," I said.

"You don't have to. I'm not saying you need to go declare your love for the weird little guy—just try to cut him some slack and be aware of the affect you have on him so you don't accidentally abuse it."

"Says the girl who has Deacon Parrish, fearer of all women, wrapped around her little finger."

"That's different," Brighton said dismissively. "And stop trying to change the subject."

"Fine, but we *will* be revisiting that topic later," I promised.

We were both silent again for a moment before Brighton's phone buzzed. She glanced at the screen and gave a little half smile.

"The boys think they found a good lead." She grabbed a few pieces of equipment and stowed them in her purse.

"Great," I said, not sure I was ready to face more of Jefferson's silent treatment. "I guess I should say something to Jefferson, huh?"

"Probably," she responded in an apologetic tone.

"That'll be the world's most awkward conversation."

"But it'll be good for you." She pulled her hair out of its ponytail and shook it to give it more body.

I pulled my black boots on over my jeans and put a yellow v-neck shirt on over my tank top before grabbing my own purse.

"Hey, Sade?" Brighton said hesitantly before we left the hotel room. "I'm not sure if you care, but no one would judge you if you did like Jefferson."

I had to laugh. As sad as it was, I was actually very concerned about the idea that people might make fun of me for liking Jefferson. It wasn't because I was some awesome catch (because that definitely wasn't the case), but just because you never knew what he might do in public and that meant I could very easily be pulled into the sideshow that was his life. I wasn't sure I was okay with being perceived as something other than "normal."

"Hey, Brighton?" I responded, matching her tone perfectly. "Yeah?"

"I wouldn't judge you if you liked Deacon," I said with a grin.

~

The Boston Public Library was a pretty gorgeous site, with its arched windows and statues guarding the doors. Much to my dismay, however, we didn't actually get to go inside. The Parrish boys were sitting on a bench across the street. Jefferson actually didn't look too out of place in his slacks, collared shirt, and vest. For once, he seemed to have found his people in this historic city.

"So, what did you guys find?" Brighton asked, joining the boys on the bench.

I opted to stand, crossing my arms uncomfortably and trying not to let my shoulders look too scrunched up. Jefferson looked up at me and smiled in a strained way, doing exactly what a normal person would do in the awkward situation and throwing me off completely.

Under normal circumstances, Jefferson wouldn't care about making accepted social efforts and he'd just blatantly ignore me if he were mad, or he'd drop a few really pointed comments that would make the entire group uncomfortable. Yet there he was, forcing a smile and making eye contact.

It was unnerving.

"There's an old house a few blocks from here that has record of an Eva living there," Deacon said.

"The Eva with no last name?" Brighton asked.

"Exactly," Jefferson put in.

It was odd to hear an even tone from him. He was either manic and joking around, or somber and sounding like an undertaker. There was no middle ground with Crazy Parrish Number One. Sometimes his voice would take on a bored, droll quality, but that was about as normal as it ever got.

"We think she's our best bet because the timelines seem to match up pretty well," he went on. "Plus, the house is within walking distance, so we can give the Jeep a rest."

"And what do we do when we get to this house?" I asked. "Just come right out and ask if the place is haunted?"

"We'll just be very upfront and honest with them and ask if they've experienced anything odd," Jefferson said, again being way too normal. It was actually kind of making me mad. The act didn't suit him at all. "If they have been having experiences, we'll offer to investigate."

"I don't know that they'll go for it but I guess it's worth a shot . . . assuming it's even the right Eva."

"That's enough of a 'yes' for me," Deacon said. He stood and led the way with Brighton by his side.

Jefferson gave me another forced smile, stood, and followed behind them, leaving me to catch up as usual.

Being short was the worst sometimes.

"Do you really think this person is going to let four complete strangers into their home?" I asked Jefferson in a hushed tone.

We were walking far enough behind Brighton and Deacon that they wouldn't be able to hear us. Plus, Deacon was currently acting as a tour guide and pointing out all of the historical sites to Brighton, sounding exactly like a textbook.

"I think it's worth a shot." He turned toward me, wearing that infuriating fake smile again.

It wasn't even the kind of fake smile that was meant to be sarcastic and make you mad. It was the kind that was meant to smooth over a bad situation, and it was awful.

"Would you stop doing that," I breathed in irritation.

"What would you like me to stop doing now, Sadie?" he asked in a sweet voice.

"Everything you're doing right now. This whole thing," I motioned to his tall lanky figure. "The fake smiles and saying what's socially acceptable in this situation we're in."

"Stop being normal?" he asked in an overly innocent tone.

He was doing this on purpose. He was acting normal to show me how annoying it was to worry about what people thought all the time.

Brat.

"Okay, fine, you made your point. I hate it when you don't act like you," I said with a roll of my eyes.

"But you also hate it when I am me, so where does that leave us?" he asked, the dismal tone back to his voice as he returned to his version of normal.

"Listen," I said, grabbing his arm and stopping our walk. Brighton and Deacon didn't even notice as they continued their mini tour. "I'm really sorry about what I said back in Tennessee. I was super tired and you caught me off-guard with that kiss, so I panicked. And then you started saying all of this stuff about the mean things I was doing and—let's face it—no one likes to be called out on something they're doing."

"Especially hot-tempered Cuban girls," Jefferson added with a knowledgeable nod.

I actually smiled a little. "Especially hot-tempered Cuban girls."

"You know you pull out the 'hot-tempered Cuban' card a lot," he said, "but from what I've learned about your sister, who's obviously also Cuban, she's an even-tempered saint."

I gave him a look to tell him the topic of my sister was off limits.

"I'm sorry for how I acted that night and can we please get back to normal?" I asked.

"So obsessed with normal," he sighed with a sad shake of his head.

"I meant our normal, which isn't normal at all."

"Yes, Sadie, we can get back to our normal." He looked down at me with those huge eyes and his lips tugged up in one corner.

I might have glanced down at his lips for a split second longer than I should have, but I quickly pretended I was just glancing at something else. Of course, I instantly regretted it when he said, "Can I still kiss you?"

"Absolutely not," I answered a little too quickly.

"But what if I really want to?" he asked again, his half smile turning into a full-blown wicked grin.

I blushed profusely.

"Really want to," he said again, being way too honest and calm about what he was saying.

"Crazy Parrish," I mumbled under my breath uncomfortably. I quickly turned on my heel and jogged to catch up with the other half of our group. I was literally running away from my problems.

I could hear Jefferson laugh behind me and I hated myself for loving the sound of his laugh.

CHAPTER 17

"Brighton is the most normal looking of the group, so she should do it," Jefferson said very matter-of-factly. He was standing much too close to me.

He smelled good, his normal cinnamon scent coming off of him in waves. Why on earth did he always smell like cinnamon?

We were all gathered on the sidewalk outside of the tiny brick home where our Eva may or may not have lived back in the 1900s. It hadn't taken us long to find the home, but now that we were there, we couldn't quite figure out how to get inside.

"You're joking, right?" Brighton asked. "Have you seen me speak to a stranger? I'm like Woody Allen."

"But look at you," he emphasized. "You're all blonde and . . . stacked."

"Stacked?" I asked with a laugh.

I mean, it was true Brighton had the body of a supermodel, but it was so awkward to hear someone like Jefferson point it out. I didn't think he was capable of noticing a female figure unless it was a ghostly reflection in a photo.

"He's got a point," Deacon said under his breath, although we all clearly heard him.

Brighton's little blush was the most adorable thing ever.

"Why can't Sadie do it?" she asked. "She's the most normal one here."

"Yeah, but she looks like she's twelve," Jefferson said. "They'll think she's selling Girl Scout cookies."

"Ouch," I said, narrowing my eyes at him.

"Deacon and I can't do it," he went on, ignoring my hurt ego. "We're too . . ."

"Tall?" Deacon offered.

"Crazy?" I added. "British? Weird?"

"Off-putting," Jefferson finished.

"Would it be too intimidating if all four of us went to the door?" I asked. "I mean, only one of us would do the talking, of course."

"Yes!" Brighton exclaimed, finding her "out" and grasping to it for dear life. "That is definitely what we should do."

I shrugged at the boys and linked my arm through Brighton's, walking with her up to the front door. There was no way this was ever going to work, but I wasn't in the mood to break into this person's house either, so we didn't have much of a choice.

"You knock," she whispered to me, grasping my hand much too tightly while the Parrish boys discussed something on the sidewalk.

They were probably trying to figure out a way to overturn the decision I'd just made for the group.

"Here goes nothing." I knocked lightly on the old wooden door. "She's probably going to think we're Mormons or Jehovah's Witnesses."

I could hear a woman inside, calling through the house to tell someone she'd be right back before answering the door. The woman couldn't have been any older than thirty and she had curly brown hair and a kind face. This might not be too difficult.

"Hello." She smiled, raising her eyebrows a bit at us in an unspoken question.

Brighton squeezed my hand even tighter.

"Hi, I'm Sadie," I began, not quite sure how to word my insane question. "Um . . . there's not really a great way to say this without sounding crazy, so I'm just going to come right out and say it."

The woman kept her smile in place, but I could see that she was now a bit worried about whatever message I had come to deliver to her.

"We're paranormal investigators and we've been working on a case recently that led us here. You may not know, but is there any chance someone named Eva used to live here a long time ago? Around the early 1900s?"

The woman's smile instantly faded as her hazel eyes widened. Now it was my turn to smile awkwardly at her as she silently stared back.

I exchanged nervous glances with Brighton, wondering if the woman was about to call the cops on us, just as Jefferson and Deacon walked up to the door.

"So, can we come in or not?" Jefferson asked with a deep sigh, being as tactless as humanly possible.

I stepped on his foot subtly, hoping it would shut him up.

"I'm sorry about him," I said to the still silent woman. "Is now a bad time? Should we come back later?"

She shook her head as if realizing there were people standing in front of her. "No, I think you should come in." She looked at the two Parrish boys a trifle nervously.

I couldn't really blame her. If two lanky, weird British boys showed up on my doorstep, I wouldn't just take them in off the street. I'd made that mistake once and look where it had gotten me.

"I'm Ally, by the way," she said, beckoning for us to follow her inside.

The old brick house was small but felt very homey and lived-in. I had a small pang of jealousy over the fact that she had such a cozy home when I was less than excited about going back to our tiny hotel room after this was all over.

Ally's fridge was covered in crayon drawings and plastic magnet letters, and down the hall, I could hear the sounds of a little girl squealing over something. She led us toward the giggling in her daughter's room.

"This is Layla," Ally said with a smile, motioning to a girl who looked to be about five years old, sitting on the floor and surrounded by dolls. "And here's the reason I don't think you're completely nuts." She handed me a stack of papers.

I flipped through them. Jefferson was practically draped over my shoulder trying to see too. Page after page held crayon pictures of two girls, one smaller girl with the name "Layla" written above it, and the other a taller woman with the name "Eva."

My mouth almost dropped open in shock as I looked up at Ally. "Did your daughter draw these?"

"She did," she said. "About a year ago she started naming all of her dolls 'Eva.' I didn't really think anything of it except that I wasn't sure where she had heard the name. Then she started telling me about an imaginary friend whose name was Eva, and how this was her house before it was ours."

Ally let out a small shudder, looking down at her little girl. Layla had already started ignoring us again, opting for playing with her dolls.

"Have you had any experiences yourself?" Jefferson asked. I wished he would change his tone to be more personable and less accusatory, but I didn't think chiding him in front of Ally would make us look great, so I stayed silent.

"We haven't had anything bad happen really, and I've never felt unsafe. But I have had times when I've thought someone was in the room with me, or times when I think I see my reflection in the mirror, but when I look over, there's no mirror beside me . . . but I swear it was me I saw out of the corner of my eye."

"Doppelgänger," Deacon murmured to Jefferson.

"Or mimic," he replied. "Which would be infinitely more fun."

"Jefferson," I said, hoping he'd take a hint and stop talking about this woman's problems like they were a gift. "Has Layla seen Eva?"

"She says she has, but you never know with kids." Ally shrugged. "Honestly, until I started seeing and hearing things myself, I still thought she was playing around."

"But you say you've never felt uncomfortable here?"

"Never," she said. "Even when I've heard things, I've never really been scared. Just startled."

"That's good, at least," I said. "I'm sure there's nothing for you to worry about. Sometimes a presence can just attach itself to a place; it's not like *Poltergeist* where the entire house is suddenly going to turn on you."

"That's reassuring," Ally said with a small laugh. "Honestly, if you had knocked on my door a few months ago I would have laughed at you. I never really believed in this stuff."

I smiled at her reassuringly. I couldn't blame her for being a skeptic. I hadn't always been so sure of the paranormal.

"I know this is probably a really weird thing for us to ask since you don't know us . . . but would you be willing to let us investigate your home to see if we can figure anything out?" I was sure that she would say yes, now that we had proven we knew our stuff.

"Preferably at night, and without you and your family in the house," Jefferson added, making me want to slap him.

Of course, he had to go and make it sound like we were asking her to leave her home so we could rob her.

Ally looked over at her daughter for a moment and then back to us, seeming unsure.

"It's just easier if there's no one else in the house who can contaminate the investigation and cause any additional sounds or shadows that we might not be expecting. Do you have a relative or someone you could stay with?" I asked, trying to smooth over Jefferson's lack of tact.

"I'm really sorry," she said after a moment. "I don't think it's a good idea. My husband, Brian, is out of town until tomorrow, and I wouldn't really feel comfortable letting strangers hang out in my house at night without talking to him about it."

Jefferson rolled his huge eyes in a painfully obvious way. He might as well have come right out and said he thought she was completely useless.

"That's totally fine, Ally," I said with a bright smile.

Crazy Parrish Number One was now narrowing his eyes at every person in the room. He was quickly descending into "Angry Jefferson."

"Go ahead and talk to your husband when he gets back tomorrow and let us know what you guys decide. We don't want money or anything; we just want to check the place out and see if we can pick up on anything that might be going on here. Here's my number. You can just give me a call tomorrow."

"I will," she assured me. She didn't sound like she was shutting us down completely, which gave me hope.

We walked silently to the front door, Brighton still squeezing the life out of my hand and the Parrish boys moping.

"Thank you for letting us into your home," I said, still not wanting to scare this woman off when we were so close to investigating our next location.

"I'll call you tomorrow," she said with a smile, closing the door behind us.

The second the door was closed, Brighton took a long puff on her inhaler and released my hand.

"Well that was an epic waste of time," Jefferson scoffed as we started walking back to our hotel room.

"Because of you," I said. "Why can't you just keep your big mouth shut and let me do the talking so you don't scare everyone away with your Jefferson-ness?"

Deacon laughed. "Oh, congrats mate, you're now an adjective."

"It's not funny, Deacon," I snapped. "I really think Ally was going to let us investigate tonight before Crazy Parrish Number One had to be himself and ruin everything."

"What is your problem, Sadie?" Jefferson asked.

"You are my problem," I answered, feeling the heat rise into my cheeks. I wasn't sure why I was getting so upset. It really wasn't that big of a deal.

Brighton looked monumentally uncomfortable with my little fit. "Jefferson's right, Sade, you need to just calm down for a second."

Of course, all that did was send me over the edge.

"Go ahead and side with him again, Brighton."

"Again?" Jefferson asked.

"Just forget it," I said.

I couldn't understand why they were calling me out for being the only normal one there.

"I'll see you guys back at the hotel room," I said.

And with that, I stormed away in the opposite direction, thinking maybe I could head back to the library to do some research, even though it was probably closed by now. Even as I was walking away, I knew I was being completely irrational. I wasn't quite sure why I had suddenly become so angry, and I felt like an idiot for lashing out at my friends over Jefferson doing what he always did, but I still couldn't help myself.

I could feel my phone buzzing in my pocket but I ignored it. I wasn't in the mood for Brighton telling me I needed to apologize to Jefferson, and I didn't want Deacon trying to smooth everything over with a joke. All I wanted was two seconds where I wasn't smashed into a small space with the three people I saw every day.

My breathing was heavy as I walked, not so much because I was walking particularly fast, but because I was so mad at everything at that moment. It didn't take me long to get downtown, and when I finally did, I stopped inside of a bookstore, thinking it was a safe place to hang around without getting strange looks. That's what bookstores were for, right? Hanging out?

Grabbing a random book off the shelf without looking at it, I sat in one of the big overstuffed arm chairs, holding the book up over my face so people wouldn't see my scowl. I had absolutely no intention of reading whatever I had picked up; I just needed an excuse to sit in silence for a moment to think about what had just happened.

Besides my sudden outburst that I really couldn't explain (even though I was completely justified in my rage), I thought about how close we had been to investigating Ally's house. I could tell she was seconds away from letting us check things out, until she saw the Parrish boys in all of their awful glory. That had been what changed her mind. Maybe if Brighton and I could go back and do the investigation alone she'd be more receptive.

I sighed audibly, feeling suddenly drained from the entire ordeal. Drained and embarrassed. I knew Jefferson was difficult to deal with, and I'd put up with a lot more from him than a few misplaced comments, but for some reason, our encounter with Ally had sent me over the edge for no reason at all. I wasn't really sure how I'd explain myself when I met back up with my friends. Lowering the book from my face, I glanced across the bookshelf-filled room to see the awful Parrish in question sitting in an armchair and blatantly staring at me.

"You have got to be kidding me," I breathed.

He stood up and strode across the room toward my once solitary space.

"What do you want?" I asked, as he took a seat in the chair beside me.

I was ready for an awkward conversation about how I was lashing out at him because I loved him so much, or about how I was too worried about being normal. Instead I got a bizarre statement . . . which shouldn't have surprised me.

"I think there was something weird going on inside of that house," he said, staring at me even more creepily than normal.

"What are you on about now?"

"There was something in that house. Like an energy or something. It doesn't seem to be affecting the family as far as I can tell, but it was definitely messing with all of us."

"And why do you think that?" I asked, finding that I actually wasn't mad at Jefferson anymore.

"Brighton said she could feel it the second we walked in. That's why she was so quiet . . . or quieter than normal around a stranger, I guess," he began. "I mean, think about it. She was all freaked out; Deacon was quiet, which is unusual for him; I was being kind of weird; and you just suddenly went off on a psychotic rage."

"You're always weird," I pointed out.

"True," he agreed. "But this time I wasn't doing it on purpose."

I thought about this for a moment, not wanting it to make sense, even if it did.

"I was unnaturally mad at you back there," I said.

"Unless you really do think I always ruin everything."

"Only most of the time," I said. "Not always."

"Sade, that lady is probably going to let us investigate," Jefferson said, propping his elbow on the arm of the chair to lean closer to me.

"But what if she doesn't?"

Jefferson thought this over for a moment, looking down at my hand on my own armrest and then looking back up at me.

"Then I'll break into her house and investigate for you," he said with a smile. He was probably joking.

Hopefully.

"But I don't think it'll come to that," he added. "So can we stop being crazy now and go back to the hotel room to go over our old tapes?"

"You make it sound so appealing," I said sarcastically.

I suddenly realized why I had recognized the name of the bookstore when I'd passed by it on my rage-walk. I stopped, my eyes widening.

"What?" Jefferson asked, and I quickly placed my hand over his mouth in a panic.

Pulling him to his feet, I flattened myself against his chest, using him as a human shield as I peeked around his tall, lanky form at a girl silently shelving books.

"No, no, no, no," I whispered.

"What?" Jefferson asked again, looking over his shoulder at the girl.

She was taller than me and had long dark brown hair and brown eyes. Her skin was a bit lighter than mine, even though we were both Cuban.

"Wait, that's not . . ." Jefferson gave me a jubilant grin.

"Quiet!" I hissed. "You have to get me out of here without her seeing me."

"You're seriously not going to say hello to your sister when you came all the way from Portland to Boston?"

"Don't sound so judgmental—you don't even like your family. Just help me," I pleaded.

"What do I get out of it?" Jefferson asked, enjoying my pain way too much.

I glanced around my human shield again to see that Michigan had almost unloaded her armful of books and would probably be walking this way at any moment.

"Whatever you want, Jefferson," I whispered, "just hide me." It was almost dark outside. If I could just get to the entrance of the bookstore without her seeing me, I could steal away into the night and be home free. Michigan and my parents would never know I had come to Boston without telling them.

"Perfect," Jefferson said. "I'm holding you to that."

He gave me a quick wink and walked right over to my sister, grabbing her by the arm and turning her away from me.

"Hello." He squinted at her name badge even though he already knew her name. "Michigan, is it? That's an interesting name."

Michigan smiled at him warmly. She was always the nice one in the family, even when faced with a creepy British stranger.

"Yeah," she said, wrinkling her nose up at him. "That was my mom's doing. She's a little crazy."

I could hear her and Jefferson laugh, but I wasted no time to stick around for the rest of their conversation. Trying to be stealthy, I tiptoed behind my sister until I passed the first set of bookshelves in the store. At that point I didn't bother with subtlety. I practically sprinted out of the bookstore, flinging open the doors into the early evening with gusto, and feeling like I had narrowly escaped a horrible fate.

I waited around the corner for Jefferson, who took his sweet time coming out to meet me.

"What took you so long?" I asked, when he finally showed up. "What were you guys talking about?"

"Your sister is completely lovely," Jefferson said, very matter-of-factly. "I don't understand what you have against her."

He was trying to get a rise out of me.

It worked.

"Ugh, she's awful." I leaned against the brick wall of the bookstore. "She's so nice and perfect and everyone loves her."

Jefferson gave me a look but didn't say anything, which I was thankful for. I didn't care that my sister wasn't the person I should have been mad at. I should have been mad at my parents for missing that day in parenting school where they told you not to have a favorite child for no reason at all. But still, it was easier to be mad at Michigan.

"Thank you for helping me," I said. I was glad that Jefferson had followed me to the bookstore even after I'd said all sorts of terrible things to him.

He was loyal to a fault; I would give him that. And if he was going to follow me around like a lost puppy, at least he wasn't the worst company in the world.

"We should probably get back to the hotel so we can go over those riveting investigation tapes," I said after a moment of silence.

"Probably," he said.

"I'll get you ice cream or something for helping me out. Just don't tell Brighton I used some of our food money," I joked.

"What if I don't want ice cream?" he replied.

"Well, it can't be much more expensive," I said. I had a scary feeling that I knew exactly where this conversation was going, and an even scarier one that I was hoping it would go there. It was safer to just play dumb. "We have absolutely no money left in our budget for today and we still haven't eaten dinner."

"It's not expensive," he said, before leaning down and touching his nose to mine, causing my head to tilt up until our lips met.

It was a shock, and I probably should have pulled away from him. He was Jefferson, after all. But I didn't. Instead, against my better judgment, I grabbed the collar of his shirt and pulled him toward me, making him stumble slightly. He caught himself by placing his hand on the brick wall behind me.

He must have been shocked that I hadn't pushed him away, because I could feel his breath catch as he kissed me more forcefully, setting off a massive explosion of butterflies in my stomach as heat spread across my cheeks.

Stupid butterflies.

I was right when I thought there was nothing gentle about Jefferson. His mouth moved expertly over mine and his free hand grasped my waist too tightly, making it difficult to breathe. Not that I cared about breathing right at that moment.

It was something of a free-fall, kissing the crazy Parrish in a dark alley and not caring for one second that I was breaking the anti-Parrish rule I had implemented from the first day I'd met him. Something about kissing Jefferson felt incredible and dangerous all at the same time, making it hard to tell if my heart was racing because he was somehow the most fantastically amazing kisser in the history of all kissers, or because I knew he was slightly psychotic and I was scared he might just switch moods at any second and do something stupid.

Either way, I kissed him for much longer than I should have before pulling my head back just slightly to create a small space between us. He still had one hand on my waist and the other on the wall behind me, while both of my hands were knotted in the collar of his shirt, which I'd most definitely wrinkled beyond help.

My chest was on fire and I closed my eyes as I breathed heavily, wishing I knew why Jefferson made me so crazy when I knew very well it was an awful idea to kiss an insane person. Or maybe I should have been kissing him all along. If this was what it was like to kiss a crazy person, I wasn't so opposed to it.

He leaned in ever so slightly so that his lips rested on mine once more.

"I told you normal was overrated," he whispered against my lips, his breath tickling me before he kissed only my bottom lip.

I looked at him now, wanting to say something, but not knowing what it was I should say. I probably needed to say something responsible about how we worked together and this would make things weird. Or maybe mention how Brighton would inevitably know something had happened and we couldn't have that.

"You bit me," I whispered, instead of the logical adult things I should have said.

"Did I?" he asked in surprise, a slight look of concern on his face as he dragged his thumb over my bottom lip, giving me more chills.

I let go of his collar and brought my hand up to meet his, pulling it away from my sore lip and placing it back on my waist. I hadn't realized he'd bitten me in the moment, but now that I pointed it out, it only made sense that he was a kiss-biter.

Only a crazy person would do something like that.

"I'm sorry," he said, not bothering to move away from me, but instead maintaining our close proximity as his large eyes roamed over my face, always coming back to rest on my lips.

I was about two seconds away from telling him that I wasn't sorry, but thought better of it. He didn't need to know that I had enjoyed our kiss as much as I had.

"Are you mad that I kissed you?" he asked after a moment of awkward silence. Those huge intense eyes of his bored into my soul, and his hand kneaded my side as if he had to stay moving to keep himself from pulling us back together.

"I'm mad that I kissed you back," I admitted.

"Why?"

"Because you're kind of a crazy person," I said.

I desperately wanted to kiss him once more, even though I would refrain.

"Isn't it great?" he answered with a grin.
I was in deep trouble.

CHAPTER 18

"We may just need to call it," Deacon said with a sigh of resignation. "We haven't heard from that Ally woman since yesterday and it's already getting dark. I highly doubt she's going to get a hold of us today, and if she does, she'll probably schedule the investigation for next week or something."

Brighton chewed on her lip from her place on the bed, surrounded by monitors. "Yeah, we definitely wouldn't have enough money to stay in town that long."

"There's still a chance she'll contact us." I pulled my headphones off for a moment and fluffed up my pixie cut once more.

Jefferson sat on the bed beside me, completely oblivious to our conversation as he listened to audio from our Queen Mary investigation with closed eyes.

I tried desperately not to be obvious, but any chance I got, I'd glance over at him or bump him with my elbow as I reached for my pen. It was pathetic, and I wasn't magically in love with him or anything, but there was something very magnetic about him all of a sudden and I couldn't seem to stay away. It was becoming a big problem.

Jefferson didn't seem to change much after we'd kissed the night before. Amazingly, he didn't drop a million hints to Brighton and Deacon like I thought he would. Instead he kept the whole thing very secret and just treated me as oddly as he always did. I couldn't tell if that annoyed me or not. On the one hand, I wanted him to keep quiet about everything because I was not ready to have that conversation with Brighton. On the other hand, I was a little offended that he didn't seem as changed by our kiss as I was.

Of course, no matter what I felt, I was incredibly annoyed with him for kissing me in the first place and bringing about all of this confusion.

"That Littlefield House was honestly and completely silent," Brighton said out of nowhere. "I mean, even for a normal house. I'm almost suspicious of how quiet it was there."

"That'd be a pretty terrible MO for a ghost," Deacon said, smiling at her. "Silence," he added dramatically, his eyes wide.

Brighton's blue eyes crinkled in the corners as she smiled at Crazy Parrish Number Two before looking back down at her screen.

I sighed deeply, half out of boredom and half out of anxiety that we'd never hear from Ally again. Brighton was watching her screens, Deacon was typing something on the laptop as he logged all of our clips, and Jefferson was still silent beside me with his eyes closed. I checked to make sure no one was looking before letting my eyes wander over to him.

His brown hair was styled in a curly mess on top of his head today, and he wore the normal slacks, collared shirt, vest, tie, and Chucks. Suddenly I found the whole Tim Burton thing very hot.

There was something seriously wrong with me. Maybe Ally's house was still having some ill effects on my mental state. That was the only logical explanation.

As I continued to stare at Jefferson, his mouth slowly curled up into a smile and he opened one eye to glance down at me.

Crap.

I looked away quickly, trying to pretend like I hadn't been staring at him creepily. That was his thing. He was supposed to be the creepy one, not me.

Luckily, my phone buzzed only seconds later, saving me from having to hide the massive blush I was sure was covering my cheeks.

"Hello?"

"Hi, is this Sadie?" a woman's voice asked—a woman's voice that sounded mercifully like Ally's.

"This is," I answered.

Jefferson removed his headphones and pressed his cheek against mine, trying to hear what was being said.

I would have expected goose bumps but instead I got a heat that started in my chest and quickly moved to my head in a distracting way. I hoped Jefferson couldn't feel my cheeks getting hotter.

"Hey, it's Ally . . . from yesterday?"

"I definitely remember who you are," I said.

Jefferson placed his hand on the small of my back, pressing his cheek more firmly against mine in his excitement.

I suddenly couldn't breathe . . . or think.

"This is going to sound a little crazy, but would you guys be willing to come over tonight to do your research?" she asked.

Or at least, I was pretty sure that's what she had said. I swear I was listening, but I was also incredibly distracted by the little brown curl from Jefferson's hair that was hanging in my eye and the pressure of his hand on my back. I tried breathing in and out a few times to make sure I was capable of breathing like a normal human being still.

Maybe I was getting sick. There was no way Crazy Parrish Number One was seriously having this effect on me.

"Sadie!" Jefferson whispered.

Brighton gave me an odd look over my lack of normalcy.

"I'm sorry, what?" I asked into the phone.

"Can you guys come over tonight? I know it's short notice, but I saw myself again, not just out of the corner of my eye but standing right in front of me."

"She saw the mimic again," Jefferson whispered to Deacon, sadly removing his cheek from mine to relay this message.

"It was only for a split second, but it was enough to make me think maybe we shouldn't delay this anymore," Ally went on.

"I completely agree," I said.

"My mom lives right across the street so my daughter and I can just go over there while you do your thing," she said.

Of course, she was leaving out the unspoken fact that she could also see us out the window so we'd better not steal anything.

I couldn't say I blamed her. I'd be wary of four strangers coming into my house to look for ghosts too. It didn't really seem like a credible way to build a professional relationship with someone.

"That's perfect," I said. "And since you'll be so close, we'll be able to come over to see you if we have any questions."

Really, we wouldn't need to ask her anything, but I wanted to reassure her we were all on the same side and we weren't insane people that she was letting into her house.

"Oh good!" she said. "So what time would be best to start this?"

"Usually later is a little better." I grabbed Jefferson's arm and looked at his watch. It was already seven at night. "Maybe ten?"

"That works for me," she said. "And thank you for doing this. I really don't think this thing wants to hurt us, but it would be nice to have some answers."

"Definitely," I agreed. "We'll see you tonight at ten."

"See you then."

It seemed like all of us held our breath until I hung up the phone, and then it was suddenly chaos.

"We need to get all of this equipment in the car," Deacon practically shouted, even though we were all in the same room and we had a few hours until we needed to leave.

"And I need to transfer these tapes to the external hard drive so we have room to film tonight," Brighton said, sounding incredibly stressed. "There's not enough time. We need to make sure the batteries are charged and do about a million other things too."

She stood from the bed and looked wildly around the room. I was assuming she was on the hunt for some anti-anxiety medication.

"Brighton," I said, jumping off the bed and grabbing her shoulders. "It's okay. We can get everything done in time."

"We haven't even eaten!" she said. "I totally forgot!"

"There are some fast food places right down the street. It's not a big deal," I said in the too-calm voice.

"But the tapes," she whined.

"I'll transfer them over," I said. "Or I can go get the food while you do that."

She looked back and forth between me and the tapes, trying to decide if she really trusted me with the responsibility of transferring our hours of hard work. Then she looked out the window with a deep sigh.

"Maybe some fresh air will be good for you," I suggested.

She looked like she'd been cooped up for far too long.

"I hate fresh air," she said.

"All the more reason to go get some."

After a moment of inner turmoil, she relented.

"Deacon, will you come with me?" she asked, being much bolder than she normally was.

"No!" I yelled, not meaning to be quite so loud. "You can take Jefferson," I quickly added, trying to be nonchalant.

Jefferson looked over at me and grinned.

He knew.

"You two seriously need to learn to get along," Brighton said, grabbing her purse and taking Deacon's hand, which was also pretty daring for her. "If you haven't killed each other by the time we get back, I'll consider that a small victory."

"Jefferson probably needs some fresh air too," I attempted desperately.

I could not be left alone in the room with him at the moment. I was too unstable.

"I feel great, actually. And I'd love to help you transfer those tapes over," he said, tilting his chin down and looking at me through his eyelashes, the wicked grin still on his face.

Normally I'd think the look was creepy, but now as I saw it, I just wanted to kiss him. What had happened to me? This was totally ridiculous.

"There you go," Brighton said, still having a minor panic attack as she looked around the room at her unfinished tasks.

I knew she didn't want to go get food. The only reason she'd agreed to go was because she knew she would have some alone time with Deacon to do whatever it was they did. What did they do? Awkwardly avoid eye contact with each other? Compare neurosis?

"We'll be back in five," Deacon said, his eyes locked on Brighton in a non-stalker way.

How was he related to Jefferson?

"But—" I began, before the closing of the door cut me off.

I glanced over at Jefferson for a brief moment, wary of being alone with him, before I sat down on the bed and began transferring our video data over to a hard drive. He gathered a few cords up and tossed them into a bag, being deliberately slow in his movements so that he could watch me.

We worked in silence for what seemed like forever. Brighton and Deacon had to be almost done getting food.

"We probably won't have time to transfer all of these tapes over," I said, trying to break the deafening silence. "But we can get enough for tonight."

"Good," Jefferson answered, finally letting his eyes leave me and actually focusing on his task at hand.

Maybe I'd actually done it. I'd shown him I wasn't interested and he was giving up.

"Plus, Brighton can always wipe more tapes while we're investigating." I was no longer looking at the computer and instead watched Jefferson as his tall form moved around the room. "If we need her to."

"Good to have options," he said, still not looking at me.

His curls fell into his eyes when he bent down to grab a piece of equipment and he furrowed his brow when he hit his hand on something. He was completely distracted as he looked down at his finger in concern, trying to figure out where he'd cut it, I was guessing. And for some reason unknown to me, I stood up, strode across the small hotel room, literally pushed him against the wall, and kissed him.

I had to stand on my tiptoes but I didn't care. I kept my hands firmly planted against his chest as I pinned him up against the wall, not thinking at all as I kissed him vehemently. Inhaling deeply, I could smell that same cinnamon scent on him and I let my kisses trail down his neck, under the collar of his shirt, before bringing my lips back up to his.

Somehow, I had a handful of his curly hair in my grasp and I could hear him hit his head on the wall behind us as I kissed him with a little too much force, not realizing how intense I had gotten.

His eyes were closed, so at least I knew he was enjoying himself, but two seconds later I heard the key card beep as someone began opening the door, and without a second thought, I sprinted back to the bed and jumped into the pile of computers, hoping I could convincingly look like I'd been working the whole time Brighton and Deacon were gone.

"I wasn't sure what you guys wanted but we're broke so I just got the cheapest things on the menu," Brighton announced as she and Deacon entered the room. "Plus Deacon had a panic attack because the person at the register was a woman, and I had a panic attack because they were a living human in general, so it took a while to decide whose neurosis were the worst and who had to order."

Jefferson was still flattened against the wall, with his eyes wider than I'd ever seen them as he stared off into the distance. His hair was a huge mess and his shirt was now untucked with the collar pulled down on one side. I wasn't sure how I'd done all of that in such a short amount of time, but apparently I'd made good use of those few seconds.

"What's wrong with you, mate?" Deacon asked, barely glancing at his cousin as he set the food up on the small table in the room.

Jefferson didn't speak, but his eyes suddenly met mine and grew determined. He began walking quickly through the room toward me with a look that said he was about to return my favor and I panicked.

"No!" I yelled, pointing at him and stopping him dead in his tracks.

Who just tried to kiss a person in front of their friends? What was wrong with him?

"What?" Brighton asked, still not looking at me.

It was a good thing she and Deacon were so preoccupied by the food or they'd definitely know what was going on.

Jefferson tilted his head to the side at an extreme angle like he always did, looking enormously confused and asking me a question with his eyes.

I shook my head at him incredulously. We were *not* going to kiss in front of Brighton and Deacon. This was why he was so weird. A normal person wouldn't have had to ask if that was an okay thing to do. To be fair, though, a normal person wouldn't have just attacked him and pushed him against a wall either. I wasn't being a very good example of "normal" at the moment.

"Sorry," I quickly amended, just as Brighton turned around to look at me. She glanced at Jefferson with a puzzled look at his rumpled clothing and disheveled hair, but didn't say anything. "I thought I had erased one of our tapes by accident," I lied.

"Wait, you didn't though, right?" she asked in a sudden panic, shooing me off of the bed to take over my job.

"False alarm," I said, trying not to touch Jefferson as I passed him to get to the food. He let his fingers trail down my back as I passed, making me shiver and also making me mad that he would be so obvious in front of everyone.

"Thanks for getting food, guys," I said in an uncomfortably tight voice.

This was so embarrassing. Not only should I not have been affected by Jefferson so much, but I also definitely shouldn't have acted on it when he wasn't even provoking me. This was becoming a problem.

"The batteries are mostly charged, so I think they should be fine by the time we leave tonight," Deacon said to Brighton, both of them still ignoring us.

Jefferson looked away from me and silently tucked his shirt back in, biting his bottom lip as he smoothed his hair back down. Why was everything he did suddenly so attractive? Had he always been that good-looking?

"We might want to brush up on our mimic research for tonight," Jefferson finally said. His eyes flicked up to meet mine for the briefest of seconds before he smirked and looked away.

I hated myself for blushing.

"Doppelgänger," Deacon corrected.

Jefferson raised his eyebrows. "I guess we'll find out who's right."

"Fantastic," Deacon said with a laugh.

"You boys need to play nice or I'll have to separate you," Brighton put in from her spot on the bed.

During the entire exchange I was silently staring at Jefferson and—not for the first time that week—thinking about how completely and utterly in trouble I was.

CHAPTER 19

I tagged my tape as I walked through the dark, quiet house holding a flashlight and a camera. "This is Sadie Smith investigating the Bray house in Boston, Massachusetts, on September ninth at 11:00 p.m."

Because the location was so small, both Parrish boys were stuck in the car with Brighton, but they were hardly complaining since Ally had brought some hot chocolate over for us. Deacon was wonderful and charming about the gift, actually managing to speak to a woman, while Jefferson just looked at it suspiciously, as though worried Ally might poison us.

I had narrowly escaped being forced into another ridiculous costume by Jefferson and was now walking around the darkened house in my normal clothing. I wasn't sure if our suddenly complicated relationship had gotten me out of costume duty or if Jefferson had unexpectedly become more reasonable. Either way, I was grateful to be free of the long flowing dresses and ridiculous wigs.

"Try reading some of the script I gave you," Jefferson said in my earpiece.

I guess I hadn't avoided all of the awful parts of the job.

"I'm not in costume. No ghost is going to buy that I'm from their time period," I said, feeling slightly irritated with him.

Before investigating, we'd all decided to be extremely aware of our emotions on this particular job, since it seemed like something was messing with them. Personally, I was almost one hundred percent sure that the weird energy in the house was where my sudden attraction to Jefferson was coming from. There was no way he'd always been that hot and I'd just never noticed. Either way, we vowed to avoid saying anything too harsh to each other while at this location, thinking it was probably a result of the house's energy and not our own opinions.

"These aren't lines for a character," Jefferson assured me. "I want you to say you have a letter for Eva from Thatcher. See if you can draw her out to talk to us."

I never liked to give Jefferson the satisfaction of knowing he'd had a good idea. It only led to overconfidence on his part, and overconfidence for Jefferson Parrish translated into being cocky and weirder than ever. That being said, his idea with the note was actually kind of brilliant.

"Here goes nothing," I said with a sigh, pulling the folded letter out of my pocket and trying to balance my camera while pointing the flashlight at the paper. "Eva?" I said to the empty room. "Is there an Eva here who might want to talk to us?"

"We should have given her a K2 meter," Deacon said from his position in the van.

"We definitely should have given her more than just a camera," Brighton agreed.

"Eva, if you're here, you don't need to be scared of me," I went on, trying to sound inviting. "We just want to talk to you and find out what happened with you and Thatcher."

"I still don't think this whole ghost hunt is about connecting the dots on a failed love story," Jefferson said.

I tried to ignore him and get back into the zone. The house was too quiet.

"Eva, I have a letter here from Thatcher," I said, holding up the piece of paper. "He had a message for you."

"Just read it," Jefferson said.

"I'm getting to it. Would you shut your mouth?"

"Sade!" Brighton exclaimed. "Remember rule number one for this investigation?"

"No snapping at Jefferson," I recited robotically.

"No snapping at a fellow team member," she corrected.

"Trust me, Jefferson is the only one I'd snap at," I assured her.

"She loves me," I heard him say to Deacon in the van, which would have been a typical thing for him to say on any other day.

Now his words just made me nervous.

"She has a funny way of showing it, mate," Deacon replied.

"Yes. She. Does," Jefferson said, injecting way too much meaning into his words.

Had I been in the Jeep with him, I would have punched him.

"Reading the letter now," I said, hoping I could cut off any suspicious questions from the more sane half of our team.

Unfortunately, because of my recent behavior, I'd allowed myself to be grouped together with Jefferson in the insanity ranking. It was never a good thing when Deacon Parrish was saner than you.

"I will breathe in your boiled-down truth and essence. If I have to retreat within my own for that solace, I will take it. I choose drowning in madness if it is but in your glory," I read in the most incredulous tone possible. "What in the world is this?" I asked, shock lining my voice.

"It's a love letter," Jefferson said.

"But where did you find it?" I looked at the paper like it was roadkill. "Brighton, listen to this." I said, reading more of the eerie letter, "So let me drown and suffocate and choke in whatever of you I can take."

"Whoa," Brighton said with a low whistle.

"It's romantic," Jefferson said, even more defensive than before.

"Wait," I said. "You didn't write this yourself, did you?"

There was silence in my earpiece for far too long.

"Jefferson?" I said slowly.

"It's romantic!" he said again, sounding very put out that I didn't like it.

"This is not romantic! This is why people get restraining orders." I said. There had to be something wrong with me that I seemed to find Jefferson attractive when he was clearly a sociopath. "Do not ever let another letter like this see the light of day or they will throw you in jail."

"It's poetic," he said.

"It sounds like you're two seconds away from making a skin suit out of this girl," I corrected him.

"It's not my fault you don't understand poetry, Sadie," he answered in a low, dark tone. He was no longer defensive; now he was just pissed. "It's beautiful."

"Okay, we're going to call it a night on the love letter idea," Brighton cut in, trying to stop our fight before it started. I could hear the sound of an inhaler over my earpiece. "Sadie, why don't you just . . ." her words trailed off distractedly.

"Why don't I just what?" I asked, tucking the creepy "love letter" back in my pocket so that Ally wouldn't find it and have us all committed.

"Wait," Brighton said, making me instantly nervous.

"Brighton, what is it?" I asked more urgently.

"You're in the living room, right?" she asked, although she knew very well right where I was since we had cameras stationed all around the house.

"Yeah."

"Because I swear I just saw you looking out the front-facing window on the second floor."

I felt my body instantly go cold at her words and I wasn't sure what to do. Part of me wanted to run after whatever was upstairs, but the investigator side of me screamed to stay still and not scare it away. I held my breath, listening for any footsteps on the wood floor above me, but there was nothing. The house was completely silent.

The rest of the group must have been holding their breath too, because nobody spoke. I took one step forward, the floor creaking under my weight.

"It moved away from the window," Brighton said, her voice airy and terrified. "Go after it!"

I didn't stop to think. Instead, I bolted up the stairs, tripping over a few of them in the process. A large hand was instantly on my back to help steady me as I skipped the last few steps, and the smell of cinnamon that hit my nose made it so I didn't even have to turn around to know that Jefferson was behind me.

How had he gotten inside so quickly?

Entering the empty, tiny room on the almost nonexistent second floor, the pleasant cinnamon scent I'd just been guiltily enjoying was overpowered by the smell of rotten eggs.

"Oh heavens!" I used my arm to cover my nose.

Jefferson lifted his lip at the smell but didn't do anything to block it.

"What's wrong?" Deacon asked from the Jeep, his voice cutting in and out over our earpieces.

"Rotten eggs," Jefferson said.

"Ha! I knew it was a Doppelgänger," Deacon said. "And you thought it was a mimic."

Jefferson looked at me and rolled his considerably large eyes toward the ceiling, making me smile in spite of myself. Only the Parrish boys could turn a paranormal investigation into a competition. Especially when seconds before we'd been panicked about a ghost.

"What's the difference?" I asked Jefferson, though Deacon was the one who answered.

"With a Doppelgänger you get that rotten egg smell." I could hear the grin in his voice. "And a Doppelgänger can usually only imitate . . ."

"One person!" Jefferson exclaimed, making me jump with his sudden enthusiasm. "Whereas a mimic can imitate anyone and any environment. So I was right!"

"Then why does it smell like rotten eggs?" I asked.

"Well, if a mimic can imitate anything, then it can imitate smells as well, right?" Jefferson asked.

"Guys," Brighton said, trying to rein us all back in. "I'm not sure that Doppelgängers versus mimics is an exact science. Can we please just say something really weird is going on in this house, no matter what you want to call it?"

"Fair enough," both Parrish boys said in unison.

"That thing was imitating me," I said, finally realizing just how unsettling that was. I looked around the dark corners of the room to make sure it wasn't still there. "Jefferson, you are no longer the creepiest thing in this house."

"His letter still is," Brighton said with a laugh. She quickly quieted herself though. Probably realizing he may not take kindly to her poking fun at his "romantic" letter.

"You're really you, right?" I asked the tall lanky boy in front of me, giving his chest a little push.

"You're really into pushing me around lately," he said mischievously. "I didn't expect that to be your thing, but I can do that. Keeps things interesting."

"What are you guys on about?" Deacon asked, just as I slapped my hand over Jefferson's mouth.

We had an investigation to be doing. I couldn't have him flirting in his own messed up way when we were supposed to be talking to ghosts.

"He just thinks I've been bossy lately," I lied.

Jefferson's huge eyes squinted as he gave the biggest smile ever under my hand and nodded his head enthusiastically. I narrowed my own eyes at him, hoping he'd behave. He kissed my palm and I quickly removed my hand. My heart skipped, but I didn't want to let him know that so I tried to look as put out as possible.

The room was much too silent to have any useful evidence anymore. Whatever had been there was gone now, so Jefferson and I walked back toward the Jeep. We'd scared off our mimic.

"If we're dealing with a mimic or Doppelgänger or whatever, is it possible Eva isn't even here? Maybe it's just someone imitating her?" I asked.

"It's possible," Deacon answered. "But if this ghost is imitating Eva, then it must have seen her before. Like maybe she did live here and now this other spirit is imitating her. It couldn't just pull the imitation out of thin air."

"So, if Eva lived here before, this should still be our third location. Even if this spirit is trying to confuse us, there's still a clue here somewhere," I said.

"Seems like it," Deacon said as we reached the Jeep, taking a seat on the tailgate. "My turn?"

"Have at it," I said, handing over my camera and flashlight to Crazy Parrish Number Two.

I wasn't sure if Brighton had really seen a mimic version of me staring out the window, but if she had, it was a solid bet that we were on the right track. It just seemed odd that there could have been a mimic around without any sign other than its appearance. Up until Brighton had spotted it, I hadn't heard anything in the silent house.

I thought back to my time in the house only moments ago, searching my memory for any signs of the mimic until it had been spotted. Had the air been cold? Had I smelled or heard anything? It seemed like the house had been totally silent. How had there not been a single trace of that thing until it appeared?

I sat on the tailgate of our Jeep with a furrowed brow, hoping we'd caught the mimic on tape. We couldn't let that kind of evidence go unrecorded.

Jefferson knocked my knee with his over and over again as I tried to watch Deacon on the monitors. He was adorable, I'd give him that, but he also had no sense of discretion.

"This is Deacon Parrish in the Bray house," Deacon said, as I leaned over and turned off his audio feed to ask Brighton a question without distracting him.

"Do you think we should be asking questions to Eva, or should we ask the mimic where our next clue is?" I asked the group. "I mean, we can beat around the bush all day long pretending we're actually talking to Eva, but wouldn't it be better to just lay our cards out on the table and figure out what we came here for?"

"Being blunt might scare the mimic away, though," Jefferson said "If we're taking away its fun, why would it help us? If we play its little game and ask it where our clue is, maybe it'll lead us there."

"Or maybe it'll just lead us in circles because it has nothing better to do," Brighton said.

"It doesn't seem to be particularly malicious," I offered. "It's never tried to hurt that little girl or the family. It seems like it just wants to hang around and be part of our world."

"You sound like a Disney song," Brighton said with a laugh.

"But if it's not malicious, why did it make you go mental on me yesterday?" Jefferson asked, sounding genuinely concerned about my outburst.

"I think it's still messing with my behavior," I told him.

"It's not," he answered back, letting his fingers creep over mine, which were luckily out of Brighton's view. "It's definitely not."

I pulled my fingers away from his and placed my hands in my lap, hoping he'd get the hint. Of course, the concern in his voice did make me feel a pang of guilt. It seemed like Jefferson might honestly be worried that I didn't actually like him and maybe my mood was being altered by something in our investigation. I couldn't really say much on the matter because I half thought the only reason I'd suddenly start liking the boy who drove me crazy was that very explanation. But I'd never say that out loud. Not when Jefferson was currently giving me puppy dog eyes and melting my heart.

"What is Deacon doing?" Brighton asked in alarm.

His mouth was moving as if he was speaking, but we couldn't hear anything.

"Deacon?" Brighton asked, but it looked like he couldn't hear her.

"Oh, sorry," I said. "The sound."

I hit the switch to turn our two-way audio back on.

"Deacon?" Brighton said again.

We heard the tail-end of his sentence, which sounded something like, "Do you mean that?"

At the sound of Brighton's voice in his ear, Deacon got very still, his eyes getting wide as he looked around the room in confusion.

"Are you okay?" she asked him.

"Sorry, I was just . . . Where are you guys? In the Jeep?"

"Yeah, we're still outside, but Sadie turned off our audio so we could strategize," Brighton said.

"Oh," he responded, sounding deflated. "I was just asking some questions . . . trying to find our clue, but I haven't gotten anything yet."

His voice sounded off as he spoke, and the three of us exchanged questioning looks in the Jeep.

"Do you need a break?" Brighton asked.

"Yeah, I think this house is messing with me," Deacon said, making a quick exit out the front door and practically throwing the equipment at his cousin. "You have a go. See if it'll be kinder to you."

"What happened in there?" Brighton asked, looking concerned.

She reached out a hand to touch his shoulder but froze, seemed to think better of it, and tucked her hair behind her ear as if that had been her intention the whole time. Deacon hardly noticed in his perturbed state.

"Nothing happened," he snapped. "I didn't even want to come to this stupid house in the first place. I was fine with staying in Portland and being jobless but you guys had to drag me out of my comfort zone to this dead-end of an investigation. We're probably going to run out of money in Boston and have to sell our organs to get back home or something, all because you guys got greedy and thought we could make money off this hobby."

We all fell silent, staring at Deacon in confusion. His accent had gotten so thick as he ranted that I could hardly understand him by the end of his tirade.

Without hesitation, Jefferson picked up the equipment Deacon had tossed at him, slapped his panting cousin on the back, and offered him a thin-lipped smile.

"Don't be so moody, mate. It's not an attractive color on you," Jefferson told him. "Besides, if you steal my thing, I won't have anything left."

"Shut up," Deacon replied with a roll of his eyes.

The house was definitely messing with his emotions. I felt bad for him but it was also a little funny to see Deacon so upset when he was normally the one cracking jokes during investigations.

"Don't wait up," Jefferson added to me with a wink before he left.

Could he be any more obvious? I was amazed that Brighton and Deacon hadn't called us out ages ago, but it probably had something to do with the fact that they were always either distracted by a case or each other.

"He's been weird lately," Brighton said seriously, trying to move the topic away from Crazy Parrish Number Two and his sudden outburst. "Even for him."

"I can hear you," Jefferson said, before disappearing into the darkness of the house.

"I know," she responded, not sounding like she cared.

The Parrish boys were the only people in the world Brighton would stand up to, even if she would never tell Deacon how she felt about him. Although apparently she'd also stand up to me, since she had been voicing her opinions on the Jefferson subject quite frequently lately. I couldn't complain though, since I was just glad she'd grown a backbone.

"Are you feeling any better?" Brighton asked Deacon with a raise of her eyebrows.

At least he'd stopped panting now.

"Sorry . . . I don't know why I got so crazy for a second there."

"It's the house," I answered. "I think it's making us all a little crazy."

"Jefferson Parrish, investigating the Bray house in Boston, Massachusetts, on September ninth at midnight," Jefferson cut in over the speaker.

I watched the black and white screen in the darkness of the Jeep, taking note of how deliberately Jefferson moved through the dark, quiet house. He was definitely in his element in the world of paranormal investigation. He seemed completely at ease, letting his large eyes roam over the walls and darkened corners of the rooms, and I couldn't help but smile.

After a moment his eyes came to rest on a spot somewhere in front of him. He didn't move for a while or say anything; he froze and watched, looking very purposeful.

"Sadie?" he asked.

Brighton and Deacon both looked over at me and I hoped Jefferson wouldn't say something embarrassing or inappropriate because he knew I was too far away to hit him.

"Yeah?" I responded.

"Perfect," he said, walking forward with determination.

He walked up the staircase and into the room where Brighton had seen my Doppelgänger, or mimic, or whatever it was, before getting down on his hands and knees. He placed the camera and flashlight on the floor and began knocking on the hardwood panels.

"What are you doing?" I asked.

He didn't respond, of course, but lifted one of the floorboards and pulled an old wooden box from the concealed space, making all three of us stare at the screen in shock.

"How did you know that was there?" I asked him.

He smirked up at one of our stationary cameras, knowing we could see him on the monitor.

"You showed me."

CHAPTER 20

Jefferson's long form was sprawled out on the bed in the hotel room while I sat on the ground, my back leaning up against the bedframe. We were so close that I could lean my head back and hit his cheek, although I hardly let that distract me at the moment. We had far more important things to talk about.

"What did you tell Ally, Sade?" Brighton asked, twisting her hair nervously around her fingers.

"I told her the truth. I said we definitely found evidence of paranormal activity in the house, but that we don't think it's Eva. I let her know that while the presence did seem pretty happy to play tricks on us and mess with our emotions, it might just be protective of the house and the residents."

"Especially since it's not bugging the family," Brighton said, as if we were talking to Ally right at that moment. "Only outsiders."

"You didn't tell her we got rid of it, did you?" Jefferson asked, his mouth so close that I could feel his breath on my neck.

I ignored my chills.

"I told her that it might be gone now that we found the box of letters, but it might still be hanging around. Either way, I don't think it's something to be scared of."

"Well done, boss." Jefferson smirked so that only I could see him as I turned my head toward him.

I looked down at his lips that were, unfortunately, only inches from mine, and his smirk grew. We were way too close.

"Now that we're no longer around civilians, tell us how Sadie showed you where the box was," Deacon said, causing me to come back to reality and turn my head away from Jefferson's magnetic pull.

"I'm curious about that too," I added with a nervous laugh.

I was turning into Jefferson. I had been thinking of kissing him in front of Brighton and Deacon like a tactless weirdo.

Jefferson smiled to himself but didn't answer us right away.

"I may or may not have seen our ghost," he said with a self-satisfied look.

"And it looked like Sadie?" Deacon guessed.

"Sort of . . . except that she was smiling at me, which was what gave the ghost away. I knew it couldn't be Sadie at that point."

"Apparently it wasn't a very good mimic," I said, giving Jefferson a taste of his own medicine. "If it had been, it would have told you to stop writing creepy 'love' letters."

"Poetic," Jefferson retorted, looking put out. "And see if I ever write you one if you keep this attitude up."

"Think of all of that nightmare-inducing prose you'll be missing out on, Sade," Brighton said.

"Somehow I'll live."

"Can we please get back to the interesting stuff?" Deacon asked. "You really, honestly saw a full-bodied apparition in the house? I mean, she wasn't see-through or shadowy or anything?"

"It looked like Sadie standing there," Jefferson said. "There were no clanking chains or glowing lights or anything. But like I said, I knew you guys were in the van, so once Sadie confirmed that over the radio, I just followed the mimic when she turned and walked up the stairs."

"How were you not scared?" I asked, somewhere between respect and incredulity.

"Why would I be scared?" Jefferson asked it so genuinely that I couldn't begin to explain to him how normal people would react in that situation. "I wanted to find our clue and this apparition was obviously leading me there." He shrugged his shoulders as if this should be the simplest thing in the world.

"You weren't even impressed by the fact that you saw a ghost?" I pressed. "You live for this stuff."

I just couldn't believe that he was being so nonchalant about actually seeing a ghost. The rest of us would have killed for that opportunity, and here he was acting like it wasn't a big deal. Only days before he'd been ecstatic over half of a muffled sentence on our audio recordings.

"I've seen them before," he said cryptically. "So the fake Sadie pointed to the floorboards, I looked down at the spot she pointed to, and when I looked back up, she was gone."

"And you just understood that you were supposed to pull the flooring up?" Brighton asked, not buying it.

"What else could she want me to do?"

"Sit down?" Deacon suggested.

"Go back downstairs," I added.

"Apparently the ghost and I were on the same wavelength," Jefferson said.

"Surprise, surprise," I put in.

He knocked my shoulder with his forehead for my comment and I turned to smile at him, too close once more.

"What I want to know is how you could have waited until we got back to the hotel to tell us all of this," Brighton said.

"I wanted to make sure you guys were actually paying attention. I'm more surprised you let me get here without forcing me to tell you what happened."

"We tried to get it out of you the entire way home," Deacon said.

"I'm very good at keeping secrets," Jefferson said in a quiet voice, so close to me that I could feel his lips brush against my ear.

Now he was just toying with me. He was awful.

"Can we read the letters?" I asked, trying to discourage any more contact.

Ally had been kind enough to let us borrow the letters for the next two days until we could figure out what we needed from them. We promised her we'd bring them right back after we'd finished with them, and I could only hope we'd be able to grasp their meaning at all.

"There are a lot in here," Brighton said, sounding overwhelmed as she rifled through them. "But they're all dated, so maybe we should split them up by chunks of time? That way we can each research a few months and piece our findings together."

"That sounds easier than all of us reading every single letter," I said. "Plus, we still have to go over the investigation tapes to see if we caught the mimic on film."

"Every letter in this box is from Eva to Thatcher, who apparently lived in New York by this point, so our storyline shouldn't be too hard to figure out if it's all from one point of view."

"Why are there a bunch of letters from Eva in Eva's house?" Deacon asked.

"Maybe they never got sent?" Brighton suggested.

"That's a lot of letters to forget to send."

"Maybe someone else was supposed to be sending them for her, and they didn't," I said.

"That sounds like a good reason to have us investigate," Brighton answered with a yawn. It was nearly three in the morning and we were all exhausted. "Maybe that's part of what we're supposed to uncover."

"I say tomorrow we start with the letters and review the tapes after," I suggested.

"Tomorrow?" Jefferson answered with a pout in his voice.

I turned my head to glance back at his form on the bed.

"Jefferson Parrish, go to bed," I ordered, my voice lined with mock authority.

He narrowed his large eyes at me, half playing and half serious.

"You win this round," he said, before lowering his voice to a whisper, "But if Deacon tries to cuddle with me again tonight, I'm switching beds."

~

Hours.

We had spent hours reading over letters from Eva to Thatcher in our tiny, stuffy hotel room, and I was feeling itchy with the desire to be outside.

Deacon had fallen asleep over the small table in our room, probably drooling all over one of the very old and possibly valuable letters Ally had entrusted to us. Sitting next to me, Brighton's eyes were bloodshot and kept drooping closed as she fought to stay awake, while Jefferson wasn't even pretending to be working anymore. Instead he was asleep on one of the beds with a faint smile on his lips as he dreamed.

"I can't do this anymore," I whispered to Brighton, trying not to wake the Parrish boys. Even if they weren't helping us, it was always better to let a sleeping Parrish lie. "Do you want to go to the park or something? We can bring the letters with us and go over them there."

Brighton's mouth instantly turned into a small hard line at the mention of going outside.

"What is it now?" I asked with a sigh.

"So many things," she answered. "Sunburns, bugs, noise, pollution, kids running around with sticky ice cream-covered fingers. Just to name a few."

"How is it that you can make a nice sunny day in the park sound so life-threatening?"

"It's my job," she said with a sad nod.

"Well, I'm still going. I can't stay locked up in here anymore. Besides, when we do figure out our last location, I'm sure we'll be spending days in the car again and I can't be that close to these Parrish boys for that long."

"You can't go to the park alone," Brighton said.

I motioned for her to lower her voice. Jefferson stirred on the bed and the last thing I needed was him distracting me.

"You could get kidnapped or attacked," she finished in a whisper.

"It's the middle of the day. I'm pretty sure I'll be fine."

Our hotel room was incredibly small, since we had to be hyper-aware of our quickly dwindling funds, and nothing was going to keep me from getting outside. Ignoring Brighton's quiet protests, I gathered my bundle of letters, placed them in my purse, and waved over my shoulder to her, closing the door to our hotel room before she could talk me out of going. I only had a few more letters to read, but I didn't care. I needed air.

It didn't take long to get to the Boston Public Library from our hotel, and there was a small park right across the street, perfect for the solitude I needed. If I was going to make any progress on extracting relevant information from these letters, I'd need my head clear.

Taking off my yellow ballet flats and walking barefoot through the wet grass, I reveled in the feeling of the sun on my skin. I was looking incredibly pale lately and definitely disgracing my Cuban heritage. Some time out in the sun would do me a world of good. Of course, the fact that the grass was wet meant that I'd be getting my jean shorts wet, and I'd probably get teased by the impossible Parrish boys.

"I brought a blanket," Jefferson said behind me, as if he could read my mind.

I didn't even turn around to look at him—I just sighed at my bad luck.

"Why are you here?"

"I needed to get out of that room too. You're not the only one who needs space."

"You being here is not giving me space." I finally turned to see that he had one of the thin comforters from the hotel room bunched under his arm. "Jefferson!" I scolded. "You can't take the comforter out of the hotel."

"Even laying it on the dirty ground in the park won't make it any dirtier than it already is," he said, quite reasonably.

"Gross."

"It is," he agreed. "But it's better than getting your bum all wet."

I looked skeptically between him and the wet ground for a moment, wondering how many weird looks we'd get for so obviously stealing a hotel comforter with its awful faux art deco pattern, before deciding I'd rather be dry than proud.

"Fine, go ahead and lay it out," I said. "But one peep out of you when I'm trying to go over these letters and you're sentenced to the hotel room again."

"Yes, ma'am," he said with a salute, laying the blanket down and making himself right at home as he stretched out on his back. It wouldn't have looked so comical if he hadn't been so incredibly tall and dressed in his old-fashioned suit. Thanks to the latter, he just looked like he belonged in a turn-of-the-century painting of an afternoon in the park. And then, of course, I lay on my back next to him in my yellow T-shirt and jean shorts, totally throwing his whole vintage thing off.

"Did you bring your letters?" I asked, glancing over at the Parrish by my side.

He already had his eyes closed against the sun, and his little contented smile was back in place.

"I already read all of mine," he said, keeping his eyes closed.

"You did not," I countered, thinking he was joking.

"I really did. I'm ready to report once you guys are done."

"What are you going to do while I read, then?" I asked, scared he was just here to bug me.

"I'm going to take a nap in the sunshine."

"You don't seem like the type to like sunshine."

"Under the right circumstances I do," he answered, his little grin growing ever so slightly.

"You're probably going to get a sunburn," I attempted in a last-ditch effort to get rid of him.

"I don't burn," he answered.

It made sense. His deep olive skin probably really didn't burn. He was probably like me, just getting browner and browner and feeling bad for people like Brighton and Deacon, who had to avoid the sun like the little kids on *The Others*.

"Just remember that I'm actually working." I pulled out one of my letters and held it above my head in one hand, my free hand right next to Jefferson's.

Not on purpose, of course.

Jefferson must have taken my hint, because he didn't respond to my "threat," which I was actually a little disappointed about. I kind of enjoyed our arguing.

Shrugging that thought off, I read through the letter in my hand at least a dozen times. It wasn't anything too special, although I had learned an interesting detail earlier about why Eva had followed Thatcher to Boston.

Apparently there had been a baby involved, which I tried not to get too hung up on until I knew more from the other letters. It was a huge detail, but I couldn't draw any conclusions just yet. But that didn't explain why none of Eva's letters to Thatcher were ever actually sent. I could understand if she was writing them as a way of getting things off her chest without ever intending to mail them, but the further along in the story I read, the more it became apparent that Eva was discouraged by Thatcher's lack of response to her letters. That meant, as far as she was aware, her letters were being sent.

"Jefferson?" I said. I got no response. I moved my fingers those few empty inches and closed them around his hand, giving him a little shake. "Jefferson?" I tried again.

"I thought you were working and I was sleeping," he answered, keeping his eyes closed.

"Who do you think was supposed to send Eva's letters?"

He sighed deeply. I guess he really had been excited to take a nap.

"Probably not a maid. She was too poor for that."

"That's what I'm thinking," I agreed. "But then why would she think someone else was supposed to send her letters? People in her class would just do that themselves, right?"

"Thatcher seemed to be wealthy . . . maybe he got her a maid," he suggested.

"Why do you think Thatcher was wealthy?"

"He got a ticket on the Queen Mary to come over and see his girlfriend, who was a maid. Sounds like a bad romance novel."

"And that makes him wealthy?" I asked.

Jefferson finally opened his eyes and rolled over on his side to face me. "All evidence points to that," he said.

I chewed on my lip, thinking about this for a moment before putting the letter back in my bag. I only had one or two more to read before I was done with my chunk, but I hardly felt like I was getting any answers from them. My only hope for this investigation rested on the fact that Brighton had the last set of letters. Maybe Eva would end her letter writing spree with a good clue.

I hadn't realized it until his fingers moved over mine, but I was still holding Jefferson's hand as I pondered our current mystery. Looking over at him, he smiled at me. An actual, genuine smile. Not like he was teasing me, or being creepy, or trying to flirt, but just like he was happy to be there.

I thought about rolling my eyes at him or making some snarky comment, but instead, feeling sleepy and less anxious about my association with the crazy Parrish in the sunny afternoon, I rolled onto my side and scooted closer to him so that we were only inches apart.

"I don't actually like the sunshine," he admitted after a moment.

I brought his large hand up so that I could rest my cheek in his palm.

"You didn't strike me as a sunshine lover," I replied with a smirk. "It was a nice try, though."

"I wanted to follow you so I could spend some more time with you."

"That's honest," I said with a little wince.

I knew it was good to be honest, but I wasn't used to having such straightforward conversations with people. Normal people didn't say things that honest all the time. They found a way to partially tell the truth so that they could still have some sort of power in the conversation. Apparently Jefferson didn't care about having the conversational upper hand.

"Do you want to spend time with me?" he asked. The question didn't sound at all clingy, but just curious. "Or do you want me to leave?"

I thought about it for a moment. I knew what I wanted. But I didn't want him to know. Still, he had been nothing but honest with me, so the least I could do was return the favor.

"I want to spend time with you, but I don't want Deacon and Brighton to know."

I thought he'd ask me why or be offended that I still seemed to be slightly embarrassed by him. Instead he just nodded, as if my statement was fair . . . which it wasn't.

With my cheek in his hand, I let my thumb run over his wrist, feeling the rapid pulse there. His heightened heart rate made me smile. It was difficult to read Jefferson, and from what I could see, he was totally relaxed and not at all affected by our close proximity. But his pulse couldn't lie to me.

"Tell me about your family," I said after a moment of silence.

His pulse sped up a fraction more.

I wasn't sure why I wanted to hear more about them, but for some reason, I was honestly interested in Jefferson's story—in what made him tick.

"Why?" he asked.

"Because I want to know."

"Why?" he asked again, obviously reluctant to talk

This was getting me nowhere. I'd have to try a different tactic.

"Why aren't you some big fancy businessman in England like your dad was?"

Jefferson's expression changed at the mention of his dad. I could tell he had a serious soft spot for him.

"I despise responsible, well-thought-of careers," he answered.

"For some reason, that doesn't surprise me."

"It's not what you might think," he interjected, piquing my interest. "My mother only married my father for his money. She thought he was too eccentric, and she loathes me for being odd. The only thing that's important to her and that whole Temple side of the family is status. They judge your character based on your career path and don't bother to look deeper than that."

"I feel like normally that would make someone strive to be more successful," I said.

"It would," he agreed. "If I gave a sod what my mum thought of me."

"Rebel Jefferson," I teased with a smile.

"See, I don't think wanting to be seen for more than my career makes me much of a rebel. And yet my whole family sees the Parrish lot as being no-good bums, despite the fact that my father was so wealthy. Even though he had the fancy career, he had to work to get it and the rest of his family, like Deacon's father, weren't successful."

"And that's bad?"

"That meant my dad wasn't worthy of being respected by the Temples. And then there's my cousin Hayden, who admittedly is a good guy but can just be such a . . ." He let his words trail off in frustration.

"Jerk?" I offered.

He gave a short laugh. "That's a nice way of putting it, but I'll stick with that so I don't offend you," he said. "Anyway, he's not a people person, we'll say, but he's the Temple Golden Boy because he's a doctor. And there's the two evil Temple twins, Dresden and Alistair, who are a million times worse than Hayden, but they have successful careers so everyone loves them."

"And then there's you, who's a wonderful person, but they don't respect you because you don't have a job?" I guessed.

"You think I'm wonderful?" he asked.

"Of course, that's the only thing you'd get from that." I laughed uncomfortably. It was so hard for me to just admit to Jefferson that I liked him. I'd spent so long being annoyed by him that it was a rough transition.

"I make it my goal to strive toward mediocrity just to make my family mad," he said, back on topic. "It's not fair that they should judge me for being a little odd, and I'm definitely not going to let them assign me a status based on something as meaningless as a career path."

"That sounds like you spend an awful lot of time not doing things just to make a point to your family," I said, feeling like the world's biggest hypocrite for my words. "How do you make yourself happy if you're putting your life on hold to make them mad?"

"This makes me happy," he said.

"Yeah, but what about when the investigation is over? You have to have something else besides all of this paranormal stuff to make your life full."

"Not the ghost hunting," he said, sounding like I was dense. "This," he emphasized, giving me a meaningful look that I definitely wasn't ready for. "Do you like me, Sadie?"

The question was simple, and it should have been easy to answer. But it wasn't.

"That's not important," I said, trying not to look at him, which was impossible when we were facing each other, lying side by side, and only inches apart.

"It's important to me," he responded. "I'm not going to make you tell Brighton and Deacon. I'm not going to make you be my girlfriend. I'm not even going to say anything has to change in the way we interact. I just want to know."

The fact that he was being so sincere and open made it so much harder to be my normal, guarded self. I still tried, but ended up failing miserably.

"You're weird," I said to him. "And kind of crazy. And the fact that you're so unpredictable and have the world's worst mood swings terrifies me."

His brows furrowed together.

"But I do like you. Against my better judgment," I finished.

He placed his free hand on my waist and pulled me closer to him on the blanket so that our stomachs were touching.

"While we're on the topic of things we really don't want to talk about . . ." His thumb ran up and down my ribcage in a motion that brought those very unwelcome butterflies back. "Why are you so obsessed with being normal? It's so boring."

"I'll tell you I like you all day long, but we aren't talking about this," I said, drawing the line and wishing my brain wasn't so fuzzy because of our close proximity.

My chest felt like it was on fire.

"That's not fair. If I have to talk about my awful family, you have to talk about the family you pretend is awful, even though they aren't."

"I don't pretend anything," I said. "My family left me to be with my sister, who doesn't even want them there."

"You sister seemed very nice," he said. He was trying to be frustrating just so I would get defensive and talk about my family, no matter how little I wanted to.

"Except for when she's making up things I never said," I countered. "She could be downright pleasant minus all the times she told my parents I'd said mean things to her that I never said."

"Even with the lying, she still seems nice," Jefferson insisted. He wasn't going to let it go.

"She is nice, which makes it even worse. She's always trying to mend fences with me and asks me why I'm so mad at her, but how am I supposed to say, 'Sorry Michigan, I know you didn't ever do anything to me, but I hate you because Mom loves you more than me.'?"

I hadn't intended to be that honest with Jefferson (or with myself for that matter), but I couldn't seem to stop myself.

"I'm an awful person, aren't I?" I asked Jefferson, feeling much too vulnerable in front of him.

"Sadie, you're a strong person," he said, which didn't really help me. "You can take care of yourself. I only met your sister for a few minutes, but she was far too nice. She's kind of a doormat. Did you ever think that maybe your parents followed her to Boston because they didn't think she could take care of herself? Maybe they knew they didn't need to worry about you so they went along with Michigan to keep track of her."

That sounded like a good solution to the problem, and I appreciated Jefferson for trying, but it just didn't solve it.

"They've always given her special treatment," I said.

"Could be for the same reason," he suggested. "But none of this tells me why you have to be overly normal."

I sighed deeply. This conversation was too exhausting. "I can't figure out why my parents don't love me as much as her. But I can make sure I don't give them any reason to dislike me. I just kind of figure as long as I'm normal, they won't have any reason to be upset with me."

"Which is why you hide the mirrors?" he asked.

I felt my stomach drop a little bit that my weird obsession had somehow not escaped his notice.

"You like to collect old mirrors, which is a perfectly normal thing to do," he began. "But you don't display them. They aren't in your room or apartment. They're shoved away in a box. I thought at first maybe it was just because you didn't like them much, but if you care enough about these old things to bring some with you on our trip, you must love them."

"How do you even know about all of this?" I asked, though I knew he'd never tell me.

He just seemed to know everything and I seemed destined to wonder where he got his knowledge from.

"I just know that you shouldn't try to hide something you love just because you think it seems . . . less-than-normal."

"I'll stick to hiding my feelings like a normal person, thank you very much," I responded, half joking but mostly serious.

Jefferson gave me a sad look.

"We're kind of pathetic, aren't we?" he asked.

"A little," I said.

"I don't think we're really affecting our families much by keeping ourselves miserable over them. I think we're just keeping ourselves miserable."

"Unfortunately, I think you're right," I said with a nod.

"You should talk to your sister."

"You should talk to your mother," I countered.

"Touché," Jefferson said with a laugh. "Normal or not, I think you are completely and utterly amazing, and your family is crazy if they don't see that."

"Too honest," I said, though his words made me smile.

"Sorry, I forgot we weren't supposed to say what we really think. I'll have to read more of my 'how to be a normal, avoidant human being' handbook."

"I'd appreciate that," I said. "Now that we've had all sorts of uncomfortable conversations, should we go back to the hotel room?"

"Slow down Sade, I have morals," he said sarcastically.

"That's never going to be what I meant," I responded.

His thumb was still running a bumpy course over my ribcage, and I could feel his stomach move against mine every time he inhaled.

"Let's just stay here and work on the letters a little longer," he said, his green eyes locked on mine.

"You don't have any letters to go over," I pointed out.

"Oh well." He wrapped his arm around my waist, eliminating any space between us so that my cheek was against his neck with my head tucked safely under his chin. The breeze kept us cool as I snuggled against him. "I'm okay with pretending to be a sunshine person for a little longer."

CHAPTER 21

"Sorry I couldn't stop Jefferson from following you to the park," Brighton whispered.

She was searching my face with an anxious look, probably thinking she'd offended me by her inability to stop the willful Parrish.

"It wasn't a big deal," I said with a shrug.

Obviously I couldn't say it was one of the best moments I'd had in a long time. That was a bit more honest than I was ready to be right then.

"I know it's been kind of miserable hanging around in hotel rooms and living on the road," Brighton said, "But how are we going to go back to normal life after this? I don't want to go back to work."

"Uh-oh. You've been hanging around with the Parrish boys too much."

"They do have an aversion to work," she agreed.

I smiled at her and grabbed my bundle of letters, ready to start our unofficial presentations.

"Sadie, do we have any refreshments for our business meeting?" Jefferson asked, his voice taking on a whiny quality. He came and stood much too close to me, putting his hand on my elbow.

Brighton definitely noticed.

"Sit," I commanded, pointing to the bed.

"So, no snacks, then?" Deacon asked, looking as upset as his cousin. "I'm feeling a bit peaky."

"Both of you sit," I said in exasperation.

Brighton rolled her eyes at the boys and took a seat on our bed, folding her legs up to her chest and watching me expectantly.

"I've called you all here today to solve a mystery," I began dramatically.

"You didn't gather us here," Deacon pointed out.

"I'm trying to add an air of intrigue, thank you very much," I said, finding that even with the Parrish boy's teasing, I was in an incredibly good mood for some reason. "But since you guys are ruining my fun, I guess I'll just tell you what my letters said."

"It was a valiant effort," Jefferson offered. The smile I sent in his direction garnered another odd look from Brighton.

"Basically, my letters were over a two-month time period, and from what I gathered, Eva was pregnant with Thatcher's baby . . . or at least that's what Eva says, although it doesn't look like Thatcher knew she was pregnant."

"It's like a soap opera," Brighton said.

"Pretty much," I agreed. "Eva wrote letter after letter to Thatcher telling him that she was pregnant. It looks like she followed him from Austin to Boston but was ill when she arrived, so she wasn't able to go see him. I'm not sure if he even knew she was here, especially since it looks like her letters were never sent."

"Someone didn't want Thatcher to know Eva was in Boston," Jefferson said.

"That's what it looks like."

He was quiet for a minute, brow furrowed as he stared at the ground. I could practically hear the gears turning in his head.

"What else did you learn?" he asked after a moment.

"Not much. She just says, 'I'm getting weaker and fear this illness may have taken root for good,' which is a little depressing. Whatever was wrong with her wasn't a common cold."

"Poor Eva," Brighton said, looking down at her hands with a frown. "And she was pregnant on top of all that."

I nodded somberly but didn't elaborate on Brighton's sentiment. There wasn't much to say. Whatever situation Eva had been in was a bad one. And what had happened to this baby she'd been carrying? With how sick she seemed in my letters, I couldn't imagine the baby had ever actually been born.

"That's about all I had in my set of letters," I said after a moment, trying to shake the heavy feeling our meeting had just taken. "That means Deacon is up."

As Deacon stood, I almost went to sit beside Jefferson before catching myself and changing course to head for the bed where Brighton was perched. Jefferson looked up at me a little sadly but said nothing.

"Mine are actually about the same as Sadie's," Deacon said. "Eva is trying to get ahold of Thatcher, saying that she's getting sicker and . . . you know . . . more pregnant. But she does thank him for putting her up in the house she's staying at and thanks him for hiring a nurse for her."

"The Bray's house?" Jefferson asked, starting to piece things together in that massive brain of his.

"Yep," Deacon replied.

"So, Thatcher did know Eva was here?" I asked. "I mean, he hired a nurse to look after her and let her stay in that house."

"Does it say she ever actually spoke to him at this point? Or was she just told it was Thatcher who was doing all of this stuff for her?" Jefferson asked.

"From the way she's talking, it didn't sound like she'd seen him since moving to Boston. So I'll go out on a limb and say she was just told Thatcher was helping her out."

"That's not suspicious at all," Jefferson said sarcastically.

Deacon sat down on the bed beside him, apparently done with his chunk of the letters.

Jefferson then took over the narrative. "My letters mentioned a friend of Thatcher's. It sounds like after seeing Eva in Austin, he went to Boston to open up a law firm with a man he sailed with on the Queen Mary. But they didn't stay in Boston for long, because a few months after Eva came here, Thatcher left to New York. I'm not sure if he was opening up another law firm or just moving his original one, but for some reason he left with his new friend Edward Meyer."

"That's the friend he met on the Queen Mary?" I asked, thinking it all sounded a bit suspicious that Thatcher would just leave the woman he loved behind, especially when he knew she was pregnant.

Jefferson looked down at a letter in his hand then nodded silently. "I mean, I can theorize about what happened, but I'm hoping Brighton's letters offer a solid answer." He turned his huge owl eyes on her.

She took an audible breath, nervous to be speaking in front of us, no matter how comfortable she was with her friends. Any form of public speaking was difficult for Brighton. I thought I was being funny when I stood in front of the group like it was an actual business meeting, but since they all seemed to follow suit, Brighton felt the need to stand as well.

"I think my letters piece things together nicely," she said. "We're still guessing at a few things, but it seems pretty obvious what happened. Eva, by this point, is about to have her baby, but she says in her letters that she's too sick and she thinks having the baby will kill her."

Brighton swallowed at that statement, seeming uncomfortable with it. She bit her lip for a moment before continuing.

"She says in the letter she's grateful that Thatcher gave her the nurse and took care of her by proxy throughout her pregnancy, and that she understands why he had to send her away. Or why he left her in the first place, I guess. It sounds like when she followed him to Boston, someone met with her and said Thatcher couldn't see her because of the disgrace an illegitimate child would bring him and how it would affect his career. But they also told her that he didn't want to shut her out completely and that he'd put her up in the house, have someone take care of her, and make sure she and the baby were taken care of."

"And Thatcher probably said none of this," Jefferson said. "Because he probably had no idea there even was a baby or that Eva followed him."

"Now who's drawing conclusions?" I asked him with a grin. He smiled back at me and I quickly looked away, not wanting to get distracted.

"She went on to say she was worried he wasn't getting any of her letters because she hadn't heard from him since being in Boston and it wasn't like him to just ignore her."

"Bingo," Jefferson said. "He never knew she was here."

"In the last letter she's only a few days from having the baby, but it looks like Thatcher had already left Boston a while back and she couldn't follow because she got too sick. But she actually does leave us with a pretty solid clue."

"Which is?" Deacon asked, sitting up and holding his breath.

Brighton looked down at the letter to read our final clue.

"I've begun to worry you've missed my letters all along. Perhaps I should have followed you to New York. Livingston and Meyer. It's such a handsome title, Thatch."

"Because with her woman's intuition, she knew he never knew about the baby," Jefferson insisted.

He really wasn't going to let his theory go easily.

"Woman's intuition?" I repeated.

"Not only that, but she was pregnant, so she had mother's intuition as well."

He said this as if it were a scientific fact and not his own crackpot theory.

At my raised eyebrows, he narrowed his eyes. "Think about it, Sade. This guy sailed over from England to be with the woman he loved. And then suddenly he just leaves her for no reason?"

"The reason was the baby. Remember?" I asked.

"He left her before she came to Boston to tell him about the baby. And I don't think there was ever a reason in any of our letters for why he left Austin in the first place," he said. "That Meyer guy convinced him to leave and start a law firm with him. Who knows? Maybe the shady little bugger even said Eva didn't want to be with him anymore and that's why Thatcher left Austin in the first place."

"Okay, now you're just being dramatic." I didn't quite disagree with his theory but he had no solid evidence.

"Either way, I think our next location is this Livingston and Meyer place," Brighton said. "I'm not sure if the actual law firm will still be there and functioning, but I bet the building itself is."

"At least New York isn't nearly as far as our other locations have been," Deacon said, sounding optimistic.

"It's like three or four hours, right?" I asked. "Give or take."

Jefferson instantly looked down at his watch. It was early in the evening and not quite dark outside yet, but we still had a lot of research to do before barging into this law firm.

"Don't even think about it," I said.

"It's such a short drive," he pleaded, turning his big sad eyes on me.

I gave in for the briefest of seconds, but quickly regrouped and held my ground.

"We've already paid for the hotel for tonight," I said. "Plus we have to give the letters back to Ally, and we don't know anything about our next location."

"And if it is still a law firm, or any business, really, it's probably closed right now," Brighton said.

Jefferson pouted but didn't argue.

I tried to dampen the blow. "We'll take Ally's letters back tonight and review the investigation tapes from her house to see if there's anything we might have missed on there that can help us with our next location."

I wasn't quite sure where Jefferson and I stood, since he didn't seem like the type to have the "define the relationship" conversation, but it felt like I was somewhere between a girlfriend and his mother, which was not a place I wanted to be.

"Who gets to review tapes?" He narrowed his eyes suspiciously like I might try to rob him of the "joy" of reviewing hours of boring tape.

"Brighton and I will bring the letters back to Ally, since you Parrish boys would just say something inappropriate and make her hate us forever."

"Fair enough," Jefferson agreed.

Brighton moaned, obviously unhappy about the prospect of human contact.

"I'll do the talking," I assured her. "You just stand there and look pretty."

"That's what I'm best at," she said.

CHAPTER 22

Brighton managed to get out of "human contact duty" because Deacon had stepped up at the last minute claiming he wanted to go to ask Ally a question. He didn't really have anything to ask her; he just knew that Brighton was freaking out about having to talk to a stranger, so he did what he could to keep her from the horrors of awkward conversation.

Of course, that meant I had to talk to Ally with Deacon as my wingman. Deacon Parrish, the amazing woman-fearing man. Luckily, he just stood stock-still during our entire conversation, and when Ally tried to hug him in gratitude for figuring things out, he let out a nervous laugh and practically ran back to the Jeep.

Now I was stuck with Deacon in traffic because of a fender-bender a few blocks up from us. We weren't very far from our hotel, but there was no way to get out of the massive clump of stopped cars, so we stared out the windows while I worried about what my attraction to Jefferson said about me.

It wasn't that he was an unattractive guy. In fact, if someone didn't know how weird he was, they'd think he was hot. He had the big eyes, olive skin, and curly hair thing going for him. The sharp features were a plus as well. And I guess he was a pretty sharp dresser . . . or at least he would be if we lived in Victorian England. But still, he was a very attractive guy.

He was just so odd. And really, if I was being honest with myself, I kind of loved that about him. But I also needed to be normal. I needed to not be the weird daughter at Christmas dinner. I already felt like an intruder at my own family gatherings with my parents doting on Michigan, and I didn't need any more reasons to be the outcast in the family.

Of course, the need for normalcy didn't really stop me from paranormal investigation; I just "forgot" to tell my parents about that part of my life whenever I saw them. You couldn't exactly "forget" to tell them about a person, though.

"You know, if I had a Portal Gun, this wouldn't be a problem," Deacon finally said. "Traffic would be a thing of the past. Just blast an entrance portal right in front of the Jeep and shoot the exit portal at the hotel."

"Who would shoot the exit portal at the hotel?" I asked, indulging his geekiness for a moment.

"We'd have done that before we left, obviously, although I'm not sure where you'd get moon rocks at this hour."

"You Parrish boys got beat up a lot in school, didn't you?" I asked with a grin in Deacon's direction.

"Actually, I did. Thanks for bringing it up," he joked. "Although I did manage to get a kiss from Alicia Tyler in grade school by promising to do her homework for a year."

"I thought you were scared of women," I said.

"I wasn't until high school," he responded. "That's when I found out I should be scared of women. Until then I lived in blissful ignorance of their terrifying ways."

I raised an eyebrow at him questioningly.

He hesitated. "There was an unfortunate incident with a fake note and the girl's locker room."

"Okay, what?" I asked with a laugh. "You have to elaborate now."

"One of the guys on the rugby team put a note in my bag, and I thought it was from this girl I fancied. When I went to meet her in the locker room like the note said, I was met with a very shocked and very angry scantily clad girl's football team."

I tried not to, but I couldn't help myself—I burst out in uncontrollable laughter.

"Oh yeah, go ahead and laugh it up, but I couldn't walk for a week after the beating they gave me! Have you ever seen a female football player? They're strong."

I wiped away a few tears that had escaped my eyes during my laughing attack. "You had a women's football team?"

"Soccer," he said in an exaggerated tone. "Americans."

I managed to get my laughing under control. "I can see why you might be scared of women," I said, trying to be sympathetic. "What about Jefferson? Was he picked on a lot?"

Part of me was simply bored from the traffic jam that hadn't moved an inch in the past ten minutes, but part of me was actually curious about Jefferson's childhood. Somehow I couldn't imagine the crazy Parrish as a child. He seemed like someone who had always been a little adult. I mean, a scary, intense adult. But still, an adult nonetheless.

"Jefferson and I didn't go to school together," Deacon said, sounding like I should have known this information.

"I don't know why I just assumed you lived close together." "We sort of did. I mean, he lived in a posh neighborhood and I didn't, but we were within walking distance. But Jefferson's mum sent him off to boarding school right after his dad died."

I tilted my head to the side in confusion, pulling the classic Jefferson move by accident. Maybe I had been spending too much time with the boy.

"He actually got in a lot of trouble at that school," Deacon said with a conspiratorial grin. "You know how a lot of schools have teacher evaluations at the end of the term?"

"Yeah."

"Well, Jefferson's evaluation of his teachers was a bit . . . intense . . . I guess."

"What do you mean?" I asked, suddenly interested.

"I can't remember the whole thing unfortunately, but he said something like, 'I would surely take such immense pleasure in crawling into your brain to explore it and pick it apart. To see the inner workings of your brilliant mind would be very satisfying.'"

"Yikes," I replied with a slightly horrified look. "Sounds like a serial killer."

"Yeah," Deacon agreed with a nod. "That's what the teacher said too. The school threatened to kick him out, but his mum donated a library wing or something to keep him in. Then they said he had to meet with the school psychologist once a week as long as he stayed there."

"Wow," I said as the traffic began to ease up a bit. "Poor guy."

"People just don't quite get him, I guess," Deacon said, putting it lightly. "Like, he freaked a lot of the kids at his school out because he would get them these ridiculously elaborate, expensive presents when he was their Secret Santa. I'm talking really personal gifts that were just a little weird."

"Like what?"

"I think he got one kid a vacation to Scotland with his family because he heard the kid saying he wanted to spend more time with his parents. Just really extravagant things like that. And while he would think he was being sweet and thoughtful, the kids and parents thought he was a complete nutter."

"That sounds about like Jefferson," I said, thinking that this picture of his younger self made perfect sense.

"I think he would even draw pictures of the kids in his class and give them to them as gifts," Deacon went on, starting to laugh at his cousin's cluelessness. "Which, you know, I could see why he thought it would be nice. But to a perfect stranger it was probably a little creepy."

"He does walk the line between sweet and creepy a little too precariously," I said with a sigh.

There was definitely something wrong with me for liking Jefferson as much as I did.

Deacon gave me a sideways glance as we neared the hotel. "I'm just glad you and Brighton are nice to him. I know he says he doesn't care, but not a lot of people are kind to him."

"He's weird and moody, but we're kind of stuck with him, for better or worse. There are definitely worse friends to have," I said.

We fell silent for a minute after Deacon parked the Jeep in the hotel parking lot. We both stared out the window, lost in our own thoughts.

"Hey, Sadie?"

"Yeah?"

"Do you fancy my cousin?"

I tried not to be obvious in my shock at his question. I didn't want to give anything away. Instead, I replied with the one thing that would shut him up effectively.

"Do you fancy Brighton?"

He narrowed his eyes at me in the darkness of the Jeep. "Well played, sir," he said.

I gave him a self-satisfied smile and got out of the Jeep. I was quite proud of myself for my little victory, although my mind was distracted by what I'd learned about Jefferson. When I'd first met him in college, I knew he was weird. It was pretty obvious with all of his staring and lack of normal responses to things. But in college, (especially in Portland), people just thought you were being individualistic when you acted weird. I could only imagine that kids at a boarding school would have been intolerably cruel to him for his quirks. Kids were mean as it was, but throw someone like Jefferson in there and it was amazing he'd survived.

Opening the door to the hotel room, I was overcome with an intense desire to run over and give Jefferson a hug, but I obviously refrained. Instead, I let my lips pull up into a little half smile when I saw him. He'd been wearing an odd expression when we'd first entered the room, although when he saw my smile, his face instantly lit up.

Brighton, on the other hand, was staring at the computer screen in front of her and Jefferson with a bright red face.

"What's going on?" I asked. "Is Jefferson making you watch more of those microbiology videos about how many germs live on your skin?"

"We were just reviewing tape," she said.

I glanced over at Deacon to see if he thought they were being as weird as I did, but his face instantly turned red as well.

"Okay, now I have to see this tape," I stated, sitting beside Jefferson on the bed and placing my hand on his back as I leaned toward the computer screen.

I could feel him tense under my touch while a small smile formed on his lips. I couldn't seem to stay far from him. It was a little ridiculous.

Brighton's finger hovered over the mouse pad on the laptop, but she didn't play the isolated clip. She just continued to stare at the screen, her mouth thin and tight. Deacon was frozen by the door where we'd entered, looking immensely uncomfortable.

"Brighton?" I asked. "Are you going to play the clip?"

Jefferson laughed softly beside me and I narrowed my eyes at him. Something weird was going on.

"I'll play it," he finally responded with a full-blown smile, hitting the play button.

The screen held an image of Deacon by himself in one of the rooms in the Bray home. He held a flashlight and walked around nonchalantly, but suddenly froze as if he'd heard a noise. Turning around slowly, relief flooded through him at whatever he was seeing.

"What are you doing in here?" he asked, and I waited to hear a response from one of us, although none ever came.

"Are Sadie and Jefferson still in the Jeep?" he asked the empty space.

I racked my brain to figure out where in the investigation this was until it hit me all of a sudden. This was when we'd turned off the volume to Deacon's mic so that all three of us could talk about the investigation. He'd been alone in the house until he got mad about something and came back out to the Jeep.

This realization made the clip I was seeing that much weirder, since Deacon definitely thought he was talking to Brighton at this point.

"Oh . . . well, good," Deacon said awkwardly on the video.

"Can we please turn this off?" the real Deacon asked, still standing by the door and looking pained.

"We're just getting to the good part, mate," Jefferson said with glee in his voice.

Deacon groaned, but didn't say anything. It was obvious Brighton had already seen whatever the clip contained.

On the screen, the recorded Deacon backed up a bit until his back was against a wall in the Bray house. He looked a bit startled, but not as if he'd seen a ghost. Whatever was talking to him had to be the mimic pretending to be Brighton.

That was just so mean.

"I mean, I definitely do, I just never thought you'd . . . you know," the recorded Deacon finished quietly—almost too quietly to hear.

This was painful to watch and I could feel myself grimacing involuntarily at the awkward situation we were suddenly all a part of.

His expression on the tape went from startled to ecstatic before he said, "Do you mean that?" just as Brighton's recorded voice cut in, calling his name.

And then the clip ended.

We were all silent. Awkwardly silent.

There wasn't really much to say. It was painfully obvious that Deacon had thought he was talking to Brighton, and that Brighton was telling him she liked him. And then, of course, Deacon had admitted to liking her as well. It was just too many levels of awkward to process, so I did what needed to be done and didn't bother with the whole "talking about this situation like adults" thing.

"Ally was really grateful we brought the letters back," I said, startling Brighton, who jumped a little at the sound of my voice.

Deacon was staring at the ground and wringing his hands, not able to look at any of us. No wonder he'd been so upset when he'd left the Bray house—he thought him and Brighton were finally on the same page only to find out it was just a mimic messing with his mind. Of course, I was desperate to talk about the fact that Deacon had carried on a full conversation with a ghost that we apparently couldn't see on the screen, but I didn't think there was a tactful way of addressing that issue at the moment.

"Oh, good," Brighton responded, trying way too hard to sound like we hadn't just watched Deacon declaring his love for her.

"Did you already map out our trip for tomorrow?" I asked her, trying to keep things light.

"I already booked a hotel," Jefferson cut in.

"What?" Brighton and I said in unison.

"Jefferson, you know you can't book the hotels," I said incredulously. At least now we had something to distract us from the clip.

"Did you remember to get a room on the bottom floor?" Brighton asked, sounding like this was a life or death situation.

"I don't remember," he answered.

"I have to be on the bottom floor," Brighton practically shouted, starting to panic.

"She's scared of falling through the floor," I whispered to Jefferson, sure Brighton could hear me.

"Calm down," he answered, exasperation dripping from his voice. "I remembered; I was just joking with you guys. Everyone here is so uptight."

Brighton's breathing was still rapid, but the small panic was effective in changing the subject away from the clip we'd just watched. Deacon finally moved away from the door, although he and Brighton were too careful about avoiding each other for the rest of the night as we all got ready for bed.

It would have been cute if it weren't so sad.

CHAPTER 23

Inevitably, Jefferson and I ended up sleeping on the floor in the small space between the two twin beds again to avoid our impossible bed buddies. I wanted to pretend like I was upset by this fact, but since Deacon and Brighton were both sound asleep, I didn't see the point in pretending around Jefferson. Instead I lay on my side and laced my fingers through his, smiling at him in the darkness.

It felt good.

"Deacon told me all of your secrets today," I whispered, pretending to be scandalized by his "secrets."

Jefferson's face remained neutral. Apparently, he didn't have any secrets he was worried about.

"What did he say?" He looked down at our entwined hands and ran his thumb over my palm. "You have the smallest hands, by the way."

I wasn't sure if he was complimenting me or simply making an observation, but either way, I ignored it, wanting to hear more about Jefferson's childhood straight from the source.

"He told me that you went to a boarding school and that you got into a little bit of trouble there," I began, now looking down at our hands as well instead of at Jefferson.

"You know, they aren't really secrets if they're things I would have told you myself, Sadie. And I would tell you anything."

I knew he was trying to be sweet, but as usual, it just came off as way too intense, making me shift my weight a bit at how open he was with me.

"How was it, having to go to the therapist when you hadn't really done anything wrong?"

I wasn't sure when I had sided with him on the whole situation, but I guess knowing that Jefferson hadn't been malicious in his teacher evaluations but was honestly just clueless about how creepy he came off sometimes made him more endearing and less weird.

"I never told Deacon the whole story," he said, swallowing hard and meeting my eyes.

He seemed hesitant, but couldn't really refrain from elaborating after just saying he would tell me anything.

"After my dad died, I would see him around a lot," he admitted, biting his lip for a moment before continuing. "We'd never talk or anything, but I'd see him standing in a room with me. I'd smile at him and he'd smile back, and that was all we needed. We didn't need to say a bunch of meaningless words. Sometimes words just get in the way. We understood each other enough to just smile."

"How often did you see him?" I asked, believing him wholeheartedly. Normally I'd think he was just crazy, but not now.

"A few times a week," he answered. "Anyway, when I went to see that therapist at the school, I felt like he was my friend and I could trust him, since he talked to me when none of my teachers or classmates would. I guess I was too young to know he was paid to talk to me."

I squeezed his hand.

"I told him about seeing my dad all the time, thinking it was a cool story that he'd want to hear about. But then I heard him talking to the headmaster about being worried that I was schizophrenic and suggesting they start medicating me, which obviously freaked me out."

"You knew what schizophrenic meant when you were that young?" I wasn't sure why I'd chosen to focus on that particular piece of the story.

"We had a big library at my house and I read the medical dictionary there . . . a few times."

I refrained from looking shocked that Jefferson had read a medical dictionary as a child. Of course he had. He was Jefferson.

"I didn't want them putting me on medication for something I didn't have, so the next time I met with the therapist I told him I'd made the whole thing up and apologized. I pretended I was joking with him and said I just had a bad sense of humor."

We were both silent. I could hear Deacon and Brighton snoring lightly still, letting me know that we were, for all intents and purposes, alone. I scooted closer to Jefferson, laying my head on his pillow and watching him, silently willing him to continue.

"I never saw my dad again after that," he said, puckering his lips tightly and furrowing his brow.

I opened my mouth and took a breath as if I might say something, but I couldn't think of what to say. Instead, I brought my hand up to his cheek and lightly stroked the spot right below his eye.

"I keep hoping if we do enough of these paranormal investigations, he'll come back. He'll see that I'm sorry for saying I didn't really see him."

"Jefferson, I don't think your dad left because he was angry. Maybe he just moved on."

"Maybe," he agreed halfheartedly. "That's a big part of why I hate the idea of being 'normal' when you don't want to be. The last time I denied something I knew was true, I lost the person I loved the most."

"How do you put up with me and my insistence on being normal?" I laughed, although the laugh was humorless.

"It gets complicated when the thing you love is the thing that wants to deny her own weirdness," he said with a small smile. "But I'm working on figuring it out."

I nodded, trying desperately to think of something else to say so that I could gloss over the fact that Jefferson had most definitely just said he loved me. It shouldn't have surprised me that Jefferson Parrish would say something like that to a girl he wasn't even dating, but it still took me by surprise. He had a bad habit of doing that. "I'm sorry people at your school didn't get you," I said, trading in being honest about one thing for being honest about another.

I wasn't ready to be as honest as Jefferson as far as our relationship went—or our non-relationship, I guess.

"Sadie, nobody gets me," he answered, sounding amused by this fact. "Except maybe you."

"Great," I said.

He wrinkled his nose at me and leaned over to give me the smallest of kisses, which I returned with a bit too much enthusiasm. I may not have said I loved him back, but it was kind of an amazing feeling to have someone tell you they loved you, especially when I spent so much time with a family I didn't think loved me at all.

Moving my hand behind his head, I pulled him closer to me, wanting to forget about everything around me and only focus on Jefferson Parrish, the weird boy I had suddenly become so attached to against my better judgment. His hands found my back and pulled me against his chest as we kissed, but it didn't take long for him to pull away from me.

"Brighton," he whispered.

"What?" I asked, slightly offended.

"Brighton and Deacon are sleeping about two inches away from us," he elaborated in a whisper. "Probably not the best place to be snogging."

This was coming from the boy who had tried to kiss me in front of them numerous times, but I didn't point that out.

"Did you want to go outside?" I pressed my lips against his once more and deepened our kiss, trying to tempt him away from the stuffy hotel room.

I could use some air anyway, and kissing Jefferson stopped me from being so uptight. It was like Brighton's equivalent of taking a Xanax.

His hands squeezed my back as I kissed him and I could tell that, at least for a moment, he was seriously considering it. But he eventually pulled away from me again. Unfortunately.

"Not a good idea," he said, our noses still touching.

"You know I'm just talking about kissing, right?" I said. "Just wanted to clarify."

"And as much as I love kissing you, Brighton and Deacon don't sleep that heavily. I'm sure they'd hear the door."

I paused for a moment, wondering why he was saying that when he didn't care at all if they knew about us.

"It doesn't bother me one bit if they find out about . . . this," he began, reading my mind once more. "But I know it matters to you."

He should have been mad that I was too embarrassed about our relationship to share it with Brighton and Deacon, but here he was, watching out for me and my pointless discretion. Jefferson was definitely different, but it wasn't in the bad way that everyone else seemed to think. He was loyal and considerate and more thoughtful than I ever was.

Suddenly, I just wanted to kiss him again, but I restrained myself.

I looked at him for a moment, admiring the boy who drove me so crazy. "Thank you for telling me everything."

"I want you to know everything," he answered, before rolling onto his back and pulling me close to him so that my head rested on his chest.

I wasn't sure what he meant by his statement, but I knew that it brought that warm feeling back to my chest.

"Good night, Sadie," he said, kissing the top of my head.

"Good night, Jefferson," I answered. I decided I'd stay awake until he fell asleep so I could move from his chest. The last thing I needed was to fall asleep in this compromising position and have Brighton question me the next morning.

Once his breathing slowed, I moved his arm that rested over my shoulders and scooted back to my side of the makeshift floor-bed. With my back against Brighton's box spring, I watched as Creepy Parrish Number One slept. Suddenly it didn't seem so weird to me that he watched me sleep at night. It was relaxing to see someone so peaceful when the rest of your life was in slight chaos.

Watching as Jefferson smiled in his sleep, I let my eyelids droop closed, and then felt his fingers lace through mine as I fell asleep.

~

I wasn't sure how I had gotten there, but I was standing in some kind of waiting room in front of a receptionist desk. It didn't quite look like a doctor's office, even though that would have been my first guess with how clean and neat everything was.

A bell chimed as the front door opened and a girl walked in. She tapped me on the shoulder, and when I turned to face her, I let a small gasp escape. I was looking at myself. Smiling and wearing a purple shirt I'd never wear in a million years. It was like the mimic had followed me to this office building and was now messing with my mind.

The girl didn't speak, but beckoned for me to follow her. I glanced at the receptionist skeptically, thinking the woman wasn't going to let us just walk into the office with no explanation. Still, I wasn't in any position to ignore this ghost. Walking behind her, we entered the back offices without the receptionist so much as glancing in our direction.

I tried to ask the mimic what we were doing, but found that I couldn't speak. Perfect. I finally got to see a full-bodied apparition and I couldn't even ask it any questions.

The mimic pointed to a safe in the office, opened the door, and handed me a large sealed envelope that was heavy with documents.

She stared at me for a long time in silence, although I wasn't sure what she wanted me to do.

I tried to open the envelope, but she placed her hands over mine, stopping me. I was quickly growing frustrated, but there wasn't much I could do when I had no voice.

"Sadie?" the mimic finally said, not sounding at all like me. Her voice was a bit deeper than mine, but still feminine. "This is important."

And then I woke up.

CHAPTER 24

The drive to New York was laughably short compared to the thirteen-hour days we had been spending in the car. It also didn't hurt that Kingston, New York, was possibly the cutest city I'd ever seen. There were historic buildings everywhere that I was just itching to investigate, even though we'd have to stick to the old law firm we'd come to find.

Because of Brighton's incredible ability to research anything in mere hours, we'd discovered that the law firm of Livingston and Meyer was still thriving in Kingston, even though the title had been changed to simply Meyer Law Offices, since Thatcher Livingston's claim to the law firm had died with him only four years after the practice moved from Boston to Kingston. Of course, Jefferson was quick to point out that this was extremely suspect, and no one argued with him, since obviously he was right.

It may have been the easy option to guess that there was some foul play involved with the whole Eva and Thatcher story, but we'd be stupid to completely ignore the facts that were staring us in the face. Thatcher loved his girlfriend enough to move from England to America for her, but they'd only been together about a year before he suddenly packed up and left. Eva followed him to Boston but couldn't get ahold of him, even when she found out she was pregnant. Then Thatcher and the business partner he'd met on the Queen Mary decided to move their newly founded business from Boston to Kingston for no logical reason that we could find. Eva probably later died in childbirth, and no records for her and Thatcher's child could be found anywhere. And then, of course, to top it all off, Thatcher Livingston died at the age of thirty-five in his own home in Kingston, New York, from "natural causes."

It was like a bad murder mystery.

"We can all agree that Edward Meyer was a bad guy, right?" Deacon asked.

He was driving through Kingston as he spoke, squinting his eyes trying to find the law firm.

"Let's hope it doesn't run in the family, since the law practice still belongs to the Meyer line," Brighton responded, looking over at Deacon.

Jefferson and I sat in the back seat of the Jeep. When I thought it was safe, I'd give his hand a squeeze or throw a smile in his direction. I'd become completely pathetic.

"Do you think the current owner knows his great-great-grandpa is a murderous liar?" Jefferson said.

He had really taken our theory on the story to heart, which meant he was determined to solve the mystery and prove that he was right. He had also taken the supposed treachery very personally, for some reason. I wasn't sure why he'd decided to become so attached to two people we'd never met, but he was definitely on their side. Had I been a completely illogical person, I would have thought Thatcher had come back from the dead to avenge his own murder.

"His name is Anthony Meyer," Brighton said, "and I don't think we should barge into the law firm accusing his ancestor of murder."

"What if Anthony Meyer is our mysterious beneficiary and he only hired us to see how easy it is to uncover the truth about his family, and once we get to the end of this trail, he's going to kill us all?" I asked, using an overly dramatic tone and widening my eyes in mock shock.

"You're adorable when you're happy," Jefferson said, and I instantly removed my hand from his and leaned away from him, praying that Brighton and Deacon hadn't heard his remark. "And not nearly as affectionate, apparently. Duly noted."

I shook my head at him incredulously. He was awful at being subtle. He just grinned right back, enjoying my discomfort.

"If that's the case, I hope he at least pays us before we die," Deacon said. "I'd really like to know what it's like to be rich, even if it's just for a minute."

Jefferson shifted in his seat at this comment but didn't say anything. He had an aversion to money.

"I don't think we should lead off with the whole ghost thing when we talk to Mr. Meyer," Brighton said, trying to keep us focused.

"Maybe we can say we're history buffs and we want to learn more about the beginnings of the law firm?" I asked.

"That doesn't sound made up at all," Deacon said.

"I don't hear you coming up with any brilliant ideas," I shot back.

"It's because he's afraid the receptionist might be a woman and he wouldn't be able to say anything," Brighton said.

"And you're afraid the receptionist might be a human being, so that would rule you out for the speaking parts," he retorted, grinning over at her.

"Touché," she said, holding her hands up in surrender.

"Sadie can do the talking," Jefferson said.

It wasn't really a question or a command; he was simply telling us what was going to happen. I looked over at him with a raised eyebrow.

"Why can't you talk to them?" I asked.

"I don't talk to lawyers."

"Or doctors," Deacon said under his breath, even though we all heard him. "Or politicians . . ."

"I'll talk to them," I sighed.

We pulled up outside of the law firm and parked along the busy street out front.

The little brick building was gorgeous and obviously very old, although it was quite a bit smaller than I had anticipated. At least our area to investigate would be manageable.

"I don't feel like I'm dressed properly to talk to a bunch of lawyers," I said. Why did I always insist on wearing my jean shorts? They didn't exactly scream "respectable."

"I have a dress you can wear," Jefferson said with a wicked grin, referring to the frumpy "period costumes" he always forced me into for our investigations.

"Hard pass on that idea," I answered.

"I think I've got a bandage dress in my bag," Brighton said.

"Bandage dress?" I repeated skeptically. "Like the ones that are all strappy and super form-fitting and . . . hot?"

"Yeah," she said.

"I think that sounds like a good idea," Jefferson said, making me want to elbow him. He still wore the wicked grin that made me blush.

"Brighton, I don't know how many times we have to go over this, but I'm built like a twelve-year-old boy. Not everyone looks like a super model like you."

"You're petite; there's a difference." She was trying to defend me. It wasn't working. "You'll fill it out fine . . . except maybe in the hips . . . and if it's too baggy on you, we can just stuff your bra or something."

"Jefferson, I want you to kill me right now," I said, completely mortified. "You can't tell me you haven't already planned how you would do it."

"Well, yeah, I've planned it out, but where are we going to get wedding clothes and goblets for a blood ritual at this time of day?"

We all stopped arguing at that statement and turned to face Jefferson. Brighton stared at him with her mouth slightly agape. I had been joking around with him. Sadly, I wasn't so sure he was joking and, not for the first time, I wondered why I liked such a psychopath who might kill me at any moment . . . in wedding clothes, apparently.

"I'll just grab that dress out of my bag," Brighton finally said, breaking up the awkward silence as Jefferson just smiled at me with his head tilted to the side in that impossible angle.

"You know I'm scared you might actually kill me one day, right?" I asked him in a low tone.

"Sadie, I would never do anything to hurt you. I'm going to spend my life making you happy, even if it kills me."

"Gross. I'm still in the car, mate," Deacon said.

I could only hope he thought his cousin was joking, although I did have to wonder how much Jefferson had already told him.

"Here," Brighton said, thrusting the dress and some shoes through the open window in the back of the Jeep.

The pastel pink bandage dress was made out of some kind of stretchy material that would hug the curves of someone like Brighton in a very attractive way. On me, it would probably just look like a baggy arm warmer.

"Where exactly am I supposed to change?" I asked.

"I'll turn around," Jefferson said much too seriously.

It was the little twitch in the corner of his mouth that gave him away.

"Yeah, that's definitely not going to happen."

"There's a gas station across the street," Brighton said. "If you can brave the germ-filled bathroom, you can change there. Just don't put your bare feet on the floor, okay?"

"I promise," I answered.

As I got out of the car and walked across the street to the gas station, I wasn't sure I really had any intention of keeping that promise, but I knew it would be better to put Brighton's mind at ease.,

It didn't take long for me to get into the dress, although it took several minutes of mental pep talks to actually leave the gas station in the ridiculous outfit. Luckily, because the material was so stretchy, the dress wasn't baggy on me. In fact, had I not known better, I would have said that it was almost flattering. Of course, that was only because I hadn't seen it on Brighton before, so I wasn't sure what it was supposed to look like.

The nude heels she'd given me to wear were incredibly high, and I almost broke my ankles five times as I walked back over to the car across the busy street. I knew Brighton was good at dressing like the normal popular girl she looked like, but I just couldn't imagine someone as clumsy and paranoid as her walking around in heels this high.

As I approached the Jeep, I could see Jefferson watching me, his green eyes even wider than normal as he did nothing to hide his shock. It was a bit insulting, really. He shouldn't have been that surprised that I could look like a girl.

"Sade," Brighton called in amazement. "Look at you! You've got a chest!"

"Please stop. Right now," I begged, hoping my cheeks didn't look as red as they felt.

"And hips," she went on, ignoring my pleas. "Who knew you had such a cute little figure under all of those jeans and T-shirts?"

"Brighton, I'm begging you."

"Wait, I'm confused. Is Sadie supposed to be seducing this guy?" Deacon asked.

"Shut up," I said, rolling my eyes at him. "I'm trying to look like a prospective, possibly wealthy client."

"Be serious," Deacon began. "You're trying to seduce him, huh?"

I laughed with a shake of my head and went to throw my clothes through the window into the back seat with Jefferson. He still hadn't said anything, but continued to stare at me, looking slightly confused. I wasn't quite sure what he could possibly be confused by.

"Should we give her an earpiece?" Brighton asked Deacon.

"I'm on it." He got out of the Jeep with Brighton to pull some equipment out of the back.

"You know, that look of shock on your face is a little insulting," I whispered to Jefferson, placing my elbows on the open window and leaning into the backseat. "I don't look that different, do I?"

"You're just . . . I mean . . ." he said, stumbling over his words in an adorable way.

As insulted as I was, it was kind of nice to have such a powerful effect on him. Maybe Brighton was on to something with the whole "dressing so people will like you" thing.

"I'll come back later, once you've found a way to stop digging your own grave," I said.

"Would you be mad if I kissed you right now?" he asked, not joking at all.

"Very," I answered, careful to quickly step out of his reach just as he leaned over to kiss me.

Unfortunately, I stepped backward into the busy street, thinking more about being playful than my very perilous surroundings. Luckily, Jefferson leaned out the window, grabbed my arm and forcefully pulled me back against the Jeep as a car came speeding by, honking at me and cursing.

"Please don't get yourself killed," he said, his tone gentle, but serious. "It would utterly destroy me."

I looked at him for a moment, wishing I knew how he could just flip on that "intensity switch" at the drop of a hat. It was a little jarring.

"Sorry," I breathed, too shocked by his sudden honesty to make a snarky comeback.

"We're going to get you all wired up, Sade," Brighton called, beckoning for me to join her at the back of the Jeep.

"Probably not something you want to shout right outside of a law firm," Deacon said, nudging her with his elbow and making her turn a violent shade of pink.

Jefferson kept his eyes locked on me and gave my arm a tight squeeze before letting me go, pursing his lips as he watched me walk away. The boy was a little too intense for his own good and I had to wonder if I'd ever get used to it.

"Earpiece," Brighton said, handing over the small device. "And mic," she added, giving me the tiny pin that I placed on the pink dress. "Don't talk about ghosts at all. These are lawyers. Just talk about wanting to submit a claim with them and casually bring up the name change that the law firm underwent. Say you noticed it when researching the firm. Maybe ask about the history in a non-suspicious way. I'll keep the boys quiet for you."

"Sounds easy enough," I answered sarcastically, giving Brighton a little shrug as I began walking toward the entrance to the law firm.

"Oh, and Sade?" she called.

I stopped and looked at her with raised eyebrows as she grinned and went on.

"You're kind of a babe."

CHAPTER 25

I was already off balance when I entered the law firm because, like a five-year-old, I had pushed the door repeatedly in an attempt to open it before glancing down at the big "pull" sign located right by the handle. Trying not die of embarrassment, I slowly pulled the door open, and walked into the front waiting room.

"Do you need me to come help you with the door?" Deacon joked over my earpiece. I was ignoring him in favor of something more pressing, though.

The small waiting room I found myself in was the exact same one I'd dreamed of the night before. I may have been a paranormal investigator, but I wasn't very well-versed in psychics and visions and things. In fact, I wasn't quite sure I believed in them at all.

But I knew that I had somehow dreamed about a room I'd never seen in my life, only to be standing in that place the very next day. Maybe I should have been a believer.

A small smile beginning to form on my face, I turned to my left and began walking toward the back offices, knowing exactly what I needed and where I'd find it. Whatever was in that large envelope in the safe was important. I'd said so myself in my dream. Now I'd just have to remember the combination to the safe.

"Um, excuse me, ma'am—can I help you with something?" the woman behind the front desk asked.

I put my hand down at my side, not realizing I had extended it to open the door I probably wasn't supposed to open. For some reason I panicked and couldn't think of a thing to say—instead I just froze there, staring at the door in front of me in shock.

"Sadie?" Jefferson said in concern. "Sadie, say something to her."

"Right," I said, shaking my head to gather my thoughts. Putting on a bright smile and turning to the receptionist, I let out a little laugh. "Sorry! I was totally on autopilot."

She was smiling, but gave me an odd look.

"This office is set up just like mine. Do you ever have those days where it's just go to work, go home, and go to bed? It's like you don't even have to think, you just sort of move. Good thing I didn't ask you for my memos, huh?"

The woman let out a breathy little laugh and the tension was instantly broken, which was great because my next plan if she didn't go for the "autopilot" thing was to make a break for it and try to run away in the impossibly high heels.

"I think we all have days like that," she replied with a conspiratorial wink.

"I almost forgot why I was here," I said, keeping my smile much too big and bright. "I was considering using this law firm for a consultation on some legal issues my company is facing."

"Well, Mr. Meyer is in a meeting right now, but I think he'll be available around one today. I can pencil you in if you'd like."

"That would be fantastic, Jenny," I said, reading the little plaque on her desk and wrinkling my nose at her. I was being way too cheesy for my own good. It was awful.

Jenny filled out an appointment card for me and updated the schedule in the computer.

"Ask her about the ghosts!" Deacon shouted in my ear.

"Are you crazy? I said no ghost talk. Just ask about the history . . . but in a natural way," Brighton said.

Their instructions were distracting.

"So, in doing some research on this firm, I noticed it underwent a name change after it was first established," I prodded.

"Did it?" Jenny asked.

"Yeah, it used to be Livingston and Meyer and now it's just Meyer Law Offices. The title was so nice before—why did they change it?"

"Oh goodness," Jefferson said in my earpiece.

I guess he didn't think I was acting natural enough.

"She's got this," Brighton said.

"No, she's going off the rails. This lady is going to kick her out."

"Jefferson, get back here!"

"I didn't know they'd changed the name," the woman continued, distracted by whatever she was finishing up on the computer.

"I only ask because I'm a bit of a history buff and I thought it might be an interesting story," I said, just as Jefferson walked into the waiting room with something in his hand.

"I'll be with you in a moment, sir," she said to him without looking up.

Jefferson, however, wasn't looking at either of us. Instead he sat on the bench behind me and began messing around with the potted plant there. I widened my eyes at him as I realized what he was doing.

Somehow, planting a camera in a law office with a live feed to our computer didn't seem like the safest thing to do. He was going to get us all arrested. Which, of course, meant it was my task to keep the receptionist distracted.

"I read that the law firm was founded by Mr. Meyer and a Thatcher Livingston," I said, repeating anything I could think of from our research to keep the woman's focus on me. "What ever happened to Mr. Livingston?"

"Sadie, stop!" Brighton said in my ear. "You sound totally suspicious right now."

The receptionist kept her smile in place as she looked up at me, although her eyes were slightly narrowed.

"What did you say your name was?" she asked.

"Don't tell her," Brighton and Deacon said together.

"For the appointment," the woman added, smiling a bit too sweetly.

I kept my eyes locked on her, feeling my heart begin to beat faster and scrambling for a fake name. Any fake name. Why could I suddenly not think of a single name?

A bell chimed as the door to the law office closed, making me jump in surprise.

"Well, I guess he was in a hurry and couldn't be bothered to wait," the woman joked, trying to lighten the mood.

She probably knew she was coming on a bit strong. Of course, that made me sound like Jefferson, thinking there was some big conspiracy and even the receptionist was in on it.

"Eva," I finally said.

"I'm sorry, what?"

I could hear Brighton groan audibly in my earpiece.

"Sadie's not allowed to do undercover work anymore," Deacon said.

"Amen to that," Jefferson agreed.

I guess he'd made it back to the car.

"My name is Eva," I repeated, taking the card from the woman. "I'll see you in a few hours for the appointment."

The receptionist didn't say anything to my retreating form, but she did get up from her desk and hightail it to the back offices with impressive speed. I guess I'd hit a nerve with the names I'd been dropping.

"Sadie, why on earth would you say your name was Eva?" Deacon asked, his voice echoing as I could hear him both in the car that was now within view and in my earpiece.

"I panicked."

"Clearly," he said with an exasperated sigh.

"Both of you be quiet. I want to hear what that receptionist is saying," Jefferson said, his eyes closed as I got into the Jeep.

"We should probably park somewhere a bit less conspicuous," Brighton said.

"Fine, but do it quietly," Jefferson said.

Deacon started up the Jeep and pulled around the corner into a little parking lot behind the building. We weren't able to drive too far away or we'd lose the signal to our camera.

"I can only catch bits and pieces of what she's saying, but I heard her mention Thatcher. I think it's safe to say she does know something." Jefferson absently placed a hand on my bare knee as he kept his eyes closed, listening to the conversation.

I wasn't sure why he was touching me, but I tried to ignore it as I stared at the laptop screen between Deacon and Brighton in the front seat. The camera was partially covered by leaves from the plant, but we had a clear view of the receptionist's desk and the door to the office spaces in the back.

The conversation going on behind closed doors was audible, but I had no idea how Jefferson was able to make out anything they were saying. His eyes were still closed and his brow was furrowed as he listened. Every once in a while he'd run his thumb over my knee and give me goose bumps, which I kind of hated him for, but I didn't dare push his hand away when he was in the zone. I didn't want to be the reason he lost track of the conversation.

"Sounds like Mr. Meyer isn't too happy about your visit, Sade," Jefferson whispered, so quietly I could barely hear him.

As soon as Jefferson finished speaking, the door to the office flew open and out stormed a tall, good-looking man in a suit. His secretary hurried over to her desk and typed something quickly into her computer as the man, who I was assuming was Mr. Meyer, stopped and looked over at her.

"When she comes in for the appointment, make up an excuse as to why I can't meet with her, and if you see her in here again, call the police and say she was harassing you," he told her. "I'll be back."

With that, he pulled a large envelope out from under his arm, placed it in his briefcase, and walked out the front door.

"That's it!" I said.

My exclamation caused even Jefferson to jump in shock as his hand grasped my knee in surprise.

"That's the envelope we need!" I explained.

Mr. Meyer walked around the corner and into the parking lot where we were currently hiding out.

"Shoot, get down," I whispered to our group.

Brighton and Deacon slouched down in their chairs and Jefferson pushed me over a little too forcefully onto the bench seat in the back, crushing me underneath him. I held my breath, listening for footsteps that I couldn't hear and praying a car engine would start up soon so I could relax a little.

A soft click let me know that Deacon or Brighton had closed the laptop, which was good, since the screen held an image of Mr. Meyer's office waiting room. That might look just a bit suspicious if he caught us.

"If I wasn't so worried about being arrested by that man, I'd quite be enjoying myself right now," Jefferson whispered, letting one long finger trace my collarbone.

"You're ridiculous," I whispered back.

"Have I told you how much I love that dress on you?" he asked, arching one eyebrow up rakishly.

"He just started his car," I said loudly enough for Brighton and Deacon to hear, pushing Jefferson off of me and ignoring the butterflies that always picked the most inopportune times to show up in my stomach. "Deacon, we have to follow him wherever he's going. We have to get what's inside that envelope."

"Why are you so jacked up about the envelope?" Deacon asked. He still followed my instructions, though, making sure to keep a good distance from Anthony Meyer's car.

"I dreamed about it last night," I informed him.

I was trying to sound natural about the whole thing, but there was just no good way to put that.

"You what?" Jefferson asked, no longer flirting and suddenly all business. "Why wouldn't you tell me about that?"

"I didn't tell you guys," I said, so that Brighton wouldn't be suspicious of our non-relationship, "because I thought it was kind of a ridiculous thing to bring up. I'm not psychic."

"Well, you dreamed about the envelope."

"And the office building," I admitted.

"Seriously, Sadie?" Jefferson asked. "Unbelievable."

"I didn't think it was a big deal," I said.

"At least we know it's important," Brighton said. "Deacon, just make sure you stay far enough back that he doesn't notice us. It looks like he's paranoid enough right now as it is. He's probably looking for tails."

"Roger that," Deacon replied, enjoying this pursuit far too much.

"I just can't believe you wouldn't tell me something like that," Jefferson said, sounding very put out. "Did you also dream about who our beneficiary is? Or maybe what the link between these four places is, and you just forgot to tell us?"

"Stop pouting—we need to concentrate on getting whatever is inside of that envelope," I said, trying not to look at Jefferson as he huffed at me.

"You probably already know," he complained.

He really was like a child sometimes.

"In my dream, I walked into the office building and then another version of myself followed me in, led me to Anthony Meyer's office, got the envelope out of a safe and handed it to me. Then she said, 'This is important,' and I woke up. That was my entire dream. I promise from now on I'll keep a detailed dream journal every morning for you."

"See, you say that, but I know you won't," Jefferson said, sounding less upset now. "And I would pay big money to know what goes on in that head of yours."

"Big money you'd have to get from your mom," I said with a grin.

His smile instantly faded as he turned to look out the window, facing away from me.

I'd unintentionally hit a nerve.

Jefferson's mood swings were always bad, but today he flew through them with impressive speed.

"I love this neighborhood," Brighton said to Deacon. "Look at all of these old houses."

"If you like old houses, you should come with me to England and see where I grew up," Deacon answered, before realizing what he'd just said and quickly backtracking. "I mean, with us. All of us. We should all go there and do some investigating or spend time with family or . . . something."

"Oh yeah. I'm sure you guys would love to meet my family," Jefferson said sarcastically, still mad at me for the comment about his mom.

"They're not that bad," Deacon said.

"The psychotic Temple twins?" Jefferson challenged.

"Okay, maybe Dresden and Alistair are a bit . . . abrasive."

"You're terrified of Dresden."

"She's scary!" Deacon said. "And Alistair is . . . well he's . . . sneaky."

"And then there's Golden Boy Temple," Jefferson went on in disgust.

"Hayden isn't bad at all. You just don't like him because he's a doctor."

"I don't like him because he insists on calling me Jeff and he's all buddy-buddy with my sociopathic mother."

"You know he's in the states now, right?" Deacon said. "Maybe we should pay him a visit."

"I'll pay his stupid fancy car a visit with a cricket bat," Jefferson muttered.

It made me laugh, although I quickly covered it up. I couldn't help but smile at his obvious dislike for his family. His upbringing was no picnic, from what he'd told me, but it was still amusing to hear the way he talked about them like they were so terrible.

"Would you please just concentrate on following this guy?" Jefferson finally said, sighing deeply and shaking his head at his cousin.

He stole a quick glance in my direction but quickly looked away when he saw me smiling at him. I guess we weren't ready to be friends again.

"I think he's stopping at that house," Brighton whispered, even though there was no possible way Anthony Meyer could hear us. "Pass the house so we don't look suspicious and then loop back around."

"Someone's been reading her murder mysteries," I said.

"They help me build my investigative skills," she answered with a shrug.

Deacon did as he was told, driving slowly past the house and then turning around and parking a safe distance across the street. We all slouched down in our seats involuntarily as we watched Anthony get out of his car with his briefcase and go into his house at a quick clip.

Brighton stared at the huge red Craftsman with white trim like it was a bottle of hand sanitizer in a public restroom. "I want that house."

"There he is," I said, pointing at a figure through the front window.

It looked like he was in a study or library of some sort. He leaned closer to one of the bookshelves there and opened the door to a safe I hadn't even seen hiding amidst the dusty old volumes. Placing the envelope gingerly inside, he looked over his shoulder and shut the safe door once more.

"At least we know where it is," Brighton said.

"For now," I added. "I don't think he's going to keep it there long if he knows someone is asking questions that he doesn't want asked."

"I knew he was a bad guy," Jefferson said.

I ignored him. If he was going to be moody and distant, I wasn't going to enable him by making him think it was okay.

"Who is he talking to?" I asked Brighton. I leaned between the two front seats so that I was positioned between Brighton and Deacon, my hip nudging Jefferson into his corner of the back seat where he seemed content to brood.

A moment later, a boy who looked to be in his late teens or early twenties left the house with a scowl, Anthony following closely behind him.

"A son?" Deacon asked no one in particular.

"Looks like it," I agreed.

The boy looked astonishingly like his father with his tan skin, dirty blonde hair, and handsome face.

"Roll the window down," I whispered to Deacon, who instantly obliged.

"Logan, you'd better go to the mixer tonight," Anthony said from the steps. "It's important to mingle in your first semester and meet new people."

"I already told you I'd go, Dad," the boy shot back, sounding very unhappy about whatever activity his father was forcing him to attend.

Without another word, he got into a red sports car parked outside of the house, started it up, and drove away far too quickly for the quiet residential area filled with mansions.

Anthony shook his head and got back into his own car before driving away, leaving the envelope safely inside of his home.

"So, what do we do now?" I asked. "Try to break into the mansion that probably has a million security systems?"

"No, silly," Brighton said. "We go to the mixer at his school tonight and talk to Logan, who hates his father and might just help us out."

"How do you even know all of this?" Deacon asked. "I highly doubt public records keep track of familial relationships."

"I don't need public records." She held up her phone to display a picture of the boy we'd just seen. "I have Facebook."

CHAPTER 26

"You did not just find that all out in the few seconds we've been here," I said as we pulled away from the house.

"He said his son's name was Logan, and we already knew his last name was Meyer," Brighton said. "It wasn't hard to find a Logan Meyer in this area who looks like that."

"What do you mean, 'looks like that'?" Deacon asked.

"Handsome," we both said, and then grinned at each other.

"Gross," Deacon said. "Do you guys want to go to jail? He's probably like seventeen."

"What are you even talking about?" I asked. "We're going to go talk to him about his father. There's nothing illegal about that."

"Plus, he's in college, so he may be legal," Jefferson said from the back seat.

"Would you guys stop saying 'legal'?" Brighton asked. "I just said he was handsome. Besides, I'm not going to do the talking. That'll be all you guys, while I sit safely inside and listen through my earpiece."

"What is this event we're going to?" I asked, finally sitting back in my seat with my shoulder touching Jefferson's.

"It's a back-to-school mixer for the State University of New York, which is actually in New Paltz, about twenty minutes from here," Brighton recited, reading off of her phone. "But the mixer is for prospective law students and is in a smaller venue here in Kingston, so we don't even have to drive far to get there."

"I still don't understand how you figured this all out so quickly," I said.

"I literally just read Logan's Facebook status," she replied. "He's not very subtle about his rocky relationship with his dad, so that part was easy to figure out, and the mixer created a Facebook event that he joined with the time and location. Everything we need to know."

"It would be so easy for me to be a serial killer in this day and age," Jefferson said. "I wouldn't even have to try. Facebook is like a menu."

"Those are the kinds of comments we keep to ourselves," I said, partially joking.

"There are a lot of comments I keep to myself," he responded, giving me one of his penetrating stares.

Why on earth was he so moody today? I thought we had gotten our friendship to a good place.

"All right, well, just keep holding it all in," I answered.

"I swear, you two fight like an old married couple." Brighton turned around in her seat to look at me. "By the way, this mixer is a semi-formal masquerade."

"Seriously?" I groaned. "How cheesy is that? This whole leg of our investigation is honestly turning into a bad episode of *Murder She Wrote*."

"If *Murder She Wrote* was mixed with *The Vampire Diaries*, where they have a formal dance every other episode," Brighton agreed.

"And they somehow all manage to pull together amazing outfits at the last second," I said, "which, by the way, how on earth will we find clothes for this thing if we aren't blessed with a magical Mystic Falls free formals store?"

"I'll figure something out," she said. "I may be fully incapable of interacting with humans, but I'm a snappy dresser and a fast shopper."

"True enough," I agreed, as we pulled into the parking lot of our hotel. "And what time does this start tonight? I'm really worried Anthony is going to go back to his house and move the envelope before we can convince his son to help us out."

"Good point," Brighton agreed, looking worried suddenly. Glancing up at Deacon, she raised her eyebrows at him questioningly.

"Oh no. You have a boring job for me, don't you? That's the only reason you'd give me that look."

"The law firm, the Meyer house, and the venue for the mixer tonight are all in close proximity to each other," Brighton began. "So, you wouldn't be out of range of the earpieces. We could still communicate."

"Just come right out and say it," he answered in a resigned tone. "What awful, boring job do you want me to do?"

"I need you to hold onto the laptop and camp out at the café next to the law firm so you can keep eyes on Anthony Meyer and let us know if he leaves."

"And you'll be where?"

"I'll be in the Jeep outside of the mixer with our home base set up while Sadie tries to get Logan to help us inside. Of course I'll be dressed for the occasion in case I need to crash the party."

"And where is Jefferson in all of this?" Deacon said.

"Assisting Sadie," Jefferson himself answered matter-of-factly. "If worse comes to worse and we can't persuade him, maybe she can just distract him while I pick his pocket for his house key. That way we aren't technically breaking and entering."

"Somehow I don't think that's how that phrase works," I said. "And I just want to point out to everyone that we're trying to steal from a lawyer and we're all most definitely going to jail."

"You're the one who said we needed the envelope," Jefferson said.

"We do," I agreed with a groan.

I wasn't sure I was really ready to believe some random dream I'd had, but if I was really listening to my gut, I knew that envelope and whatever it contained were of the utmost importance. We had to get our hands on it. I could only hope that whatever it contained was important enough to justify stealing it from Anthony Meyer.

"Then what's the plan for right now?" Deacon asked.

"Obviously Sadie isn't going to meet with Anthony," Brighton said, "but unfortunately, we're going to need eyes on him right now so we can be sure he's actually at his office, which means we need to drop you off at the café with the equipment."

"What am I supposed to say if someone walks up and asks why I'm watching a video of a receptionist?"

"Have it in a small window in the corner of your screen and pretend you're writing the next great American novel or something. Just keep your headphones in so you can hear what's going on in the office."

"Headphones and an earpiece—that won't get confusing."

"You'll manage." Brighton smiled, which made Deacon grin involuntarily and quickly look away. "And the three of us need to get semi-formal clothes with almost no money."

"And masks," I said.

"I live in semi-formal clothes, so I don't need any," Jefferson said. "I'll get us masks and leave the shopping to you two."

"Probably a good decision," I agreed, giving him a look that said he was not being very friendly today.

I didn't care if he had mood swings, but he didn't need to take out his angst on me for no reason at all. He looked at me with slightly narrowed eyes for a moment before sighing deeply and looking away again.

I almost wished we were alone so I could ask him what his problem was, but at the same time, I was grateful I wouldn't be forced to deal with his crazy when we were just about to pull off an impossible task that I wasn't ready for.

"Deacon, we'll drop you off at the café and take the Jeep to the mall," Brighton said.

I wasn't sure when she'd become such a leader.

"We still don't have much money," I said, hating to be the bearer of bad news.

"We have enough," Jefferson said, still looking sullenly out the window.

"Since when?"

"I told you guys my mum gave me less than she did so that we would try really hard to keep it within our means; then when we inevitably went over budget, we wouldn't be stranded somewhere," he said.

He still wasn't looking at me.

I opened my mouth to scold him for not telling us about the extra money when we'd been eating the worst and cheapest food imaginable for the past week, but thought better of it and just shook my head.

"Well, that solves that, then," Brighton said. "After we drop Deacon off, we'll head over to the mall and plan to finish up in an hour?"

"I wish we had watches to synchronize or something," Deacon said with a laugh. "Make things so much more official, don't you think?"

"Do you at least have some cool gadgets for us, Brighton?" I asked. "You know, like an exploding pen or dental floss that . . . does something?"

"Doubles as an explosive wire?" Jefferson offered, coming out of his funk ever-so-slightly.

"Sure," I agreed.

"I'll work on that for our next investigation," she said. "Until then, let's just stick with earpieces and try not to mess this up too badly."

CHAPTER 27

Brighton hadn't been kidding when she'd told me she was a fast shopper. My guess was that it had something to do with hating to be around other people. The second she saw a salesperson approaching her, she suddenly became very efficient and developed an inhuman ability to find cheap, cutes clothes in seconds.

It was a gift.

I knew she'd said it was something she had always been good at, but even with her anxiety around people and her dislike of being in public places, I had to give Brighton some respect. Since we'd left on this trip, she'd managed to come out of her shell a bit more and get the job done, even if it meant putting herself into an awkward situation. I wasn't sure she would have been able to do half of the things we'd done these last weeks if we'd stayed in Portland in our boring jobs and boring lives.

As we sat outside of the mall waiting for Jefferson to come pick us up, I riffled through my bag. Even though Brighton had insisted on dressing me for the mixer, I hadn't made out too badly. I had been worried she would stick me in some awful pink dress, but she actually listened to me when I told her yellow was my favorite color, and I'd ended up with a yellow knee-length dress.

The bodice was all sequins, which I kept trying to pick off, hoping there was some normal material under there. Brighton slapped my hand every time I started pulling the dress apart. A yellow satin sash was tied around the waist and the skirt was a full yellow tulle skirt that poofed out way too much for my taste.

"I'm going to look like a lemon cupcake," I said, still trying to pick the sequins off of the bodice.

"A gorgeous lemon cupcake," Brighton reiterated, slapping my hand.

"What's gotten into you? You're so . . ." I paused, unable to think of a good word. "Leadership-y."

"Leadership-y?" she asked with a laugh at my made-up word.

"You know what I mean. Why the sudden take-charge attitude?"

"I'm just feeling good," she answered with a shrug.

She was being elusive on purpose.

"Any particular reason? Or you just suddenly feel good?"

She glanced from side to side for a moment, as if someone might be listening in on our conversation even though we were the only people outside of the mall. Then she looked at me with a wide grin.

"I think Deacon might like me," she finally said, as if she were revealing a big secret.

I wasn't sure if I should play along or laugh at her for making such an obvious observation.

"And?" I asked.

"And I think he might actually like me," she said, thinking maybe I had missed it the first time.

"Brighton, everyone knows that Deacon likes you. I mean, literally everyone. This isn't exactly a revelation."

"No, we always thought he might like me, but we didn't know," she said, careful to differentiate.

"I take it back—everyone but you knows this," I said. "We've talked about this already. How could you really not know?"

"Did you hear what he said on that recording last night? He thought he was talking to me, and he was all embarrassed when we watched the video. It was so cute."

She was actually sounding like a normal person rather than her anxiety-ridden self. It suddenly all made sense how she could have possibly missed the not-so-subtle hints that I didn't hate Jefferson quite so much anymore. I had been worried that Jefferson and I were being too obvious, but in reality, Brighton and Deacon couldn't have cared less because they were caught up in their own thing.

"So, what are you going to do about it?" I asked, raising my eyebrows at her.

"Oh, absolutely nothing," she said, giving her head a fervent shake.

"What?"

"I'm really happy that he likes me, but I have no idea how I would even go about talking to him about it," she said as Jefferson pulled up.

"You're not going to do anything?" I asked.

She shrugged with the wide, happy smile still in place, and then got into the back seat of the Jeep, forcing me to take the front.

"Did you have fun, ladies?" Jefferson asked.

"So much fun," I deadpanned. "Did you get the masks?"

"For you," he said, handing a black feathery mask back to Brighton in case we needed her backup at the party. "For me," he added, pulling out his own simple black mask that would cover only his eyes. "And for you."

He handed me a beaded black and yellow mask.

"You knew to get me yellow," I said. It wasn't an accusation like it probably would have been a few days ago. Now the gesture actually brought a small smile to my face.

"We've got about two hours until we need to be at the mixer," Brighton said. "Do you think we should check on Deacon to make sure he's not losing his mind on surveillance duty?"

I glanced back at her with a meaningful look, trying to wordlessly encourage her to stop being a coward where her feelings were concerned, even if I was the last person to be handing out that advice.

"You should definitely check on him," I said in an overly serious tone.

"Never mind, I'm sure he's fine," she said. It only took her a moment to get back to being her normal self as she wrung her hands over the thought of an actual conversation about her feelings for Deacon. "Let's just head back to the hotel and get ready."

"I'm ready," Jefferson said, driving away from the mall.

"Don't you have an older, dustier, three-piece suit you can wear?" I asked, being sweetly sarcastic and batting my eyelashes at him. "I don't think this one is quite old enough."

"I could always use the suit they buried my grandfather in," he said, furrowing his brow. "But there's still some dirt on it. That was a fun night, though."

"Why are you so creepy?" I asked, not expecting an answer.

"I'm not creepy, I'm passionate—which you, of all people, should know."

My mouth dropped open at his blunt observation and I turned around in my seat to make up some excuse as to why he'd said that, but Brighton was looking down at her phone and smiling. I squinted at her screen and saw Deacon's name on her text message.

Jefferson was lucky she was preoccupied or else I would have broken his fingers.

Really, Brighton probably always tuned us out once we started arguing, so it made sense that she was still in the dark about our "relationship."

"I'll take your silence as avid agreement that you enjoy my passion." He smirked, not looking at me.

At least he was in a better mood, even if he was being totally inappropriate.

"If you ever want me to enjoy it again, you'll stop talking right now," I whispered.

"What are you guys fighting about?" Brighton asked, not really sounding interested.

"Nothing," Jefferson began innocently. "Sadie was just telling me how much she enjoys—"

"Investigating . . . with you guys. And being out here on the road. It's been great, right?" I asked, sounding like a crazy person.

"It has been," she agreed. "And tonight we'll get that envelope from Anthony's house and figure out what all of this investigating has really been about."

"And we'll get our reward so we won't be so ridiculously poor anymore," I added. "Maybe you and Deacon will be able to pay your own rent after this."

"You only paid it once," Jefferson said "And I'll be paying you back soon."

"All I know is that I'm buying tons and tons of fruit when we get back home with our money," I said. "I'm going to get scurvy from all this fast food."

"Deacon would think you're going to get botulism," Brighton added.

It was a little ridiculous how manic she was just because she'd found out something we all already knew, but it was pretty adorable, if I was honest.

"Do you think you can rein in your happiness well enough to make me not look ridiculous in that dress tonight?" I asked.

I was still skeptical.

"I'll make you look like a little ball of sunshine," she said, in a way that had the opposite effect of what I'm sure she had intended.

~

The mixer was in a beautiful historic building in downtown Kingston, although that shouldn't have surprised me, since the entire city was full of beautiful historical buildings. It probably would have been a more impressive feat for them to find a modern building to hold the mixer in.

Brighton, who was decked out in a black, silk, floor-length dress, opted to stay in our beat-up old Jeep, keeping ears on us and Deacon at the same time, while Jefferson and I crashed the party together.

Ever since I'd emerged from the bathroom where Brighton had styled my pixie cut into a curly pomp with an Audrey Hepburn-esque quality and made my eyes look five times bigger than they were using the magic of fake lashes, Jefferson had been throwing me secretive little looks and grinning to himself. I would have been flattered if I could be absolutely certain he thought I looked nice. As it was, I was half convinced that he was internally making fun of me, and that every time he smiled, it just meant he had thought of some new joke.

I would have come right out and asked him since I knew he was into the whole "brutal honesty" thing, but we had earpieces and mics on and I didn't really want Brighton and Deacon listening in on that particular conversation.

Jefferson and I walked arm in arm into the mixer. I'd expected it to be very quiet and slightly boring since it was for future law students, but it just resembled every other college party with its too-dark interior and too-loud music. The only difference was that this particular party took place in a beautiful old building.

"I thought this was put on by the school," I said, looking around at the rowdy college students in formal wear.

"It's put on by a student organization within the school," Brighton clarified in my earpiece. "So it might be a bit . . . loud."

"I don't envy you guys right now, even if I do have the most boring job," Deacon added from his position in the café. "Oh, and Anthony still hasn't left his office. Looks like he's making his secretary work late too. We must have really thrown this guy off balance."

"That's why we need to hurry up and get that envelope," I said. "I think he's trying to figure out a way to destroy whatever is in it."

"A fire would be more effective than whatever he's plotting in his office," Jefferson said beside me.

Despite what he'd said at the mall, he actually had ended up changing his clothes. He was now wearing an old black three-piece suit with a black skinny tie. The thin black mask over his huge owl eyes was actually kind of attractive, although I'd never tell him that.

"Maybe he has to legally destroy it. Not literally destroy it," I said. "I don't know; I'm not a lawyer."

"Obviously, or else I wouldn't be talking to you," Jefferson said.

"What do you mean?" I asked. "And why have you been so . . ." I let my words trail off, almost forgetting that we had earpieces in.

"Why have I been so what?"

I looked around the room, knowing we didn't really have time for me to ask Jefferson a million questions about his odd behavior when we had more important things to do.

"Never mind," I said. "Just try to find Logan."

"Already did," he said.

I gave him a questioning look.

"I'm tall," he added with a shrug. "He's standing over by the wall being about as social as I feel right now."

"I guess we don't have to worry about getting him alone," I said. "I'll go talk to him."

"Whoa, calm down there, Sade," Jefferson said, moving his arm so that it now encircled my waist as he led me toward the center of the room where a few brave students had started dancing when the music slowed. "It's going to look suspicious if you get to the party and instantly go talk to him."

"There are a million people here—I highly doubt he saw me come in," I argued, trying to fight back when Jefferson turned me toward him.

I was not a dancer.

"Almost everyone here is wearing black," he said. "You're in a bright yellow dress and you look gorgeous. I'm sure he saw you come in."

I tried to be mad that he'd called me gorgeous when Brighton and Deacon could hear, but I just couldn't muster the anger, even if I had wanted to. Instead, I used all of my energy to fight against the smile that was threatening to break over my face. He was weird. But it kind of worked for him. And I kind of liked it.

Jefferson placed his hands on my waist and, having no choice, I put my hands behind his neck as we began dancing. I kept my eyes on Logan, although I'd look away when I thought he might glance our way, not wanting to obviously stare at him.

"Werewolf," Jefferson said.

"What?" I asked, looking up to see that he was staring intently at me with a small half-smile on his face.

"The song," he elaborated. "It's called 'Werewolf.' By Cat Power. Good choice, random irresponsible student council member." I wasn't sure if he was actually talking to me or to himself, but I just let him ramble, figuring it was better to not interrupt a Parrish unless you wanted a long, drawn-out explanation. I could only hope he hadn't bribed someone to play his weird music when we barely had any money left.

I tried to look over Jefferson's shoulder to keep an eye on Logan, but Jefferson blocked my view, reaching out and plucking the hidden microphone off my dress. He did the same to his own tiny microphone and flipped the almost invisible switches on both of them so that they no longer picked up sound.

"Brighton?" he said into the small mics.

I listened in my earpiece but didn't hear anything from her.

"Good," he said, taking both of our earpieces as well and placing them in his pocket before returning his hands to my waist. "Do you want to know why I've been a little odd today?"

"Today?" I asked.

He gave me a look that said I wasn't funny.

"Not really, no. I'd actually really like to talk to Logan and get this thing figured out."

"I realized that I might not have you," he went on, ignoring me.

"Have me?" I asked. "What does that even mean?"

"I kind of thought after we'd kissed and we'd started opening up to each other, that maybe I had you. Maybe I didn't have to worry anymore about how you felt or that you'd suddenly leave. Like maybe we belonged to each other. But I don't really have you, do I?"

I was a little nervous about where this conversation was going since I knew Jefferson was a notoriously intense person. He didn't do casual relationships as far as I could tell. He seemed more like the type of person who would see a girl and either be friends with her or marry her. There wasn't much of an in-between for someone so extreme. I really wanted to play dumb so we didn't have to get into this right now, but I knew it wouldn't work. He had me trapped on the dance floor and I was going to have to take my own advice and face my feelings.

"Jefferson, we really need to talk to Logan," I said. "Maybe we can talk about this later?"

"Sadie, I don't care about being normal and I don't care if it's weird to have this conversation. I don't care if I feel too much. The idea of losing you makes me violently ill."

"Okay, way too much," I said. "I'll have this conversation with you if I have to, but you need to keep the crazy contained a little bit better and dial it down about fifteen notches, got it?"

"I'll try again," he said. "I know you're embarrassed by me. Basically, everyone is. I'm the running joke in my family and I'm fine with that."

"I'm not embarrassed by you," I said, half truthfully. "You're just . . . more intense than most people."

I adjusted the black and yellow mask that had started to drift down my face.

"I love you in yellow, by the way," he said out of nowhere. "You're like a little spot of sunshine."

I just sighed at his statement. I couldn't fault him for all of the weird things he said—that was just Jefferson, and I'd known that getting into this non-relationship.

"I'll try really hard not to be too intense. But I can't help it when I lo—"

I pressed my fingers urgently to his mouth. I was definitely not about to let Jefferson Parrish say he loved me. Not when there were so many other things that were important right at that moment. Granted, he'd basically already said it before, but before, I was able to dance around it. If he said it outright, I'd have to address it right this second.

"You can be honest with me. Just don't say that. At least not now," I said.

"You want me to be honest? What do you want me to tell you? I'll tell you anything."

"That's not what I meant," I said, but it was too late. I'd opened Pandora's Box by telling Jefferson to be honest—something he didn't have a problem with as it was.

"My family hates me. The Temple side, at least. My father was the last person to ever really love me and then he died."

"Deacon loves you," I said.

"He does," he agreed with a furrowed brow. "Deacon is a good person."

"And your family sounds awful, so I wouldn't worry about what they think of you."

"My cousins . . . the evil Temple Twins? They call me the Little Orphan," he said with a mirthless laugh. "Dresden says I don't belong on the Temple side of the family with my mum and the rest of them, and my dad died, so I'm just the Little Orphan, stuck at the grown-ups table at family reunions."

"Well, she sounds kind of like the devil, and when I meet her, I'll punch her for you," I said, trying to lighten the mood.

It was a futile effort, of course. Even talking about his awful family couldn't distract Jefferson from his task.

"Please just tell me how you feel so I know if I should let myself trust you, or if you're going to leave," he said, not begging, and oddly not sounding like a desperate, clingy boyfriend. There was something about Jefferson's sincerity that made words that would normally sound crazy instead sound incredibly genuine. He was frighteningly vulnerable for someone that everyone seemed to be put off by.

I took a deep breath, knowing honesty would be the only way out of this intimate situation.

"I'm not going to leave," I said with a small shrug, not quite sure where my words had come from. "I know what it's like to be left, too, and it makes you feel unwanted and small. And maybe I'm crazy, but I don't feel that way when I'm with you. Maybe you are too intense and maybe I am too stubborn, but your family shouldn't treat you the way they do. I hope you take me to meet them one day just so that I can say that to them and tell them how awful they are for treating you like less than a human being.

"I'm sorry that it's going to take me a lot longer than it's going to take you to be honest. I'm sorry that I'm going to get mad at you for probably every romantic gesture, but it won't be my fault because you need to learn what's a normal display of affection and what's grounds for getting placed into a mental hospital. I want to be with you, but I don't want Brighton and Deacon to know yet because I feel like this is new and special and I want it to just be ours for a while without having to explain it to anyone else.

"Also, this is probably the last time I'll ever be this honest with you, or with anyone for that matter, so I'll just tell you that I have no intention of leaving you because, as crazy as you make me and as intense as you are, I really like you. And I don't want to leave. So yes, Jefferson, you do have me."

Honesty had never been my strong point, and I couldn't really figure out why I'd picked that particular moment to let all of my pent-up thoughts come bubbling to the surface in that rare moment of sharing, but I wasn't mad that I had done it. In fact, I felt really good that Jefferson now knew exactly how I felt, even if that got rid of my power in the relationship or whatever the reason was you were supposed to be dishonest with people you liked.

Feeling this exposed was liberating.

"I have you?" he asked again, clarifying even though he really didn't need to.

"You have me," I said.

"But I can't say . . . it?" he asked.

"Not yet."

I'd excuse a lot of his intensity because it's just how he was, but we weren't going to throw around the "L" word quite yet.

"Why not?"

"Just because," I said. I didn't really have a good reason.

"Well, I'm thinking it. Just know that."

"Okay," I said, with a small smile, shaking my head at him and rolling my eyes.

He smiled back at me slowly, his big green eyes squinting behind his black mask. Leaning down, he gave me one long, deep kiss that I didn't pull away from, even though I knew Brighton might see. I allowed myself that one stolen moment with Jefferson Parrish on the dance floor at a cheesy masquerade that I'd cringe over when I thought back on the cliché of it all. But for just that one moment, I enjoyed it. I even enjoyed Jefferson's weird music that the DJ had somehow magically known to play.

When I pulled away from Jefferson with a lazy look of happiness lining my face, he brought my head down to rest against his chest. I listened to his heart beating faster than a humming bird's despite his calm exterior, and I had to smile to myself. I'd done that. "Brighton," he suddenly said, breaking the spell and pulling away from me ever so slightly so that we were at an appropriate dancing distance.

Seconds later, Brighton was by my side with an incredulous look on her face.

"I've been talking to you guys for ages with no response," she whispered. "We need to get on this! Deacon said Anthony looks like he's wrapping up for the night."

"Sorry, I was just—"

"I made her dance with me," Jefferson said, with a what-can-you-do look. "Crazy Parrish," he stated simply, pointing to himself as if that explained it.

It kind of did.

"We don't have time for this." Brighton took a puff on her inhaler before shoving it down the front of her dress. It disappeared quite effectively into her cleavage. I was slightly jealous.

"I'm initiating a code red," she informed us gravely. "Just know that when I end up in the hospital from my massive anxiety attack . . . you two put me there."

And with that, she walked away.

CHAPTER 28

"That sounds ominous." Jefferson turned back to me with a sort-of smile. It was more like he had tightened the corners of his mouth and puckered his lips out. Whatever it was, it was adorable, but far from appropriate given our current situation.

"Where were we?" he asked.

I gave him a look of disbelief.

"Seriously?" I pulled out of his grasp to get a better look at Brighton. "What is she doing?"

Not waiting for a response, I shoved my hand into Jefferson's pocket and retrieved the mic and earpiece, quickly turning it on and replacing it in my ear. The second the bud was back in, I could hear Deacon panicking.

"Guys, what is she doing? Can you see her? She stopped talking."

"I've got eyes on her," I said.

"Very official." Jefferson put his own earpiece back in and gave one last longing look at the dance floor.

He hadn't ever struck me as a dancer. Who knew?

"I'm over by the south wall and Brighton is near the refreshments table, closing in on Logan," I informed Deacon.

Logan stood by himself near an ice bucket full of cans of soda.

"Brighton," Deacon said. "Whatever you're doing, make it quick. Anthony just sent his receptionist home. I think he'll be leaving soon."

"Sorry, can I just reach behind you there?" Brighton asked Logan. Although we were across the room, I could hear her perfectly in my earpiece.

"Yeah, sure." He gave her a once-over, not doing much to hide it.

Brighton, amazingly, looked completely relaxed as she giggled and reached behind him, brushing her shoulder against his in the process.

"Thanks," she replied with a coy smile. "I'm Brighton, by the way."

"Logan."

"So, what is this party for anyway? I sort of crashed it," she said conspiratorially.

"For freshmen who are looking to get into the law program at the State University of New York."

"Isn't that in New Paltz?" she asked, not missing a beat. "Why are they having the party in Kingston?"

"No clue." He laughed, shifting his weight toward her and leaning against the table.

"I got all dressed up to go out with some friends tonight but my plans fell through," she lied easily. "So I saw that there was something going on inside of this beautiful old building and had to check it out."

"At least she had the good sense to take off her mask before she lied about crashing the party," Jefferson said.

"First, she can hear you," I said. "And second, she didn't lie about crashing the party. That's exactly what we're doing."

"Is this the 'hot' guy?" Deacon asked, sounding uncomfortable. "I don't like him. Let's just figure out some other way to get the files."

"I love old buildings," Brighton said loudly. She was wordlessly telling us to be quiet so she could concentrate. "All of these old houses around Kingston are just gorgeous, but you can't exactly sneak into a house like you can a public building." She laughed. "I bet they're full of character."

With all of the smiling and giggling, I would have thought she was totally comfortable hitting on a complete stranger, but the white-knuckled grip she had on her soda can gave her away to anyone who was really paying attention.

"Sorry." She rolled her blue eyes at him. "I'm being such a history nerd right now, huh?"

"No, I like the historical architecture around Kingston too," Logan said, a little too enthusiastically.

Over our earpieces Deacon scoffed. "What a bunch of bollocks."

I was just happy he wasn't actually here to witness Brighton turning on the charm. He'd either be enraged with jealousy or ruin her whole ruse by running over to kiss her right then and there.

"Actually," Logan began. And with that magic word, we all held our breath, hoping he was really about to say exactly what we needed him to. "I live just a few minutes from here in this little old Craftsman house."

"Little," I said with a snort.

"I mean . . . if you're not too invested in this party you aren't technically supposed to be at anyway, I could show you." He grinned at her in a charming way.

"Really?" She placed her hand on his arm, her entire face lighting up. "You mean I wouldn't have to get arrested for breaking in just to satisfy the history buff in me?"

He laughed.

Oh, she was good.

"We can avoid any possible arrests tonight." He smoothly placed a hand on her bare back and led her toward the exit.

"Are they leaving?" Deacon asked.

"Don't worry, Deacon, we'll be right behind them." I laced my fingers through Jefferson's to pull him out of the room and into the cool night air.

"Um . . . no . . . just . . . I'm fine," Deacon said out of the blue. "Don't need anything. Thank you. Just . . . working on my computer like a totally normal bloke. I'm. Um. Just going to stick with coffee."

I raised an eyebrow at Jefferson. "Waiter?"

"Female," he guessed.

"Can you still see her?" Deacon asked only two seconds later. He was now apparently talking to us since the danger of speaking to a woman was gone.

"No, but we know where they're going so we'll catch up, plus we can hear them," I said.

"Unless that boy is a psychopath like his father and he's actually taking Brighton away to murder her," Jefferson said, quite unhelpfully.

I didn't even bother to respond, knowing he was just in a bad mood because our investigation had gotten in the way of his "feelings" time.

"Wow, this is a really nice car," Brighton said, her voice starting to sound strained.

I was almost positive her change in tone stemmed from Jefferson's less-than-appealing prediction for Logan's true intentions. Brighton wasn't the kind of person who just let a thought like that pass over her. At that exact moment, I was sure she was calculating every possible way Logan could kidnap and murder her.

"Brighton, you're fine," I said. "You're doing great! Just keep up the small talk."

"I'm going to throw up," she said. "Don't worry, he's walking around the car to get in. He can't hear me. But I'm definitely going to throw up. This was a terrible idea, Sade! I can't do—"

Her words cut off abruptly as I heard a car door open in my earpiece.

"So, are you going to school?" Logan asked. He started the car and sped away toward his father's house.

"I'm taking a semester off," she said, sounding less charming.

"Keep it together, Brighton," Jefferson warned.

"But I'll be starting up at the State University of New York next semester," she added in a much nicer tone. "History major. Surprise, surprise." Her breathing was speeding up.

"Good. Joking is good," I said, trying to keep her calm.

Really, I was surprised it had taken her this long to realize she was flirting with a boy. She'd held it together much better than I thought she would.

Hoping I could be a sneaky tail in our huge Jeep, I started the car and began driving toward Anthony's house.

"Ask him why he's going into law," I said.

"So, Logan, why law?"

"My dad is a lawyer, so I think he just kind of expects me to follow in his footsteps," he said as they neared the house.

"Do you want to be a lawyer?" Brighton asked.

"Not really," he admitted. "Having an office job where you argue with people all day sounds terrible to me."

"Amen," Jefferson said from the passenger's seat.

We still hadn't caught up to Brighton and Logan enough to see his red sports car, but I knew we were nearing the house, so we couldn't be far behind.

"Wow," Brighton said with an appropriate amount of awe in her voice. "This is your house?"

"My parent's house, I guess," he clarified.

"It's absolutely gorgeous."

At least she didn't have to feign her love of the house, no matter how anxious she was.

"This way," he said.

"Anthony is turning off lights in the office," Deacon said, clearly uncomfortable. "So basically, we're going to be arrested because we aren't out of Anthony's house in time, and Brighton will have been assaulted for no reason."

"He's not assaulting her," I said.

"You can't even see her! And they've stopped talking."

"We're right outside of the house, Deacon. Stop trying to steal the title of Crazy Parrish from your cousin."

"Yeah, I don't appreciate it at all," Jefferson said very seriously.

"Anthony is leaving his office," Deacon said. "Get Brighton out of there."

"Would you shut it?" Jefferson snapped. "We're so close. Besides, if Anthony comes home before Brighton gets out, she can just keep pretending to be interested in the little bugger. It's not a big deal."

Deacon made an annoyed sound, but didn't say anything to disprove his cousin. He knew he was right.

A light popped on in the front room of the house where we'd seen Anthony hide the letter earlier.

"Would you like a drink?" Logan asked.

"This is feeling very *Rear Window* of us," Jefferson whispered.

I elbowed him hard to shut him up. Brighton didn't need any more reason to think she was about to be murdered.

"I'd love one." Brighton gathered her hair to one side of her head so that her long neck and bare shoulders were exposed.

At least she knew that when words failed her, she had the body of a model to distract boys.

"I'll get some ice," Logan said with a much too devilish grin in Brighton's direction.

The second he was out of the room, her sexy posing melted away and her shoulders hunched as she grabbed her stomach and began breathing rapidly.

"Oh my gosh. Oh my gosh. Oh my gosh," she repeated over and over again. "I can't do this, Sade. I can't keep this up. I'm going to vomit all over this desk that probably costs more than every possession I own."

"Brighton," Jefferson said forcefully. "Take a deep breath, turn around, and tell me if you see a safe."

She didn't take a deep breath or stop whispering "oh my gosh" to herself, but she did turn around and scanned the bookshelf where Anthony had hidden the envelope.

"Anthony has officially left the office," Deacon said.

"I can't do this," Brighton whispered. "Sadie, I think I'm going to pass out."

"You're not going to pass out, Brighton," Jefferson said, before I could respond. He actually sounded soothing, which was surprising. "You're doing a wonderful job. And we wouldn't have gotten this far if it weren't for you. Now just tell me what you see on that bookshelf."

Brighton placed a hand against her forehead to calm herself and looked once more. Even from our position across the street, I could see how tense she was. She seemed like she might burst into tears at any moment.

Brighton turned to look over her shoulder at some unheard sound. "Is he coming back?"

I tried to locate Logan through the other illuminated windows in the large Craftsman. "I'll watch the rest of the house—just do what Jefferson says."

"I see some obviously fake books," Brighton said, her voice tight and uncomfortable. "The safe is probably behind there."

"Move the books to see," Jefferson said with practiced patience.

"I can see Logan in the kitchen, Brighton. You're fine."

Unfortunately, no matter how fine I said she was, she seemed to be frozen in place with one hand on her forehead and the other on her stomach.

"Move the books," Jefferson said again.

"I've lost sight of Anthony. He drove away and you geniuses took the car so I can't follow him," Deacon practically shouted. "Sod it. I'm jogging to the house."

"Brighton," Jefferson said, speaking evenly. "Just take two steps forward and move the books."

I couldn't hear her rapid breathing now, but I suspected it was because she was holding her breath. It seemed like it took her hours to move, but eventually she unfroze, reached into her bra, and pulled out a pair of surgical gloves.

James Bond Brighton strikes again.

Utterly impressed with her foresight—or the benefits of her germaphobia—we watched as she pulled on the gloves, reached out to the bookshelf in front of her, and swung open the fake façade of a handful of books.

Unfortunately, as she did that, a few more books fell off of the book shelf above her, nearly hitting her in the head.

At first, I thought she'd disrupted the books by opening the safe. But even after she froze under the avalanche of books, a few still dislodged themselves without any help from Brighton. As if they were pushing away from the bookshelf of their own accord.

"You guys are seeing this, right?" she asked, her voice high and tight.

"Someone doesn't want you in there," Jefferson said, as if that was really helping this situation at all. "Maybe Meyer."

"Are you saying there's a ghost in here trying to keep me from the safe?" Brighton asked, a new level of panic washing over her

"I don't see anyone," Jefferson said. "You should be fine."

"Of course you wouldn't see them," Brighton said. "They're ghosts."

"You'd be surprised what I can see," Jefferson said. "Now just tell me what you see."

"There's a safe," she breathed, barely audible. "It requires a code."

"Which we can't exactly ask the little boy for," Deacon said, his breathing heavy.

Apparently, he hadn't been joking when he said he would jog to the house. I would actually pay money to see his awkwardly tall frame sprinting across town while clutching a laptop to his chest.

"Try 9780451," Jefferson said.

"And while you're at it, try 89432," I said. "We don't have time for this, Jefferson. We need to figure out how she can get the code from Logan before he gets back and sees her having a meltdown."

"It worked," Brighton said, before slapping a hand over her mouth to quiet herself.

I raised my eyebrows at Jefferson. "I know you're not in the business of answering questions, but how?"

"You gave me a piece of paper with the code on it," Jefferson said, sounding like I'd lost it. "You told me to hold onto it until a code was needed. Very cryptic of you, by the way."

"Jefferson, I never did that," I answered.

This conversation was strongly reminding of the many times my sister Michigan had sworn I'd said things to her that I never did.

It seemed to be a reoccurring theme in my life.

"Well, then apparently I'm psychic," he said, although I didn't think he really meant it.

He was just trying to avoid an argument with me. He was really actually convinced that I'd given him the code to the safe. And when we weren't in an actual life or death situation, I'd have to question him more about it.

"I can't hide this folder in my dress," she said. "Sadie, get over here so I can give it to you through the window."

"I'll do it," Jefferson interrupted.

Unfortunately, like his cousin, he was too tall to be subtle. I, on the other hand, was very stealthy with my twelve-year-old boy's build.

"Watch my back, Jimmy Stewart." I gave him a quick wink, before stealing out of the car and darting across the darkened lawn. I was definitely cursing myself for the bright yellow dress on a covert mission.

"What is she talking about?" Deacon asked, still sounding winded.

"*Rear Window*," Jefferson explained with a smile in his voice.

As crazy as he was, we understood each other. I would wait until I wasn't on a time-sensitive mission to explore the depressing nature of that fact.

"I'm under the window, Brighton," I whispered. I tried to duck down in the bushes in case Anthony came home.

"How long does it take to get ice?" Deacon asked.

"Logan's putting on cologne," Jefferson said. "I can see him in the bathroom."

"I can't get the window open," Brighton said. "Oh . . . wait . . . I'm just an idiot."

I heard the window pop open above me as the scent of flowers wafted strongly from the interior of the house. Brighton poked her head outside and looked down, her curtain of blonde hair obscuring her face. She handed me the files and her gloves, looking pale and miserable.

"Just let me climb out the window with you," she begged. "My eye is twitching and I can't feel my feet and I think I might be having a stroke. Can you smell burning feathers?"

"You're not having a stroke, you beautiful mess of a woman." I grasped the envelope tightly against me. "Get back in there, put on a brave face, tell him you don't feel well and need to go back to your car, and I'll buy you all the hand sanitizer and Xanax you could ever want."

"I can't. Please let me out." She really sounded like she might pass out.

"Get back inside, Brighton. He's coming," Jefferson said. "And close the safe."

With one last pathetic whimper that broke my heart, Brighton closed the window just as headlights cut through the front yard.

I flattened myself against the ground behind the bushes, pressing my cheek against the mud and hoping Anthony wouldn't catch me. I still wasn't sure if I believed Jefferson's theory that his ancestor was a murderer, but I didn't want to take my chances just in case that trait ran in the family.

"Anthony is here," Jefferson whispered, as if that fact wasn't painfully obvious. "Sadie, stay down. Deacon please refrain from jogging up to the house when you get here. And Brighton, take a breath and try to be charming."

CHAPTER 29

"Oh great," I heard a slightly muffled voice say in my earpiece.

"What's wrong?" Brighton asked, her voice somewhere between flirty and panicked.

It was an odd combination and she just ended up sounding a bit shrill.

"My dad's home," Logan said. "We should probably get going."

"And that's your out," Jefferson said. "Just keep it together while he drives you back to the party, then you can escape and we'll never make you be social again."

"It's all right, I was actually feeling a little lightheaded anyway," Brighton assured Logan.

Understatement of the year.

I heard a car door shut and knew Anthony would be entering the house at any second, but I didn't dare look up or say anything to my friends using my microphone. Despite my rational thoughts, I had started to worry that maybe Anthony was some kind of psychotic murderer who would kill me if he found me hiding in his garden with the files he was trying so hard to keep secret.

"I'll tell you when it's safe to move, Sade," Jefferson said in my earpiece. "Just stay down until I tell you to come back to the Jeep."

Apparently, I wasn't the only one who was worried this guy might be a serial killer.

"I'll go get my keys," Logan said a moment later, leaving Brighton alone in the library once more.

"No, you tosser," Jefferson said. "You can't leave her alone in there."

"I'm going to freak out, you guys," Brighton whispered through gritted teeth.

I was just assuming Logan was out of the room by that point. It was either that, or Brighton had completely given up on our charade.

"Anthony is in the house," Jefferson said. "And walking toward the library."

"Go get her out of there," Deacon said, still breathing heavily into his mic. "I'm almost to the house."

"I can't believe you ran all the way here," I whispered. I was still pressed against the wet ground in my dress. "Jefferson, can I leave yet?"

"Stand by."

"Excuse me, but what are you doing in here?" Anthony's voice came through Brighton's mic.

"Sorry . . . I was just waiting for Logan," Brighton said, her voice sounding shaky.

Things were falling apart.

There was silence over my earpiece for a moment, and even when I held my breath, I couldn't hear what was going on.

"Jefferson, what's happening?" I whispered.

"He's walking toward her." He sounded like he was holding his breath as well. "Brighton, the books that covered the safe didn't close all the way. Don't turn around and look. Just keep eye contact with Anthony and try to say something normal."

"You must be Logan's dad?" Brighton asked.

Silence again.

"What are you doing in this room?" Anthony asked.

"Just waiting for your son," she repeated, sounding much too guilty.

"Brighton, has he broken eye contact with you to look at the safe?" Jefferson asked. "If you think he's noticed the safe, I want you to touch your hair."

I held my breath, wishing I could see what was going on through the window just above me, but there was no way I was going to risk getting caught.

"Right," Jefferson said. It didn't sound like a good response. "We need to get Brighton out of there. I don't think she's safe."

"Hey, Logan?" Brighton called.

I jumped at the suddenly loud shout in my ear.

"Deacon, where are you?" Jefferson asked.

"I'm two seconds away," he said. "Take this."

I heard a quick exhale and saw a tall shadowy form running from the Jeep across the street up to the house.

"Deacon just threw his computer at me," Jefferson said.

"Sorry, sir, we were just leaving," Brighton promised.

"I'm coming, Brighton," Deacon said, looking more heroic than normal.

"What could you possibly do?" I asked.

This was exactly why we investigated places where people had been dead for years. Living people involved a sense of rush, and apparently, we didn't work well under pressure. The loose plan we had come up with was quickly unraveling and we were descending into chaos.

I could hear Deacon's frantic knock on the door and suddenly Jefferson whispered, "Run Sadie," into my earpiece.

I wasn't quite sure what was going on, but I didn't hesitate to obey. I jumped to my feet, still clutching the large envelope to my chest, and sprinted across the wet lawn. Jumping into the passenger's seat of the Jeep, I managed to get mud all over the car interior but didn't really care as I tried to catch my breath.

"You have the files?" Jefferson asked, echoing in my earpiece.

I swallowed hard against the dry lump in my throat and held the envelope up with a muddy, triumphant grin.

"Now we just have to hope Brighton and Deacon don't get killed, or we'll be asking their ghosts for signs of the paranormal."

"Not funny." I leaned over Jefferson to get a better look at the scene unfolding at Anthony's house.

Deacon was still standing at the front door, but Anthony didn't seem to be making a move to answer it. He stood uncomfortably close to Brighton in the library, having some sort of staring competition with her, as if he could intimidate her into revealing her secrets to him.

Logan finally came into the room. "Dad?" he called, making Anthony jump. "Are you going to get the door?"

"You know you're not supposed to be in my office," Anthony said coldly to his son.

He raised his eyebrows. "Sorry, I was just showing my friend around the house." He sounded like a typical teenager talking to his father and not like a rich future lawyer talking to a possible descendant of a murderer.

"Well, I think it's time for your friend to go home," Anthony answered, still standing too close to Brighton.

She was managing to keep her face pretty neutral, considering her tenuous circumstances.

Deacon knocked on the door again, this time much louder, causing the three people in the study to jump at the sound.

"Deacon, come back to the Jeep. Brighton's going to get out just fine now, and we don't need you screwing this situation up any more," I said.

But it was too late. Logan was leading Brighton to the front door with Anthony following close behind them. Deacon was already raising his hand to knock again, when the front door opened. Logan and Deacon stared at each other for a moment in silence.

"Say something," I whispered frantically into my mic.

"Brighton," Deacon said, sounding very odd with his fake American accent, "Mom freaked out when she saw that you weren't at your friend's house like you were supposed to be, so she sent me to get you."

"What?" Logan asked in confusion.

"GPS on the phone," Deacon explained. "Our mom is a little on the crazy side."

"Why are you all sweaty?" Logan looked like he didn't quite buy that Deacon and Brighton were siblings.

Brighton, though silent, looked like she might kiss Deacon for rescuing her.

"Sorry, I just came from a party. It was a little stuffy." He turned his attention back to Brighton. "Hurry up. I've got my friends waiting in the car and I don't need to be chauffeuring my little sister around all night in front of them."

When did the people in our little group become such amazing actors?

"I can take her home," Logan said.

Anthony was standing behind the pair in the doorway and watching the whole scene unfold, which was lucky for us. If he'd been alone in the study, he would have definitely looked inside of his safe and found his documents missing. Then we'd really be in trouble.

"It's all right, I'll just go with him," Brighton finally managed to say. "My mom will freak out if I don't get back home now. But thank you so much for a lovely night. We'll have to do it again sometime." She didn't bother to point out that he didn't have her number or any way to reach her.

Brighton walked quickly through the front door, passing Deacon and making a beeline for the Jeep. She hardly managed to keep herself from running across the street as Deacon followed close behind her.

"Everyone keep it together for five more seconds and I'll get us out of here," Jefferson said.

As Brighton and Deacon hopped in the back seat, I looked back at the Craftsman house. Jefferson started up the car as Logan and his father argued about something, but as soon as Logan stormed upstairs, Anthony headed into his study.

"Jefferson, he's going to look in the safe," I said. "You need to get us out of here now."

Luckily, Jefferson didn't need to be told twice to speed away from his crime scene. Taking too much joy in his excuse to drive fast, he hightailed it from the home and back toward our hotel room.

"As soon as we get to the hotel, run inside, grab all of our stuff and bring it back into the Jeep," he said. "We can't stay there tonight in case Anthony's looking for us. We need to stay somewhere a ways out of town. I don't want to risk getting murdered by that guy."

"Agreed," I said.

"Thank you for saving me back there," Brighton whispered to Deacon in the back seat. "I didn't know what to do. All I could do was stand there and try not to pass out."

"That's the story of my life, so I knew a kindred spirit," Deacon joked, although I knew he was basking in Brighton's adoration like a cat in a patch of sun. "And for the record . . . in case anyone is wondering. Books flying off shelves means I've seen the error of my ways. Ghosts are real."

I rolled my eyes at his revelation. "You think?"

CHAPTER 30

"Should we open the envelope to see if it really warranted breaking and entering?" I asked Jefferson. I was still clutching the muddy envelope to my ruined dress.

"Not yet. I want to focus on getting out of Kingston before we bother going over the contents of the envelope," he said. "Besides, Anthony seems like a pretty powerful man. I only want us to make one trip to and from the hotel room so we can get out of here as fast as possible. I don't know how long it'll take him to figure out who we are and where to find us."

"Would you give the whole 'murderer' thing a rest?" I said. "Just because you think his ancestor might have been a murderer doesn't mean Anthony is a horrible guy."

"Says the girl who hid in his garden because she was afraid of what he might do to her if he found her," Jefferson answered.

I was about to make up an excuse about how Anthony was a lawyer and I was more worried about the legal ramifications of what I was doing, but Jefferson would see right through that lie.

Pulling into the hotel parking lot, we all did a wordless scan of the surrounding area before hopping out of the Jeep, sprinting to our hotel room, and emptying the contents back into our Jeep. It was amazing how efficiently we worked when we were all scared for our lives.

Brighton eyed my mud-stained dress but didn't comment on how I'd ruined the one nice thing I owned. I think she was just grateful to not be stuck in Anthony's library anymore. She continuously shot Deacon little smiles when they passed each other with armfuls of equipment.

We were able to get our things out of the hotel room in record time, and after Jefferson dropped our room keys off at the front desk, we sped away from Kingston, hoping Anthony wasn't as connected as he seemed to be. It was a good thirty minutes before Deacon finally broke the tense silence that had fallen over us.

"You know, Brighton, in another life, you would have made an excellent gold digger."

Brighton let out a relieved little laugh. "I'll keep that in mind in case I ever need a career change," she said.

Jefferson shook his head in the driver's seat but said nothing to the exchange happening in the back.

"We're going to need to stop and get gas soon," I said. "Maybe we can look through the envelope too?"

Jefferson stayed silent but let his eyes scan our current surroundings from what little we could see in the illumination of our headlights. We were in Palenville, about thirty minutes from Kingston, and while I didn't think we were nearly far enough away from Anthony to really feel safe, I was dying to look inside of the envelope. In my hands, I held the one reason we had gone to four different locations around the United States on the word of a letter from who knew where. All I wanted was to see what all of the trouble was for.

Jefferson pulled into a small parking lot of an old building with a sign identifying it as a library. There were no other cars in the lot, but Jefferson cut the lights and engine on the Jeep, casting us into darkness and hopefully taking us off the radar of any crazy, vengeful lawyers covering up a murder from the 1900s.

Jefferson turned to me with a hungry look of excitement in his huge eyes, illuminating the inside of the Jeep with his phone. "Let's open it. I want to know why we were given this mystery."

Grinning back at him and feeling slightly giddy at the prospect of actually solving a mystery using our paranormal investigating skills, I opened the envelope and pulled a large stack of papers out.

"A bit anticlimactic," Deacon said. "Why couldn't you open the envelope and have a trillion-dollar bill fall out?"

"Not sure that's a real thing," Brighton said.

"Still, who wants to go through all of this to solve a mystery and then find out they have to sort through a stack of paperwork as well?" Deacon went on. "Not very exciting is all I'm saying."

I looked down at the stack of papers in my hands with pursed lips. It definitely wasn't an exciting prospect to have to sift through documents to see if we'd committed a crime for no reason at all. Holding the weighty stack, I almost wondered if we'd all been crazy to go on this ghost hunt in the first place. It could have very easily been an elaborate prank.

If that were the case, though, we wouldn't have found evidence of the paranormal at every location, linking this historic story between Eva and Thatcher. I was almost positive no one could have faked what we found at the Bray house, no matter how elaborate their prank was.

"Let's just split it up and go through it like we did with Eva's letters." I gave everyone in the car a small stack of papers. "The second you find something that proves we were justified in breaking into Anthony's house, let me know. Otherwise, we might need a lawyer."

"I wouldn't last in jail," Brighton said with a shudder. "They'd eat me alive. Plus, I don't know that they'd let me sanitize my cell before moving in."

"Jefferson can just call Alistair if we really need a lawyer. I'm sure he'd love to help," Deacon said.

"He wouldn't love to help," Jefferson assured us. "But I know enough of his dirty little secrets to get him kicked out of the Temple family, so he'd help us whether he wanted to or not."

"Your family sounds wonderful," I said sarcastically.

I was already flipping through my own stack of documents that seemed to consist of contracts and agreements regarding Thatcher's share of the law firm between himself and Mr. Meyer.

"They're something," he responded, also lost in his own stack of papers. "Just hope you never meet them."

We went quiet, the sound of ruffling papers the only thing breaking the silence.

"I think I might have found something," I said after a moment. "It looks like Jefferson was pretty much spot-on with his theory, from what I can tell."

"Did you ever doubt me?" he asked.

I rolled my eyes. "The only way Mr. Meyer would take possession of the entire law firm was if Thatcher had no children to inherit his portion of the firm, or if Meyer bought him out. I found several accounts of failed financial offers to buy Thatcher out, but it looks like he wasn't budging. He didn't want to get pushed out of his firm."

"And he did have an heir," Jefferson said.

"That somehow Thatcher didn't know about because Meyer covered the whole thing up, let Eva die, and had the baby put up for adoption," I added. "So the only way for Meyer to take control of the whole law firm—which was doing quite well by that point—was to buy Thatcher out."

"But Thatcher didn't want to be bought out," Brighton said.

"So, the only way for Meyer to get the law firm was if it was willed to him."

"I'm guessing Thatcher wouldn't will it to Meyer," Jefferson said. "I mean, unless he really wanted Meyer to have a good motive to murder him for his share in the firm."

"Unless Meyer somehow changed his will and then killed Thatcher," I said. "If he did that, it would look like he had inherited the law firm through completely legal means. Although, unless you guys are finding more direct evidence, these offers to buy Thatcher out still aren't enough to go on. We're kind of grasping at straws."

"There is the fact that my so-called obsession with Korean dramas might have paid off," Brighton added from the back seat.

"What?" I asked

"You guys thought I was crazy when I said the necklace we found in Texas was relevant. But look what I found." Brighton held a paper in front of her with a triumphant smile. "A letter from Eva Castillo to Edward Meyer refusing his marriage proposal. As in E.C. and E.M. from the necklace."

"No way," I said, refusing to believe our mystery was that much like a soap opera.

But as I read over the letter written from Eva, I couldn't deny that this whole thing was starting to look more and more like a romance novel turned murder mystery.

"E.C. and E.M.," I said with a short laugh. "Meyer knew Eva. And proposed to her at some point either before or after Thatcher knew her."

"I'd say greed is already a pretty heavy motivator for murder," Deacon said. "But greed, love, and revenge is even better."

I looked up at Jefferson for his take on the matter, but he was staring at his own stack of papers with a furrowed brow, looking overly concerned about something. His large eyes flicked up to mine in a searching way, and then back down to the papers.

"What?" I asked.

He looked up to meet my eyes once more. "Sade, what did you say your mom's maiden name was?"

"Vasquez," I answered. "Why?"

"Does the name Dante Vasquez sound familiar to you?"

"Not at all," I said, understanding where he was going with this. "Let me guess, Dante Vasquez is Eva's child's name?"

"His adopted name, yes," Jefferson said. "What about Diego Vasquez?"

"Jefferson, stop it." I knew he wanted a good mystery, but now he was really stretching to find an answer.

"Do you know that name?"

"That's my grandpa's name," I said, albeit reluctantly. I didn't need to give him any more fuel on the fire of crazy he was currently burning. "But it's not that uncommon. It's like John Smith for Americans."

"Sadie, I think there might be a really good reason we were set on this trail," Jefferson tried again.

I wasn't having it. "The name thing is a pretty amazing coincidence, I can admit that. But some typical Cuban name in our mystery doesn't automatically link it to my family."

Brighton and Deacon were watching the exchange with concerned looks on their faces, and I could tell the insanity was spreading. Jefferson was slowly convincing our group that I was Eva's long lost great (many-times-over) granddaughter. I needed to stop his crazy.

"I'm sure the name is very common," Jefferson agreed. He was trying to appease me at least a little, since I'm sure he could see the annoyance growing in my features. "But then why does Anthony have pictures of you and Michigan in his file?"

I ignored the chill that traveled down my spine. "Give me that."

There was no way this mystery was linked to my family. It was too much of a coincidence.

"Where did our letters come from?" Brighton asked.

Jefferson handed me the picture. It was an older picture of Michigan and me that my mom had taken. I'd guess that Michigan had posted it online. It was either that, or Anthony was much creepier than he was already proving to be and had somehow gotten it from our personal files. In the picture, Michigan beamed her perfect smile as she stood with her arm around me. I had long hair and was wearing an awful camouflage shirt to go along with my forced thin-lipped smile. It may not have been recent, but it was definitely us.

"Someone who knew Sadie was Eva's heir had to have dropped the letters off at our apartments that night," Deacon said.

"But why would they remain anonymous?" Brighton asked. "Why not just tell us who they were and what they were trying to accomplish?"

I interrupted her. "If my mom is the rightful heir to Thatcher's fortune and half of his law firm, and Anthony knew about my family this whole time, then he also knew the truth and knew where his money from his family was supposed to go?"

"And he said nothing," Jefferson said.

"When that letter we got said we'd be compensated financially, they meant my family would inherit the money they were supposed to get back in the 1900s after Thatcher died?"

"I'd guess so," he answered with a nod. "I'm not sure if Anthony knows about the murder plot. But I'm sure he knew enough to know that his family fortune had been obtained through some shady dealings. Things that would look bad for him if they came to light. Which is why he hid the documents all these years."

"Ignorance is bliss I guess," I mumbled. "And he had a lot of bliss to comfort him in the form of my family's money."

"But don't you have aunts and uncles as well?" Brighton asked. "Why, out of all of the descendants of Eva and Thatcher, would this random person pick you to give the letter to?" She paused, as if realizing she might have questioned my importance in this matter, and then quickly added, "No offense."

"Most of my aunts and uncles are on my dad's side. I have a few on my mom's side, but the Vasquez family has been pretty unlucky in the family arena. They just never had many kids . . . which I guess is kind of odd, given our culture. You'd think my mom would value family a bit more since she doesn't have much of one. But that still doesn't answer the question of where the letters came from. Who gave us this mystery in the first place?"

"Thatcher's ghost," Deacon said, with an overly dramatic quality to his voice.

"That's as good a guess as I have," I said. "I mean . . . obviously it wasn't his ghost, but it might as well have been since the sender left us absolutely no way to locate them."

"Maybe it was a good Samaritan," Jefferson suggested.

"So, Sadie, you're kind of rich now." A grin broke out across Brighton's face. "You don't have to be a waitress anymore!"

"Let's not get crazy," I said, stopping her in her tracks. "First off, I probably won't see any of this money since it'll go to my living aunts and uncles and my mom. Michigan and I will have to wait to inherit it. Second, we don't even know how to get these documents into the right hands. Who would believe us if we told them this story? How would we even go about getting the fortune without getting arrested for breaking into Anthony's house in the first place? We'd need a pretty good lawyer to keep us out of jail."

Deacon raised an eyebrow. "Jefferson?"

"I'm on it," he answered reluctantly. "We should probably take these documents and start heading home before Anthony catches us and kills us. I can see this much money and the fact that he possibly knowingly covered up the truth like his dad and his grandpa being enough motive for him to be very unhappy with us."

"So, we'll start heading back to Oregon," I said, "but we still don't know how to get these documents in the right hands."

"I'll take care of it," Jefferson said, although he didn't look too happy about it. "Just know Sadie, that you owe me big for calling in a favor with my awful cousin Alistair."

"It's true," Deacon said. "If you thought the way he always talked about Golden Boy Hayden Temple was bad, just wait until you meet Alistair Temple. He might actually be Satan . . . but he's a whopping good lawyer."

CHAPTER 31

It had taken way more driving than I'd ever wanted to do to get us back to Portland in a decent amount of time, and with only one more day of driving ahead of us, I was starting to get a little sad.

Our trip had been miserable. We'd eaten the world's worst food, stayed in the world's worst hotels, and had nearly gotten ourselves killed by a lawyer and his murderous-ghost ancestor.

But part of me would also miss the trip. I'd miss being out on the road with my friends, doing what we loved to do. And if my calculations were right, our financial situation wasn't about to change because we'd discovered the mystery of these four locations. My mom and her family would be happy. But my friends and I, for all of our efforts, would still be poor and stuck at dead end jobs.

Except the Parrish boys. They'd probably keep getting fired from their jobs.

Brighton and Deacon had left on a mission to find the cheapest food they could, and Jefferson had been on the phone with his cousin Alistair for hours, trying to get him to fly out and help us with our legal situation. It looked like his cousin was relenting a bit, but Jefferson didn't exactly look happy by the time he hung up the phone.

He sat in a chair beside me and rubbed his temples. "That man is completely impossible to work with."

"But he's going to help?" I asked, trying to keep the hope out of my voice.

"He's going to help," Jefferson confirmed.

"Now if only you had a cousin who was an expert in figuring out where ghostly anonymous letters came from. Then we'd be set." I closed my eyes and leaned my head back against the wall.

I was exhausted.

We all were.

Being on the run from a crazy lawyer whose property you'd just stolen would wear a person out.

"I don't need a cousin who's an expert," Jefferson said. "I have me."

"The all-knowing Jefferson Parrish," I said with a dramatic flair.

"I'm serious," he went on. "But you might not like it."

"You really think you know who sent us those letters?" I asked

He pulled a letter from his coat pocket and handed it to me. "Look at this."

I turned it over in my hands a few times, trying to find whatever magical clue he seemed to think was hiding in it.

"Looks about the same as it always has," I said.

"Now look at this." He handed me a small ripped piece of paper with a series of numbers written on it.

The word "code" was written above the numbers.

In the same handwriting as the letters we'd received.

"Where did you get this?" I asked him.

"Sadie, this is the code you gave me," he said, watching me to see if I'd freak out over his accusation.

"You think I wrote the letters?" I asked incredulously. "This isn't even my handwriting. I think I would remember doing that. Do you think I'm lying about all of this?"

"I don't think you knew you did it," Jefferson said. His tone was heavy with practiced patience in an attempt to keep me calm.

He then handed me the note we'd found in the pool room on the Queen Mary. The note that had bothered me so much because it was an old letter, written on new paper.

The note was the same writing as the other two pieces of paper.

"Because it's totally normal to go around writing letters and giving them to people without knowing you're doing it." I looked back and forth between all of the papers. Even I couldn't deny that it was all the same writing.

Still, that didn't mean it was *my writing*.

"The more you tell me about your past, the more I think it might be normal for you," Jefferson said. "You say that your family always accused you of saying things you never said. Your sister would be mad at your for getting into arguments you don't remember having. You don't remember giving me this code to Anthony's safe."

"Jefferson, how would I have even known that code?" I asked. I was starting to think maybe he'd finally lost it, even though a small part of me was also wondering how all of this might just make sense.

"You dreamed about yourself. You sat and had a conversation with yourself," he said. "Tell me, what were you wearing in the dream?"

"I don't see why that's important," I mumbled, not liking this conversation anymore.

"What color were you wearing?" he asked again.

"I was wearing yellow. Like I always am."

"And what color was your other self wearing? You said they looked just like you. So, they must have been wearing yellow as well."

This gave me pause.

I stopped and thought about the dream again for a moment and furrowed my brow.

"Well . . . no . . ."

"She was wearing purple, wasn't she?" Jefferson asked.

I felt my stomach drop. How would he ever know that? I hadn't told the group what my other half was wearing in the dream. And I highly doubted Jefferson was psychic, no matter how much he joked about it.

"She was wearing purple," I confirmed in a quiet voice.

Jefferson nodded slowly. "You were wearing purple when you handed me this note," he said. "I remember because I thought it was odd. With the exception of those pajamas you've got, I've never in my life seen you wear purple. Black, or grey, or yellow, or even green. But you never wear purple."

"Which of course you know from your close observations of me," I joked.

Well . . . half joked.

He definitely watched me a little too closely.

"If you watched me closely enough you'd know I don't have purple pajamas," I said.

"Makes sense," he said. "Late night chats."

I narrowed my eyes at him. He'd talked about my apparent late-night chats with him in the past. I'd thought he was joking. Maybe the truth was even more bizarre. Some purple-wearing version of myself felt the need to talk to Jefferson in the middle of the night because I was, what? Schizophrenic?

"What are you even trying to say?" I asked, wishing any of this made sense. "You think a dream gave you that code and said all of those horrible things to my sister when I was little? You think a dream planted letters in our apartments and put a note in the pool room of the Queen Mary?"

"I have to know how open-minded you're going to be right now," Jefferson said.

"Just say it." I was tired of waiting for his big revelation.

"I think you're a Doppelgänger."

I paused for a moment. Long enough to give Jefferson a look that said he was totally off his rocker.

He and Deacon had harped on and on about the Doppelgänger versus mimic conversation for hours. That was probably why Jefferson had Doppelgängers on the brain, which had led him to this crazy conclusion.

When I didn't say anything, he went on. "I think Deacon and I were both wrong about what they are. I think it's like another part of you. But I don't think it's you. I think it's a completely separate entity from you. It can do things for you while you sleep. I think it may even take a separate physical form from you. It's a part of you that does and says what you won't or can't in order to get things done."

"Because yelling at my sister and ostracizing my family is getting something done?"

"Maybe it thought it was protecting you," he said. "It may be misguided, but I think everything you've done without knowing you're doing it, hasn't been you at all. It's been this Doppelgänger version of you. The version that gives us clues to help us right a wrong in your family's past."

"Pretending for two seconds that you aren't completely crazy and this is true, how, pray tell, would my Doppelgänger self know about the mystery in the first place?"

"It may be tapped into the other side," Jefferson said, as if this were a completely normal conversation we were having. "Which would explain how it knew the code to the safe. And if it really is a separate being from you that can manifest and dissipate at will, it could have gotten into the pool at the Queen Mary without anyone knowing about it."

I shook my head and took a deep breath. Jefferson was known for having far-fetched theories on the paranormal. But the thing that was unsettling me the most was how much sense his theory made. How perfectly this idea fit into the years of fighting against my family over things they claimed I did. Things I had no memory of.

It explained Jefferson thinking I'd ever in a million years come over to his apartment for late-night chats.

It explained how we got the code to the safe. How we got the letters in the first place. How a letter from the 1930s could have shown up on the Queen Mary on a brand new piece of paper.

I'd written them out and placed them in our bags when no one was watching me. I'd put the letter in the pool room.

Or at least my Doppelgänger self had.

But as much sense as everything made, I still wasn't sure I was ready to just accept that I was some sort of paranormal being. Or half of a paranormal being.

First off, it was just too creepy to even imagine. And second, it was so far-fetched that I had a hard time wrapping my mind around it.

"Listen," Jefferson said. "I know it's a lot to take in. And maybe I'm wrong on this. But I don't think I am."

"I don't even know what to do with this." I answered.

I could feel a knot growing in my stomach because, against my better judgment, I was actually believing this crazy theory.

"We'll do more research when we get home." He took my hand and gave it a squeeze. "I know it's weird. And I know it's not the 'normal' you're looking for. But if you figure out a way to mend fences with your family, isn't it worth it?"

I scoffed. "Because they're going to think this is so normal. They'd have me committed."

"Then maybe you don't have to tell them the whole Doppelgänger thing if we decide that's what it is. This just gives you a little of their perspective. Maybe it can facilitate you possibly talking to them again. You can pretend to be normal and say you were just a troubled youth or something. But knowing the truth for yourself has to help."

"Since when is your idea 'pretend to be normal?'" I asked

"This trip may have taught me that sometimes, under the right circumstances, it's better to rein in the more eccentric parts of my personality in favor of getting a job done." It looked like it physically pained him to say it.

We both sat in silence for a moment.

I wasn't sure I bought the whole Doppelgänger theory, no matter how nicely it explained everything. It would probably take months of research and running our own version of paranormal tests before I'd even start to believe it.

But if it was true, somehow it would fix so much. It would fix the sister I thought was a pathological liar and the parents I thought disliked me for no reason. It would fix the eerie feeling that came with thinking a ghost had placed a letter in my purse to start us off on this crazy journey.

It would still be a new form of being broken, since I had no idea what a Doppelgänger entailed. But if we could figure this thing out, it would be worth it.

"You okay?" Jefferson asked, being more normal than he had been in a while.

Possibly because he knew I'd just received news that may or may not cause me to come unhinged.

"I'm compartmentalizing," I said. "Putting this information away for now until I have the energy to really think about it."

Jefferson nodded, his hand still in mine, before he leaned over as if he might kiss me.

Of course, Deacon and Brighton, with their eternally perfect timing, opened the door to the last hotel room of the trip, and I instantly dropped Jefferson's hand and went back to leaning my head against the wall.

My mind was swimming with so many possibilities, but right now, we had a job to do. And we had very little time to do it before Anthony figured out where his files went.

272

CHAPTER 32

"It only ends up being $2,500 for each of us," I said with a monumental sigh.

I was lounging on our ratty old couch back in our apartment in Portland.

"How much was the inheritance again?" Brighton asked.

She and Deacon were sitting beside each other on the couch, but very carefully not touching. I could barely hear them over the torrential downpour that was beating our window in a constant relentless stream. Jefferson had fallen into one of his moods and was nowhere to be found. It was just as well, since I didn't really want to tell him how little money we were getting out of this investigation.

"A lot more than $2,500," I answered. "That stupid letter writer was a liar. I thought he was supposed to make our financial burdens go away."

I neglected to mention the fact that Jefferson was now 100% convinced that I was the letter writer in question. I didn't really want to tell Deacon and Brighton that I may or may not have a Doppelgänger version of myself running around doing things. Because until I could confirm the theory, it sounded like a good excuse for Deacon to "borrow" money out of my wallet and say it must have been my Doppelgänger who gave it to him.

"Should I bring Alistair back?" Deacon asked. "Maybe he can sue your mum."

"I don't see why Jefferson hates his cousin so much," I said with a shrug. "I thought he was nice."

"That's because he was hitting on you to make Jefferson mad," Deacon said. "Trust me, Alistair is not someone you want to fall in with. This is one of the rare moments where Jefferson isn't exaggerating. In fact, he's a little blinded to Alistair's true evil."

"You Parrish boys are so dramatic," Brighton said.

"No matter how 'evil' Alistair is, he did an amazing job of sorting things out." I divvied up the cash that unfortunately wouldn't fill up a briefcase like one of those crime shows. That would have been a nice touch. "I'm not too thrilled about the fact that Anthony managed to weasel his way out of a jail sentence though."

"Yeah, that guy is definitely going to kill us all one day," Deacon said with a laugh, sounding much too cavalier about our impending doom.

"He is a lawyer, Sade," Brighton pointed out. "I would have been surprised if Anthony hadn't prepared for the day someone found out about his family's secret. Although I'd hope he wouldn't actually try to kill us over it. It's not like we were in the wrong."

"Somehow I don't think he'd care about following a moral compass in this situation," I said. "But it's not like he's not still rich. Even with the law firm and the inheritance going where it should, he's still loaded."

"But he lost his license, so he's probably pretty pissed about that," Deacon said.

Unfortunately, he was right. I couldn't imagine that we'd heard the end of Anthony Meyer. It wasn't every day that a group of twenty-somethings stole your money and job from you . . . although in our defense, it wasn't his money or his law firm to begin with. It was hard to steal what was already yours.

The only thing that helped me to sleep at night was the fact that if anything ever happened to me or my friends, Anthony Meyer would be the first person the cops would question, and no matter how well he covered his tracks, he would always look guilty. He had way too much motive now.

"And here's your amazing financial reward," I said sarcastically. "Two months worth of rent. I hope it's worth looking over your shoulder for the rest of your life."

"Even if we ended up not getting that much money, it was still pretty amazing that we were able to solve a murder from the 1900s using paranormal evidence, right?" Brighton asked.

"True," I admitted. "But more money still would have been nice."

The inheritance from the Livingston fortune had been placed with its proper family after some fancy lawyer shenanigans from Alistair that I couldn't begin to understand. Somehow, we hadn't gotten arrested for breaking into Anthony's house and stealing his private documents. But he also hadn't gone to jail for concealing a murder and basically stealing an inheritance that wasn't his.

Still, the large fortune that had been divided up amongst the Vasquez family was a nice consolation prize for having their fortune stolen in the first place. After it had been divided between my aunts and uncles, great-aunts and uncles, and my mom, there wasn't really a "fortune" to be had, but it left each of them with more than enough money to keep them happy and comfortable for the rest of their lives. Of course, being two generations removed from the oldest living Vasquez family member, I wasn't entitled to get anything, but my mom, in her infinite generosity, gave her daughters a (very) small portion of the money, saying that it was a "living inheritance."

I got $10,000 for the trouble I went through to discover the fortune for our family, and Michigan also got $10,000 for being the favorite daughter. Had I known I didn't actually have to do any work to get some of the money, I might have skipped the whole "almost getting caught by a psychotic lawyer" part of the trip.

The only problem with receiving $10,000 of the large sum my mom received was that I felt bad for my team. We had taken the job thinking we'd be financially rewarded and now we didn't get anything. So I did the only thing I could do and split the money evenly four ways between us, hoping it would make up for the fortune we'd lost out on. I guess at least we had gotten to prove ourselves as paranormal investigators and had righted a historical wrong. That had to count for something, right?

"Are you thinking about Michigan again?" Brighton asked. "You have that angry look on your face."

"It just makes me so mad that she got money and she didn't even do anything," I said.

I knew I was whining and being unreasonable, but I sort of didn't care.

"You seriously need to work out your sibling rivalry, Sade. It's not healthy," Deacon said.

"Speaking of not healthy," I began, "I guess I'd better go deliver the disappointing news to Jefferson about our 'vast fortune'."

"He's off being a crazy person in our apartment," Deacon said.

"So, he's being himself," I said over my shoulder.

I closed the door behind me and walked across the small hallway to Jefferson and Deacon's apartment.

I knocked on the door but received no answer, which wasn't surprising given the classical music that was blasting through the door. Until that point I hadn't even been aware you could "blast" classical music.

Sighing deeply, I turned the knob and entered the apartment, only to find complete and utter chaos on the other side of the door.

Jefferson was wearing his normal slacks, a white collared shirt with the sleeves rolled up to his elbows, and suspenders. His "white" shirt, however, was covered in dirt and soaking wet, and in the middle of the hardwood floor in their living room, sat a piano. Or half of a piano.

Wood pieces and piano keys littered the ground, and Jefferson was running his hands through his curly wet hair, staring with his mad, wide eyes at the broken piano in front of him.

"What are you doing?" I yelled, my voice barely audible over the music.

Jefferson turned quickly at the sound of my voice. Apparently, I had startled him. He had a manic look on his face, which was just as smudged with dirt as his shirt, and he grinned as I walked over to him.

"Look what I found in the alley downstairs!" he exclaimed.

"How on earth did you get it up here?"

"One piece at a time," he said. "It's brilliant! It's just what we need in here! I'm going to fix it up and put it right against that wall there. Don't you think it'll look amazing in here?"

"Do you even play piano?" I asked. My voice was quickly tiring from all of the yelling.

Jefferson looked indignant for a moment.

"I play beautifully," he said.

His lips pouted out a bit. Probably because I didn't keep a running fact sheet on his talents like he did for me.

"Can you please turn down the music?" I yelled. "It's ridiculously loud."

"It's Danse macabre!"

"I didn't ask what it was; I asked if you would turn it down," I shouted once more.

"I can play this on piano, you know," he answered with another manic grin. "Brilliantly."

I guess if I had to deal with one of Jefferson's extreme moods, I was just lucky it was a good one today.

"That's great," I said, as I scanned the room to find out where the music was coming from.

As if willing the music away, however, it suddenly stopped, taking the lights with it.

"You blew the power," I said in the sudden quiet.

"I think the storm blew the power, Sadie," Jefferson responded.

He was probably right, although I didn't tell him that.

Wordlessly, Jefferson gathered a few candles from junk drawers in the kitchen and lit them, giving us at least a little light in the messy apartment.

I sat on the old couch, shivering against the chill in the room. "Can you really play the piano?" I asked after a moment.

Jefferson lit the last of the candles and then joined me on the couch. "I come from a snobby elitist English family—of course I can play the piano."

He was definitely in a good mood. Sadly, I would have to ruin it when I told him how much money we'd actually be getting from the investigation that had taken up so much of our lives the past few weeks.

"Sadie?" he asked, before I had a chance to hand him the small sum of money.

"Yeah?" I figured he was going to bring up the whole Doppelgänger thing again, even when I told him the topic was off limits until I had some time to think it over.

"You said I have you," Jefferson began, actually looking very hesitant all of a sudden.

I sighed deeply.

"I think the phrasing is creepy. We need to change that around to something less slave-ish, but yes, you have me."

"You like me?" he asked.

I wasn't sure why he had gone from "let's build a piano" to "let's talk about our feelings," but I humored him—only after looking around the room to make sure Brighton and Deacon couldn't hold this against me later, of course.

"I like you, Jefferson."

He was crazy. He had terrible mood swings. He was way too honest and often confused romantic gestures with something a serial killer would do. But for some odd reason, I liked him. We understood each other and we filled something in each other, no matter how weird our relationship seemed to be.

"Do you love me?" he asked.

"Too intense," I said, cutting off his question. "The only way this relationship will work is if I tell you when you're being way too intense and you tell me when I'm being too obsessed with normalcy."

"Fine," he said, looking very put out. "You don't have to say it yet. But you do like me. I mean . . . me. Right?"

"I'm confused," I said. "I already told you I like you. What else would I like?"

"I don't know," he admitted, his huge owl eyes now avoiding mine. "I'm just trying to sort it out."

I shook my head at him and tilted his chin so that he was forced to look at me.

"I don't know what's going on in that overactive imagination of yours, but I can promise you that I like you." I leaned in tentatively and gave him a slow kiss.

We weren't really at the point in our relationship where I felt like I could just kiss Jefferson whenever I wanted, but something told me he wasn't going to pull away. He placed one hand on my waist and the other on my cheek, drawing me to him and deepening our kiss. I still sort of hated that I had no control over the burning feeling in my chest when I was around Jefferson, but right at that moment, I loved it.

I loved that he smelled like cinnamon and that his curls tickled my forehead when we kissed, and I loved the way everything was so deep and intense when we were together. Everything seemed heavy.

Knowing that I couldn't avoid telling Jefferson about our "financial reward" by kissing him forever—as appealing as that sounded—I pulled away slightly, biting his bottom lip lightly with a grin.

"That's payback for the first time we kissed," I said. I was still grasping his collar that I hadn't realized I'd grabbed. "You bit my lip and made me bleed."

"Oh, I remember," he whispered, his eyes closed and a smile on his lips. "I love you, Sade."

I opened my mouth to protest his words, but he quickly cut me off.

"And I forbid you to say it back to me right now. When you say it—and you will—it's going to be out of the blue and because you feel like it's the right time to say it and not because you feel obligated to return the sentiment."

"What makes you so sure I'm going to say it?" I asked with a challenging raise of my eyebrow.

"I just know," he answered.

Maddening.

At least if he had to say the "L" word, he'd still given me a definite out. I knew I liked Jefferson. In fact, I liked him a lot. But I wasn't ready to just throw that word around when we hadn't even really established that we were together.

"Now," he began, breaking the tense moment and quite obviously changing the subject. "You were about to tell me that you aren't marrying me for my money, right?"

I wasn't sure where his joke had come from, but it was pretty spot-on.

"First off, we aren't married, or engaged, or anything close to it," I said, feeling it was important to stop his over-the-top behavior before it started. "And second, you're about to receive some very bad news about your financial situation, so I can't really be marrying you for your money."

"My financial situation?" he asked, puzzled.

"Remember how we were supposed to receive financial compensation for our investigation and instead it turned out my family got the inheritance, but still I assured you guys that we were getting some money back?" I asked.

I never knew how Jefferson would react to something.

"Yes," he said.

"Turns out we only get $2,500 each." I pushed the small wad of bills into his hand. "Which is about two months of rent for the world's crappiest apartment."

Jefferson looked down at the money in his hand and actually laughed before placing the money back into my hand.

"I don't want your money, Sadie," he assured me.

"Just take it," I said. "I'm tired of paying your rent."

"It was one month," he said in exasperation.

We'd had this argument so many times that it was old-hat now. Leaning my shoulder against the couch back and draping my legs over Jefferson's lap so that I sat parallel to the wall, I rolled my eyes at him.

"One month is a lot of money," I said. It was the same argument I always began with.

Jefferson draped one arm over the back of the couch so that his long fingers could play with my pixie cut, giving me chills as he continued to smile at some secret joke only he knew.

"I told you I'd pay you back," he reminded me.

"Is that what this is?"

"Sadie, my father wasn't an idiot," he said.

I didn't follow his thought process at all. "What does that have to do with anything?"

"He had pretty well guessed that my mum was a gold digger before he died," he said. "And he could see how cold she was to me. It was obvious I'd never get a pound out of her unless it was to help me move to the States and get as far away from her as possible. Have I mentioned that my mum can't stand me?"

"Once or twice," I said in exasperation. I wished he'd stop joking around and get to the point.

"My father left me a hefty trust fund," he finished. "So again, I don't want your money."

I sat in silence for a moment with a furrowed brow, trying to understand what Jefferson was saying.

"Wait," I began. My anger was rapidly building. "Are you telling me you're rich?"

"That's a vulgar word," he answered distastefully, still playing with my hair. "But yes. I suppose I'm rich."

"Seriously?" I asked. "Why on earth have I been paying your rent if you're rich?"

"One time," he said again with practiced patience. "And I told you I'd pay you back. I just wanted to see if you'd actually do it. I'm a bit wary of gold diggers, as you can imagine."

"I wasn't even trying to marry you, you psychopath!" I yelled, pulling out of his grasp. "I didn't even show any interest in you!"

"I can see that I've upset you for some reason," he said. He was still trying to be calm, although the look of panic on his face was overriding any of his other emotions.

Of course Jefferson Parrish would be confused over why this would upset me.

"Why were we scrounging for food money during the entire trip?" I asked, my voice much louder than I had intended. "Why were we staying in the sketchiest of hotels where I was lucky to not be kidnapped? You didn't even ask your mom for the money we used on the trip, did you?"

"I wouldn't ask my mum for money if I were dying and her money was the only thing that would save me," he said.

"Does Deacon know?" I asked, wondering just how betrayed I should feel.

Jefferson winced. "More or less."

"More or less?" I repeated in a dangerously low voice.

"He knows I have money, but he thinks I can't touch it because it's in a frozen bank account."

"And why would he think that?"

"Because that's what I told him," he said with another wince.

"Jefferson Parrish! Why are you such a crazy person?"

"I just wanted to make sure the people in my life were there for the right reasons," he said. "Besides, I thought you'd be pleased I had money."

"Why would I be pleased?" I asked, mimicking his accent.

I wasn't really sure why I was so upset. Mostly it just seemed a bit hypocritical that he was all about being honest with me, yet he had hidden this huge secret. Although, given his upbringing, I guess his reasoning was sound.

Still, that wouldn't stop me from being outraged at him for no good reason.

"Because what's mine is yours," he said, as if this should be obvious.

"We aren't married!" I shouted at him.

He narrowed his eyes at me, as if I was putting a damper on his crazy idea of our impending marriage that he had somehow decided was happening.

I tried to slow my breathing down and not let my rage get the better of me. I really couldn't feel too justified in being mad at him, since his financial situation was really none of my business.

"You said you would always be completely honest with me," I accused. I was bringing my voice back down to an acceptable indoor level.

"You never asked."

As he said it, I could see that he realized how terrible that reasoning was.

We were both silent for a moment, my legs still draped over his lap as I absently played with one of his suspenders, reasoning the whole thing out in my mind.

"Well, I'm definitely keeping your portion of the investigation money," I told him. "And you owe me for one month of rent."

"Which I will pay you right away," he promised.

We fell silent again. I wasn't really sure what to say.

"Now I'm going to marry you for your money just to teach you a lesson."

"That's an acceptable punishment," he agreed with a fake, somber nod. "Because even if I trick you into marrying me, eventually you'll come around and figure out that you love me."

I rolled my eyes at him, still not smiling, but refraining from yelling at him as well.

"I'm sorry I lied," he finally said.

"Are you sorry you made me sleep in awful hotels and eat the worst food known to man?" I asked, the joking lilt returning to my voice ever so slightly.

"I am," he said. "And I intend to make it up to you."

"And how exactly are you going to do that?"

He grinned his large manic grin once more, his owl eyes crinkling in the corners as he stared at me.

"Fancy doing an investigation in England?"

ACKNOWLEDGMENTS

The Husband and I are notorious nerds. And we just happen to love *Ghost Hunters*, the month of October, scary movies, haunted houses, and basically anything creepy. Because of this, it was only natural that I'd write a book about a group of ghost hunters. So I feel like the biggest acknowledgment should go to The Husband for indulging and encouraging my love of all things creepy.

Jackie Hicken. You angel. You perfect specimen of an editor/friend. Just thank you. Thank you for everything. And thank you for putting surgical gloves in Brighton's bra. That was my favorite.

My critique group (Mikki Kells, Heather Ostler, and Lisa Harris) needs the biggest shout out of all because they've been reading this story for the past year and promising me that Jefferson's intensity is endearing and not off-putting. Which was helpful, since I was starting to think I was the only person in the world to think it was romantic. Creepy is the new cute, right guys?

A huge thank you to Hayley Mitchell for being my consultant in all things British. I'm sorry Deacon and Jefferson have non-British names, Hayley, but I promise it'll make sense in the second book!

A big giant hug and thank you to Ashlee Wille who loves these characters almost as much as me. She kept sending me AU scenarios about them and #CreepyJeffersonTexts that just made my day. Plus she let me text her as Jefferson sometimes to really flesh him out. It was fantastic.

Of course all the love in the world to my family, who encourages me, and my friends who don't think I'm crazy, and the amazing writing community in Utah.

And more thanks than I'll ever be able to give to my Heavenly Father who blessed me with an ability to write and a twisted sense of humor. I'm quite fond of that combination.

ABOUT THE AUTHOR

Shannen Crane Camp was born and raised in Southern California, where she developed a love of reading, writing, and anything having to do with film. After high school, she moved to Utah to attend Brigham Young University, where she received a degree in Media Arts and found herself a husband in fellow California native Josh Camp. The two now live in Utah with their miniature schnauzer Hemingway. Shannen's true love is Young Adult Fiction though she often dabbles in New Adult, Paranormal, and Mystery. She takes any opportunity to include her love of film and video games in her writing and you might just find a nerdy Easter Egg or two hidden in her works.

Shannen loves to hear from readers, so feel free to contact her at Shannencbooks@hotmail.com or visit her website for more information: http://shannencbooks.blogspot.com